COLD-COCKED
ON HOCKEY

COLD-COCKED

ON HOCKEY

Lorna Jackson

BIBLIOASIS

FIRST EDITION

Library and Archives Canada Cataloguing in Publication

Jackson, Lorna Mary, 1956-
Cold-cocked : on hockey / Lorna Jackson.

ISBN 978-1-897231-30-2

1. Hockey—Social aspects. 2. Hockey. 3. National Hockey League.
I. Title.

GV847.J33 2007   796.962'64   C2007-903769-0

**Canada Council
for the Arts**　　**Conseil des Arts
du Canada**

We acknowledge the support of the Canada Council
for the Arts for our publishing program.

PRINTED AND BOUND IN CANADA

for
Rex
and his crew

CONTENTS

THE GAMES BEGIN

True obsession depends on the object's absolute unresponsiveness.
– Barbara Gowdy, "We So Seldom Look On Love"

*Only the spectator can appreciate the abstract beauty of the game – the ebb
and flow of bodies drawn this way and that by the puck, like iron filings
arranging and rearranging themselves around an elusive black magnet.*
– Bruce Kidd and John Macfarlane, *The Death of Hockey*

Versus Edmonton, I took Lily. The rain was warm, the city fully itself:
grey and wet and hunkered between the Strait of Georgia and the Coast
Mountains. Vancouver raised me and curled my hair with its weather systems,
and I'm not bothered by its moods or newer sparkles and instant ethnicities.
Downtown, I hung out at the auction house with my father when I was ten; I
wandered curio shops on my way to work in Stanley Park when I was sixteen;
at Georgia and Granville, the cheapskate owner stole my tips at a pimp-heavy
all-night Greek café when I dumped university at nineteen. At the Blackstone
Hotel one Halloween night, I watched from the grimy stage as young dudes in
suits stole a homeless woman's beer change, their hands rough under her
sweater.

No harm done. Versus Edmonton, across from our hotel was the Salvation
Army hostel and Lily suspected everyone carried a hypodermic – that guy
sleeping in the shopping cart in the alley, for example – ready to poke and kill
us. In another year, she'll feel the same about cougars in Metchosin – they're
stalking our stolen territory, desperate to claim their own, all around us. I
don't feel her fear. The city's dark side has always lurked behind the curtain of
rain, a key rule of feng shui overlooked by Captain Vancouver or the sappers
who drew the port's angles. Bright and glimmerous and foreboding and enclosed: Vancouver's dominant characteristics.

Mine, too. Maybe it's this simple: the moods, the flash storms and quick
clearings I have – in technicolour these days – mean I'm coming home.

My fifteen-game Ice Pak features weekend games only. For six months, I'll travel from my Metchosin farm on southern Vancouver Island, ferry to the mainland to Vancouver, where I heard foghorns and seagulls, the heavy sigh of trolley busses and the lawnmower of the cute religious boy down the block as I lay in bed at night; where I ran and fell on snowy streets and cracked my kneecap; where I drove upriver with my father every October to watch salmon wrestle gravity to spawn, played country rock in sticky bars, lived and drank hard until I was thirty. Travel – drive north to ferry terminal and park the car; board bus on ferry; bus to downtown; walk four blocks to 1898-built boutique hotel – will amount to seven hours each game, but so what: time plus contemplation equals insight. It's good to think.

I am forty-seven and my daughter is twelve. We may have only a minute to go in the game before sarcasm, heckling, and the brick wall of adolescence shut me out, before the comic opera of "the change" makes me her fool. Meantime, take her to hockey games, be a hero. End of last season, Lily moved from exclusive crushes on Tom – her father – and our black lab, Max, to a painful one on dazzling d-man, Ed Jovanovski. Jovo, this 2003/4 season, is a huge character: fighting with an already fat lip, skating fast and hard, scoring, joking that you can't count on forwards for puck protection, for anything. During televised games, she berates and encourages him when he winds up for what is more Crazy Canuck slalom than sensible end-to-end rush – "What are you doing, Jovo? Stay in your end! Stay at home! NO!!" She retreats to her calm blue bedroom if the game's too close or out of reach to speak gently to his photos and crank up nouveau hockey-rockers, Nickelback – *You're like my favorite damn disease.*

Vancouver is a hockey town though easterners don't see it that way and never have. We fill the seats at the Garage night after night, and still a player or owner or Toronto broadcaster crowns Toronto the country's hockey mecca and claims the game for themselves. We are told that hockey fans grew up playing on frozen ponds, that hockey as Canadian identity stems from the bitter cold winters, the ice and snow, the flatness of landscape and the vast horizon of winter. Fuck that noise. Joe Sakic, Brendan Morrison, Paul Kariya, Scott Hannan, Cam Neely, the Courtnalls, not to mention players who found ice elsewhere in this temperate province – Port McNeill, Kelowna. It's a little like claiming country music only lives and breathes in Nashville: good for Nashville, but a lie. Ask Keith Urban from Australia. Ask Ian Tyson who grew up on Vancouver Island. You want ice? Thirteen thousand years ago, it was

1500 metres deep where downtown Vancouver stands, but the ice age ended. We moved on.

Here's what Montreal poet Doug Beardsley wrote in his *Country on Ice* in the mid-eighties. At forty-five, he'd taken a bus from Victoria to see an NHL game versus the Bruins in Vancouver and stops to read the city and its team through an easterner's pretensions, assumptions and prejudices:

> The city of Vancouver looms ahead, sprawling, disconnected, gorgeous in its mural landscape, yet a city lacking in human compassion. A city of free enterprise but without human dimension, a place where you live by the sword or you don't live. A cold city but not cold enough for hockey, a city that houses a team that used to fly about the league in its own private jet, the only NHL team to do so. This is the luxury of free enterprise but it produces a comfortableness in the players that carries onto the ice. The high salaries and creature comforts have turned out coddled, incubated athletes who think of their talent as a profession rather than an art, and play accordingly. On no team is this more evident than the Vancouver Canucks.

I'd like to watch him say that to Tiger Williams, face to face, on skates.

Versus Edmonton, Lily and I walked a few blocks in the rain, down the hill from the hotel to the rink. Her long legs urged us to stride fast. She wore her Jovo-white jersey like a new boyfriend, her hoodie draped out the back, concealing parts of his name but establishing her as not too girlie, sleeves turned up a couple of flips. She's taller in that jersey – already has four inches on me – and that night she possessed a power I've never seen before. Why do women wear them? To honour players, like exchanging love beads in the late sixties to broadcast a commitment to love and peace. Or it's sex: to wear the sweater is the closest thing to intimacy – to fucking – they'll get with these untouchable gods. For $1250.00 I could score a game-worn Jovo jersey from the NHL's online store and it might even smell like sex. Seconds out of the package and it would be up to her nose, then across her pillow. Free enterprise, indeed. Or it's flirting: there's a chance the player will notice from the ice – *Hey! That bubble-boobed babe's wearing my number! Let's get it on!* But my daughter is twelve; it's not so much that she's plagiarising Jovo's power or begging his attention, more like she's lending her own to him for the night, to make him strong like she is. This may not be potlatch, but there's a ritualistic exchange happening when city folk hurry down the hill to the rink, another person's name and number big on their backs. A way to identify physically with the players, sure, but we're more than some egghead's research in *The Sociology of Sport Journal.*

I LIKE RESEARCH that pokes at hockey through the bars of cinema and television studies, in which *getting off* on a game is more properly called *spectating pleasure.* Brainiacs like Laura Mulvey have said that either a viewer gets pleasure from that which is viewed, or she gets it from imagining herself in the image, from relating the image to her own life.

When the camera allows us to secretly observe players talking at the bench, or cooking pasta in their homes, or riding stationary bikes after the game, we get an illicit thrill. Parts of the game – the sudden punch, for example – invite voyeurism, too. Joyce Carol Oates has likened boxing to porn: "in each case the spectator is made a voyeur, distanced yet presumably intimately involved, in an event that is not supposed to be happening as it is happening." The thrill of voyeurism's different from the charge we get when the pan flute music starts to throb before each Canucks game and the players bound down the tunnel and toss themselves onto the ice. Fetishism needs a fetish, and pro sports, by paying so much attention to numbers and increments – player salaries and bonuses, statistics and percentages, height and weight, play by play – invites us to look hard and assess and evaluate players as commodities, as objects. Instant fetish. When television repeatedly shows Marty McSorley's stick thwack Donald Brashear's skull, and superslows the whapping of Brashear's helmetless head on the ice, our looking – if we look, and I do every time – is both voyeuristic and fetishistic.

Fetishism is pulled toward narcissism when we go from a preoccupation with things to imagining ourselves as part of those things. We see the human body, or parts of it, and we see ourselves. Some suggest that when "commentators tell stories about the players and the game; [when] they create colourful personalities for the athletes, and they construct myths and legends about the sport itself," and when a broadcast is full of "references to the athlete's hobbies, family life, and background," we get the "symbolic raw materials for identification." They're like us! Gotta love 'em!

Maybe because it moves so fast, because it's such a hyper game, I have those three pleasures simultaneously. As a voyeur, I like it when the camera catches a player throwing up at the bench having gone too long and hard; or when players groove on goals – Markus Näslund looks God-ward or Todd

Bertuzzi flips the monkey off his back when he finally scores; or the way Näslund leans forward on one arm – eyes up on the play – to recover his wind. I have a fetish for the ritual of the faceoff; I sing the national anthem; I stay for the three-star selections. And though they are bigger and hairier and manlier than me, I see myself in players: I cheer Brendan Morrison because we grew up in the same town, we both went to post-secondary school, and we both own retrievers. Occasionally – thanks to the helmetless pre-game skate or the shirtless interview – a sexual component is added ("When looking at sports as sexual, it is always illicit and therefore voyeuristic."). When Lily wears Jovo's sweater, it is part fetish and part narcissism: the object is the source of the thrill and sometimes a synthetic proxy for the man, but when she wears it, they exchange identities and she relates to her man, absorbs him through her skin.

At the rink early, we took the crowded stairs to ice level for the 6:30 warm-up, three rows from the glass, a couple of voyeurs in borrowed seats where the rink's curving corner sweeps around to the end boards. The CBC's lights and cameras made a bright mock-world around ex-goalie commentator Kelly Hrudey; his black suit glinted with a hint of sheen behind the goal. The players spun close. Jovo stopped right there, goofy grinning, dark hair curled and maybe frosted at the tips, close enough without a helmet for Lily to crash harder in love. To me, Näslund was favouring his leg or groin; Mattias Ohlund, who without a helmet resembles Peter Tork of the Monkees, looked sturdy on his new legs; Brent Sopel: you call that skin tone? We were so close to their heads.

Bertuzzi took up a position on the blue line, his back to the boards. I'll see this every game: he bends over – stick across his big knees – and wiggles his enormous butt side to side like Baloo the bear in *The Jungle Book*. The kids with their delighted faces pressed flat slap and rattle the glass with their palms. Bert dings pucks off the shaft of his stick, over the glass, for them to catch. A sneery teenager grabs one and Turbo Todd doesn't like it: *that's for him*, he snarls and growls, teeth awry, and points at a hyper eight-year-old, *give it to him*. He's head counsellor here at Camp Happy, in the skin of a lion.

The game was a little dull, a notch this side of pre-season exhibition faux-intense. It's early enough in the year to be interesting: new moves – Näslund plenty physical, where'd this come from? – and new lines – Magnus Arvedson, Matt Cooke, Trevor Linden are the shut-down line and they do; Daniel and Henrik Sedin are with rookie Jason King on what a clever newsie has called "The Mattress Line" (two Twins and a King). Newbie goal-tender, Johan Hedberg, is in net for the first time, signed to put a scare into Dan Cloutier. Even at this pace, Edmonton doesn't have a hope. Shawn Horcoff and Ryan Smyth, with his fractured finger and formerly fractured everything else, seem real; Steve Staios – the league's other hand-some Macedonian – is gritty as road base, but the Oilers look ridiculously unskilled.

Midway through period two, Linden – the night's best player with two set-ups – is tripped going into the Edmonton zone along the boards. While he's gathering himself to stand, Brad Isbister checks his head into the boards – *he's already down, asshole! It's October!* – and gets called. Isbister shrugs and raises his stupid gloves at the ref *Whaaa? Whaddid I do?* like a teenager on Sunday morning *Geez, Dad, I dunno what happened to the passenger door, it was there when I drove it home, sweartogod.* To which Jovo takes serious of-fense, arrives out of nowhere, drops his gloves and pummels his head. Jovo's face, down there below us on the ice – we're not so far away after all – is en-raged and unable to stop itself. He is awash in chivalry, setting the fucking tone, drowning in chivalry.

Lily stands and cheers him on, shrieks his name, thrilled. I'm standing, too, but not cheering. You idiots: what about his hands and their role in the rest of the season? I want to cheer but can't, given the level of violence. Also, I know he'll be turfed for instigating, but Lily's not fluent in the game. She admires what he's doing and she's right. That was a fuckwad hit on a player who mat-ters to hockey, to them all, and the Oilers are being badly out-everythinged. A penalty would not be enough to correct it. A cheap shot later in the game would not provide the instant humiliation, the logical consequence, that the scene requires. Someone had to act, right now, and Jovo was the only menace-man on the ice.

Or there's another way, one that doesn't implicate my daughter in a vio-lent act, that doesn't seduce her into cheering her boyfriend for something other than a brilliant outlet pass, or a whistling snapshot from the point, or a deft deflection off a Swede's wrister. He could score. Or he could make the de-fensive zone so hard and tight they're afraid to squeeze through and cough up the puck instead. Am I motivated by non-violent principles, or is this a fan's self-interest?

But Jovo is led like a bad dog on a short leash to his bench by the official; he's not to be trusted. Gone for two, for ten, for the game. Lily blames the ref.

It must have been a mistake, someone else's fault. Her boyfriend's in jail. She believes Jovo is proud of himself today.

While she's idealized his character over the past few months, I've kept parts of Jovo from her. I haven't told her he was known as Special Ed prior to his draft year to reflect his lousy grades at school, his half-speed cognitive processes, his aggressiveness. Or my theory that he grew up in a home where English wasn't spoken much during his childhood and that he has the quick eyes and measured diction of smart but panicked ESL students I've known and admired. I haven't told her that in his post-draft year, he and two teammates were charged with sexual assault, that the charges were dropped a couple of months after young Eddie negotiated his first contract with the Florida Panthers for $7.8 million over four years. Jovo's career began darkly, but she doesn't need to know that, given the sparks spitting off him now. Also, I haven't told her that his wife – who resembles a soft, pre-Hefner Barbi Benton – thrills to hear her Ed speak Macedonian. A rushing defenceman.

Bobby Orr talks about what happens when a blue-liner goes on a rush: hits. And those hits go to the knees. Orr's pain is constant. In a 2004 hospital interview with the *Toronto Star*'s Damian Cox, recovering from surgery to finally replace his left knee, fifty-six-year-old Orr says, "I just hope I can go for a long walk." His wife, Peggy, says, "It would be nice if we could ride bicycles." Orr: "I just want to be able to get up from a table and not have to push myself up . . . I don't need to play tennis or skate. I just would like to be a little more comfortable." Cox captures the seasons of Orr's pain – past and present – captures the touching optimism in a marriage that must have known sharp silences; captures Orr's wit; describes the many painful incarnations of "the left knee that betrayed us all, Canada's most famous knee." The last wonky line, though, veers into a sweeping generalization, a trite display of narcissism – "It all only means that we're growing old, too."

When I visited Toronto's Hockey Hall of Fame in 2003, I was touched to see Orr memorabilia/fetish objects, the sticks and sweaters. But then I rounded a corner and spotted a weird looking contraption in a Plexiglass case: plastic and steel bars, hinges and rivets and bolts, hefty enough to wrap around Secretariat's sore fetlock. The knee brace Orr had worn during that flying goal in St. Louis. I choked up but not because I felt his pain in my own knee, or I suddenly realized "Yikes! I'm ageing, too, poor me." That object proved his pain, his heroism. It was a detail missing from the story of that goal;

it explained that suspended second of gleeful flight and what it felt like to come down, and it made the story better. Not my story: Orr's.

Jovo's body will no doubt seize up in significant ways as he ages, but now he reminds me of a sturdier, curlier version of Steve Nash, his pass so hard, fast and precise, he makes forwards look supremely gifted. He can also look like a useless knob when passes get picked off, as they do several times a game. And like Nash, by deciding to join the rush, to fight, to take and give hard hits, Jovo must know he's risking his body and kissing goodbye a long career. Al MacInnis is out, probably for good, with wonky retinas: too much time in the corners and in front of the net, too much Scott Hannan's renegade stick. And yet Jovo looks so determined already this year, no ego or fear. I remember his face, a boy's pure happiness, when he returned from the 2002 Olympics with his medal. Imagine his face if he wins the Cup.

Bertuzzi's different, too. He's not scoring much, but he's playing more defensively, pulling his game away from ego, away from the forty-six goals last year, and toward team. Goal-suck fans with their gluttonous hockey pools will not like it. They'll denounce him any minute now, and the press will concur. Caution at the red line will be read as laziness and unwillingness to move his big butt. Bertuzzi, though, is a matured version of last year's brilliance. They're getting first goals in every game. They're not having to scramble back in the third. They're still not playing sixty minutes – is this even possible in hockey? Desirable? – but they're closer.

Hockey looks different. It could be me who's changed in the off-season, but last week Nashville had nine fighting majors against Detroit. Fighting is up 29%, goal scoring slightly down. Ah, the meaningless stat. I'm more immune to fighting than I was when I watched with my dad in the seventies, not offended or disgusted and I don't turn away. The spectacle of men trying to hurt each other with their hands has charm. But I'm not having as much fun. It's early in the season, but the game has gone serious. Bryan Allen slashes Henrik Zetterberg and breaks his leg. Doug Weight highsticks Henrik Sedin to the head and face, cherry chiclets clatter onto the ice and a cut – so close to his eye – opens and he's suddenly a pugilist at rest, face down on the ice, horizontal, hurt and writhing. Keith Tkachuk is suspended for three games for a stick to the throat of another player. Last year, with him, the same: menace, intimidation, grotesque malice. Why make another player feel such pain, possibly feel that pain for a lifetime? Beauty lives here, but I'm not loving it. Or the promise of watching a player's knee explode via the dirty hit, or a vertebra crushed from a crosscheck, or a head concussed, the brain swimming in skull. These men have children to hold and hedges to trim and crossword puzzles to finish: futures. How can such a beautiful game be allowed to behave so badly?

We have imagined already this season the most awful horizontal: Dany Heatley walks away from his Ferrari – shattered jaw, concussion, bruised organs, torn tendons in his legs – and then falls to the ground on a warm night in Atlanta. Last year we watched him be vertical – gap-toothed, greasy curls, so Canadian – and score four goals in the All-Star game. Gretzky visited the locker room between periods to say, *go ahead, kid, break my record, score five.* A teammate mock-groused, *He should at least wear his teeth if he's going to score like that.* Hockey is so vertical: players are upright and fast, they resist and taunt gravity, never letting it pull them down when the turn is tight; they stay up. Heatley walked from his Italian jet and went down. Dan Snyder – his buddy, his less-talented teammate – lies horizontal in a coma and will soon die. Hockey should never look like this: long muscles deteriorating every hour he is unconscious, cell by cell, the athlete turning back irresistibly into a boy. The athlete's brain growing softer, losing muscle, going back to the minors, to Junior when everything hurt too much and the toughness set in, the teeth flew with adolescent glee.

Will I stay with the game? Of course. These diversions from the season's simplistic plot – that is, who will win? – raise the stakes of the story for everyone, including those who denounce the sports culture that matches a young man's testosterone with RPMs, that pays him millions to play a game and then sets him loose to buy the world with obscene cash. We're more interested when the unexpected happens, when we aren't prepared for the game's sad surprises.

I AIM TO ENTER hockey's orbit. I'm not interested in writing as an alien, a stunned onlooker, a girlie fan in a baggy jersey, or a robot guided by the television camera's morbid fixation on the puck. If, as players insist, anyone who hasn't played pro sees only half of what's on the ice, television takes that 50% and cuts it further. The thrill I'm feeling is wide and deep and there's nothing left to learn from Pay Per View and *The Hockey News.* But I'm not interested in writing as an insider, either. I want to resist the pull of standard hockey words, the predictable structures, the linearity of plot, he shoots he scores, the inevitable seven-game series with its final protracted seconds ticking down.

The familiar shapes and patterns of sports writing don't interest me. I want to mix it up, but right there, have I slipped into lingo? I'll orbit from cheap seats far above Planet Canuck and some miracle of physics, a benevolent centrifugal force, will pull me closer, so close I can talk to players about the game, how it's changed and why I'm suddenly spinning so fast my brain's mangled. I must have connections to get me in the room.

Hello Chris,

I've e-mailed a couple of times about interviews for a book I'm working on. Here's another one.

I'm coming over for games on Nov. 22 and Dec. 6 and Dec. 14. I understand that Näslund and Linden may be outrageous requests; I might get suitable responses from others. I'm needing an astute and articulate Swede, one who might have given some thought to how his nation has influenced the culture of the NHL and its players. I'm also after a veteran who has witnessed (what I see as) the shift from the stereotype of the meathead steak-eating bruiser of the 80s to the current good citizen/good father/good body version of player. Maybe Ohlund and Keane?

Is it possible to set something up for any of the days I'm over?

This week I was first in the pool but BRUISERCRUISER keeps taking over. I dipped to fourth a couple of times but today I'm back up to number two, thanks to Martin St. Louis and Ziggy Palffy. FUKT (writer Bill Gaston) draws close but stays in ninth. Tom, my personal xenophobe, has taken my team list and marked each with an F for Foreigner or a C for Canadian; he suspected I'd been naughty and chosen too many Swedes and was ready to berate me. But he's wrong – two Swedes, a Russian, a Finn, a Slovak and a Czech – although he unwittingly names Patrick Elias a Canadian.

Hi Lorna,

Sorry that I've been so bad at getting back to you.

I'd like to help you with the interviews for your book, but gamedays are usually not too good for interviews outside of game material. Will you be in Vancouver on either of these days, before or after the games? The Toronto games will be really difficult just due to the media numbers covering the games.

I think the best Swede for you to talk to would be Johan Hedburg. He's probably the best Swedish interview on the team and really thinks about his an-

swers. Brad May might be a really good interview for the other topic.
Talk to you soon,
Chris

November 18 is retro night on television and the stick-on-ice jerseys look ultra-Swedish. The more handsome players arrive at the rink in a vintage convertible, waving and posing, encouraging sales. Coach Marc Crawford says the jerseys resemble a Viagra pill. Your point? That the boys haven't been winning in OT because they're not pumped? That they can't last? That they've lost their drive, their balls? A dumb metaphor – like a penis on pills – can go on forever.

On the ice, the boys look clean and bright. Even grunger Sopel looks feminized and sanitized, less Neil Young circa *Harvest* and more like he's wearing a birthday present to please Mom. He is Vancouver's most improved player over the last couple of years, and Tom and FUKT have crushes on him ("He's the team's quarterback," says Tom. "His face has all the right parts to be classically handsome," says FUKT.). Sopel suffers for the new look. In the third period, behind his own net, he turns into the play along the boards. His head is down, his body angled when Richard Zednik checks him hard off the puck. The top of Sopel's head drives into the boards, and he goes down and out, face on ice. Näslund scoots to the bench for a trainer. Ohlund is on one knee trying to get through the chemicals misfiring in his teammate's brain. Sopel is motionless for so long. A boy in a pretty uniform, trying to come back. He does. He slides to the bench, a toddler in new skates, head hung and hair everywhere, not able to lift it. How many concussions does that make? None reported.

Jovo says this makes hockey different from other sports: the will that players have to come back into the game regardless of pain. It's what draws fans to players, he says, what we admire. On Sopel's first shift back, he misses his man. Two Montreal players criss-cross behind Cloutier, and Sopes can't keep them straight for the split second it takes Zednik to get into the slot – he's so open – and score. A few shifts later, Sopel falls in his own end, no one close. Next shift, the booing starts and so do the hits on Zednik. Bert throws a lovely, clean and hard one that puts the trespassing Slovak on his ass. *There*, I assume, *there's that done*. But it's not. Cooke throws another and then skates after Zednik to lift an arm and elbow up into his face. Jovo hits him hard at centre (Canucks website: "Zednik fiddles along the train tracks with the puck in his skates." About the hit: "It was a chest-caver. Full marks to Jovo."). Sure, he's scored two goals and needs to be stopped, but so many times?

In the 2002 playoffs, after the Olympics brought me back to hockey, Zednik had also scored goals, and Kyle MacLaren clotheslined him at the blue line, knocked him cold with an elaborate stick to the face. He lay unconscious for several minutes – the game still did this shit? – was taken off the ice on a stretcher and zoomed to Montreal General: concussion, broken nose, lacerations on his throat and near his eye. According to *Sports Illustrated*, Zednik remembers nothing of the hit and little of the two days in hospital. When he goes to watch a playoff game two weeks later, the noise in the arena makes him tired and woozy by the third period. Tapping his fingers on the table in front of him is way too loud. In May, he fails a routine post-concussion memory test. In July, he starts light workouts but can't ride the bike; his head hurts. He says he holds no grudges.

And after the game on Tuesday he warbles, "lots of goals, lots of hits. Is good game for fans and fun to play." The Canucks had no groove for most of the game – those jerseys looked dumb in period one when the passes missed and the skating slogged. The team was dolled up for the dance and then sat by the stage, looking pretty but static, shut down and closed off. The game ended in a tie and in overtime, Bert took control, passing to himself through his skates, Mario-esque, spinning a long slow circle around the goal, drawing two defenders (website: "Like wasps to a picnic") like sculpins to a whale, and slipping a pass to Ohlund who'd come from the boards and shot low from the slot's outskirts through José Théodore's glove. "Bert told me to try that," he grinned post game.

Zednik's horizontal of two years ago prevents me from full-out victory pride. I'm not ready to see him as an opponent yet. He's a boy on the ice in another realm, his brain pinballed because one Canadian asshole took a stupid, reckless shot at his head. His brain. Zednik's hit on Sopel doesn't change it. Coach Crawford: "They all responded and sent the message that you don't do that in our building. They got a lot of good licks on him. That was a good response." Must we?

IN *Pain: The Science and Culture of Why We Hurt*, Marni Jackson writes, "work against pain, and you lose. Work with pain, and the struggle lightens. The body is not the enemy." It's taken more than thirty years to attend to my knee. I've tried time and again to come up with a program, to get help. I've filled those baggies with sand and draped them on my ankles; I've paid too much for ankle weights and then purged them at bitter garage sales; I've tried to swim lengths in many pools only to feel the resistance pull my kneecap sideways; in a psychiatric ward on Vancouver Island, recovering from the kiss of death and knee surgery (cut the tendon and re-attach with a stainless steel screw, full leg cast, an operation that today would be done arthroscopically and without fuss), I asked for daily physio and got it but my stay wasn't long enough. I cheered up too soon. At home, I was useless with pain. The weakness in my right leg made me walk crooked and the quad muscle further degenerated. I remember the pressure and turn of the screwdriver when the surgeon removed the screw at St. Paul's Hospital in Vancouver because after several months I could feel it in there, or thought I could. By my mid-twenties my back was twisted and unreliable; vertebrae would pop out, ribs, too (Cox on Orr: "his back had started acting up because he had been compensating for the near uselessness of the left knee.") and every time I tried to build muscle, I ran from the pain caused by rehab. And when Lily was born – I was thirty-five – the pain bloomed. I couldn't stretch in bed in the morning without coming apart, literally. I wept in the chiropractor's office, Lily a chubby year old and crying over in the corner to see me laid out on the funny bed, wanting to be in my arms, and the doctor angry with me: "Why are you crying?" he snarled, "Because of the pain or because of her?" Please fuck off, I thought. Pain meant danger, failure, and something more complicated. At my first appointment last year with the physio in Victoria, I tried to suggest I had been inept at my rehab for years; I attempted to blame myself for wussing out. Calm in his linen and leather, he pretty much said move on, let it go, there's lots of reasons to give up. So what?

Ronald Melzack is co-author of *The Challenge of Pain*, "a modern classic in its field." Marni Jackson believes the most important aspect of Melzack's study of pain is "an interest in language," in the words we use to define pain and how we communicate about it. "Because," Melzack told her, "what that pain means to you is critically important. You can't tack meaning onto the sensation. It's what it means to you that makes it a big pain or a little pain. Or an intolerable pain."

Melzack's changed the way I feel about my knee. I don't question whether I can carry on with the program. I can redefine the meaning of pain. The old pain meant failure, weakness, debility, laziness, danger and maybe death. The old pain said "stop!" The new pain means a little arthritis low on the inside but so what; it means muscles building fast and having a nasty twitch when they do; it means effort, growth, renewal, perseverance, accomplishment, fatigue, work, power. The pain doesn't last, how bad can it be? As always, the language saves me. Pain is just my brain's opinion of my body.

One night in November, though, I lay awake and feeling the knee sore for no reason, feeling old and pathetic for wanting the world of the locker room, for having a crush on a golden young man who wasn't even born on the coast of Sweden when I graduated from high school in Vancouver, I said the word "despair" aloud to Tom's sleeping back, to express what I felt. "Despair," I whispered.

"Dat's what you use when you get da flat," he mumbled.

LILY AND I ARE BACK for the November 22nd game against Toronto. We arrive at the hotel at two and watch the Heritage Classic on TV. Our room is on the ground floor: twelve-foot ceilings and wide-planked fir floors under thick lamination. They are the original floors and the grain is tight, though the wood has shrunk in the hundred years since it was nailed down. A dark wood sleigh bed, oak armoire. I always look better in heritage mirrors. Satin duvet, cotton sheets. We stretch on the bed and eat fancy city pizza (artichokes). Fifty-eight thousand people are sitting in -20 weather to watch Wayne Gretzky, Guy Lafleur et al play two fifteen-minute halves (the mythic number three foregone): Oilers versus Habs, nostalgia and national pride. There has never been an event like this and it is so right in tone, visuals and sentiment. Players and commentators link this outdoor event to the way these men learned to play. Gretzky orates about the way Junior hockey now takes away imagination. When kids play unstructured hockey, they use creativity and learn the game the way he did. When they are told where to position themselves, whom to check, how and when to shoot and what patterns to use to set up plays, a kid doesn't learn what he can do, for himself and by himself. Imagination is shut down.

The fans are far from the rink – constructed especially at Commonwealth Stadium in Edmonton: a backyard rink 200 feet long, eighty-five feet wide, several kilometres of piping to circulate calcium chloride to keep the ice frozen, 1400 gallons of the coolant, sixty-five truckloads of sand, 120 layers of misted water laid over forty-two hours – and the rink is a private zone, an imaginative space where men can be themselves, support each other. The camera's POV is close to the ice and that's beautiful, too. The light – blue and clear sky – is stunning on the players' faces. It's like we've been watching them in movie theatres and now they're live. Paul Coffey as himself. Russ Courtnall, forgetting everything – his sad father, his concussed career – gets great shots away, a better version of the player he was because he's here. When Marty McSorley scores, it's a poignant moment that says, *It's okay now, you're with us. With us, you can score. With us, there's no stick to Brashear's head, no trial, no shunning.* In the second half, Gretzky removes his toque. His hair is frozen.

In the second game, a regular season one between Edmonton and Montreal, José Théodore has griped about conditions but he looks great, a bleu-blanc-rouge toque low on his head. Zednik scores two goals for the Habs and is delighted: "Some day I will tell my kids I scored two goals in that game!" He is Slovakian, but so Canadian. His pink face, the smile that won't stop. Like McSorley: one moment you're a goon who aims to injure, the worst thing about the game. Then presto: you're a hero who scores lovely goals and loves that even more. A complete player, they call you.

And then through the streets of downtown Vancouver, Lily in her Jovo skin, to our own game. Watching the warm-up, behind the glass at the Canucks end, I'm breathless at how close they are, how fast and big and human. Bert is grinning and loose. He picks up a practice puck in his big glove and flips it over the glass, aiming for a woman about my age sitting with her sleek teenaged daughter. The woman catches the puck and, delighted and giggly, shoves it like a dirty joke into her black handbag. Bert catches her eye and sends a small nod her way. The woman's tougher than me; her hair colour is brassier; she's in a pricey black leather fitted jacket; she's sitting in a seat that doesn't belong to her. Bert is amused and aroused by his game and surprises buddy Brad May with a pass he must take and shoot at Cloutier. May skates over to Bert, and they have a whispered laugh. It seems to be about the woman with the puck in her purse, but I must be jealous. How did he know she was there? What am I? Plywood? I wish to flirt, too, but can't. I want to be noticed, too, but am under the radar. Or is puck chick a joke shared by two hot young assholes who know they have the power to excite and arouse, to tease a woman they don't want or need? The joke is that a woman like her will never have men like them. They've thrown her a shitty little bone, out of nostalgia for her sexuality. It's the heritage classic, but not the real game.

I must be eighty in hockey years. Bring on da funk.

CHAPTER ONE

IN THE FIELDS AND
IN THE STREETS

There are in a sense two dimensions of Time abruptly operant: while the standing boxer is in time, the fallen boxer is out of time. Counted out, he is counted "dead" – in symbolic mimicry of the sport's ancient tradition in which he would very likely be dead.
　　　　　　　　　　– Joyce Carol Oates, *On Boxing*

Serious sport has nothing to do with fair play. It is bound up with hatred, jealousy, boastfulness, disregard of all rules and sadistic pleasure in witnessing violence: in other words it is war minus the shooting.
　　　　　　　　　　– George Orwell, "The Sporting Spirit"

Sport is a liberal form of war stripped of its compulsions and malignity; a rational art and the expression of a civilized instinct.
　　　　　　　　　　– George Santayana, *Reason in Society*

Barnacled to the southeast curve of Vancouver Island, Victoria was once the busiest seaport north of San Francisco: shipyards, sawmills, fishing and sealing fleets. A century of de-industrialization has left the working waterfront crumbling and the city a web of rusting steel rails. For those who live and work here now – civil servants, pensioners, poets, the Salishan First Nations peoples – these and other vestiges of British colonialism, such as afternoon tea at the Empress Hotel, which still occurs daily, are echoes to outrun.

According to Statistics Canada, more than a third of Victorians engage regularly in kinetic activity – low-impact weeding to iron man triathlons. That makes us almost twice as active as residents of any other Canadian city.

Winds off the Strait of Juan de Fuca, the good rain, Douglas fir oxygen: we are braced by these stimulants. Canadians who have endured prairie drought or eastern ice storms move here for golf and primroses in January. Our climate is bizarrely Mediterranean. In colder and wetter Vancouver and Toronto, downtowners might spend an occasional lunch hour sparring with an ex-boxer in a flashy subterranean gym. Here, winter does not exist; we are pushed outside every day.

Imagine a Bruegel the Elder peasant scene with slimmer waistlines and tighter tights. And instead of his bustling Flemish town square, picture a sixty-kilometre linear park built along a rail line once used for business. The Galloping Goose Regional Trail honours a cantankerous 1920s rail car that shunted mail and passengers between Victoria and nearby Sooke. The new Goose uses that original line – minus rails – along with others, their spurs and trestles, and connects seven Greater Victoria communities (pop. 304,287) across neighbourhoods, landscapes, economies, histories.

The urban section of the Goose is asphalt: trousered cyclists commute to work; parents push strollers (standard and jog-friendly); university students and off-duty cabbies rollerblade through warehouse-stacked back streets. The trail's gentle grade is hyper with serious walkers. Seniors lean on canes and leashed terriers; a posse of high school girls – midriffs and cleavage absurdly bared to winter – struts alongside the Trans-Canada Highway. In early spring, Portuguese-Canadians fill creels with herring hooked along the Goose's Selkirk Trestle.

Head south from the city – not far – and locomotion is less manic, more rural. The flora turns lush: fir and balsam and red cedar, alder and cotton-wood, arbutus – the only broad-leafed evergreen native to Canada and found only here; cherry trees sprouted from pits spat out a rail car window. Loose dogs form packs, leave the trail, run sheep on bordering farms to barbed-wire deaths. Also, cougars. Still, when the leaves are off the maples at the back of my acreage in Metchosin, a century-old hayfield, I can see and hear horse riders (no pavement on the Goose here), power cyclists like hornets on wheels, and the swing and hustle of strutting off-duty moms.

Near here, women row hi-tech shells in waters once plied by the T'Sou-ke and Esquimalt peoples in cedar dugouts. To build strong legs and lungs and hearts, the rowers extreme-walk the Goose. I know women who learned to run on its humousy surface. The first hot flash of peri-menopause is like a starter's pistol: they run for their lives.

Metchosin is a comma at the southern tip of Vancouver Island's long line. It's a pause between the urban sprawliness of Victoria on the island's east side and its west, where weather is big and so are waves and trees. Sir James Douglas came in 1842, looking for a good spot for a trading post: "a very pretty

Place, and has a small fresh water Run near it. There is, however, no Harbor, and the Anchorage is exposed and must be insecure in Rough Weather." Douglas got more rhapsodic in 1873 when he was back to lay the foundation stone of St. Mary's Anglican. He wrote to his daughter in England: "Metchosin looked its best, the beautiful slope, the richly tinted foliage, the bright clear sky, the warm sunshine, the glassy smooth sea and the grand mountains in the distance, formed a combination of indescribable beauty. I felt an exhilaration of mind which led me to wander away through the woods towards the white cliffs bordering the seas from whence I contemplated its placid waters with delight." The foundation stones of Douglas's summer retreat can still be found near Taylor Beach where we run our dogs, cook autumn dinners, and occasionally help a shepherd friend chase bad dogs that chase his sheep down to the cobbled beach and into the Strait of Juan de Fuca. The mountains are Washington State's Olympic range. Raymond Carver wrote "Cathedral" right over there.

Metchosin holds on to rural: Hereford cattle, Dorset and Finn sheep, berry farms, a cornfield expertly cultivated by a guy, a former aristocrat, who once did time at nearby William Head Prison for trafficking pot, a Knights of Columbus garlic patch now ready for bulk sales, a log booming ground, a gravel pit, hay, organic farm stands, the Goose Trail our property backs onto, a trout pond, the horsey set and their rings and paddocks and dusted and vacuumed trails. Population skips around 5000. The beauty marks of anti-development persist here and average lots are more than two acres by bylaw. In a greedy world short on cash, we await the pressures of developers who see nature as business opportunity instead of last chance.

But there's no such thing as pastoral any more, so let's not get choked. Last night, I tried to sleep through street racers, barking dogs and barn owls hissing in the tall balsam outside my window. Our dogs fret and pant and click around the house when the wind blows through open windows and against the maples, which is most of the time. Today, I wrote at my desk in our 1920s cabin – built by the era's local shoemaker – and heard the intercom from the nearby concrete pipe plant beckoning, "André: line *three*. André: *line* three." I heard kids across the road imitating my rooster, I heard a convoy of screaming sportbikes taking on and taking down the posted speed limit, I heard sirens heading out to scrape another kid, no doubt, off a power pole, I heard ravens practising their range of imitations, horse riders' cheerful chatter on the Goose, and the municipality's brush cutter once again try to cut back the vine maples and alders and blackberries fingering onto the roads. The bored moan of the ride-on lawnmower, the ecstatic shriek of the machine shop, the hip-hop rhythms of the hay baler: these are rights of manhood in Metchosin and they make a music not enjoyed in the city, or by me always.

My favourite bit of local history. I love the way the Victoria paper covered it. On a clear and starlit February morning in 1866, the steamer *Emily Harris* left a wharf in downtown Victoria to ferry 130 excursionists – boxing fans – to a secret location near Weir's Farm in Pedder Bay (just down the road from here) for the first ever boxing match – contraband – on Vancouver Island, a contest between Joe Eden and George Baker, who were also on the boat and who "moved amongst the crowd greeting their acquaintances with a full faith in their own ultimate triumph." They anchored, and "with the assistance of some persons who were acquainted with the district," picked a secluded, level, soft piece of turf in a hollow on William's Head and erected a ring and then "a long discussion ensued with reference to the men fighting with spikes in their boots." They decided against. The plucky pugilists threw their caps into the ring just after ten A.M.

At seven minutes to eleven, the men prepared to fight and Eden stripped first: "his flesh presented a firm appearance, and the muscles of his arms and legs indicated great power." He was six feet and weighed 165 pounds. Baker was compact and well built and "although there was an unhealthy pallor on his countenance, he eyed his adversary with an air of firm determination."

Imagine the clean, cold air, the lushness of salal and evergreens, the breeze off the water and the whispers of cougar and deer, the moss under the fighters' feet.

First knockdown was in Round 1, first blood Round 2; from the 6th to the 14th, the tactics were similar: "Eden punishing his opponent's face with severity, Baker getting home some powerful drivers with his right hand." Neither boxer gained any advantage until the 40th round. Though he had taken control of the fight, in the 46th round, Eden hurt his left hand "which rendered it almost useless for the remainder of the encounter." By the 63rd both men were exhausted, and still Eden delivered terrific "right-handed stingers." Finally, in the 128th round, a powerful right-hander from Eden "knocked Baker out of time, upon which the sponge was thrown up at 7 minutes to 1 o'clock. Eden as a proof of his gameness jumped twice over the ropes with ease." One hour and fifty-two minutes.

Everybody back on the boat, let's go home. They were in Victoria by four o'clock. Imagine the bars.

IN THE FIRST round of the 2004 playoffs, I turn off the sound, shocked by the pro-Calgary gusto and anti-Vancouver skepticism. The experts are so unschooled. Since October, pundits talked of Vancouver as a so-called elite team and now they're bent on discounting them, bent on hexing the winner-vibe. Calgary is Cinderella, sure, but made up of ugly stepsisters: the hyper-consonant Krzysztof Oliwa, and Chris Simon and Denis Gauthier. The Flames have been admirable all year. Tough and mean and high speed, they finished close to Vancouver. But: come *on*. They are not evenly matched. Vancouver hasn't been giving everything. They've been holding back and conserving bodies and energy and spark. Rough and sticky play, a million penalties called. But Vancouver wins 5-3 in an excellent four-line effort.

Next game, I hate hockey.

In bullfighting the unanimous waving of handkerchiefs symbolizes the audience's respect. In Vancouver, too, the playoff white towels are stunning. Lily will keep hers forever. Vancouver goes down by two early: Jarome Iginla scores when Cloutier is interfered with; the second comes when the puck drops mysteriously from Sami Salo's sweater in front of a startled Cloutier and a horseshoe-assed Flame bats it into the net.

A nice man, my age plus, tilts his head: "Where'd we get Bergevin? How was that a call? Did you see how open Salo was?" and doesn't mind that I'm female, or that I notice more on the ice than he does. He's a rookie, having trouble twirling his towel, appalled by the price of beer, unable to take in everything on the ice or wipe the fat grin off his face. He follows the puck sliding to a stop in the corner while I watch Liberace-coiffed Kerry Fraser at centre pantomime a melodramatic hook and trip followed by a sissy dive. Smirking Fraser – "Hairdoo" the nice man now chants – loves his own dance. His arms are everywhere.

"What?"

"Same call," I tell my confused neighbour.

"Again?"

"Yup. Four on four." But there's still no room to rush. The Calgary trap slides into place and clangs shut like cell doors.

Näslund gets one back in the second as Jovo interferes with Miikka

29

Kiprusoff. They're losing, so Lily gets surly and over-reacts when playoff beer is spilled on her adolescent arm. Bye-bye mirth.

After the game, though, the faces are happy out in Vancouver's blossomy night, delighted even. We've lost but everyone had a blast, still jaunty with optimism.

Not me. Vancouver looked small and vulnerable. Newbies Geoff Sanderson and Martin Rucinsky were repeatedly wiped out along the boards; Morrison was roughed up and head-checked and man-handled. The Swedes didn't look hard. Näslund seemed to be saving his body. Only Jovo was able to wax a few guys and still play precise and smart. Vancouver can dump, chip and scramble and they did fine, but not fine enough with Prince Placid in goal stopping everything.

The nine A.M. ferry home the next morning is sunny, calm and bloated with languages and bodies. I untangle cross-stitch threads for Lily, listen to a car-alarm shriek on the upper deck. Everyone has a rattling and persistent cough. Their sleepy heads loll against the high seats and then they wake to cough and loll again.

We get home cranky by noon. Tom's in the driveway to tell me, hurry *up*, I have to meet a courier at a dumpster at a mall at one o'clock if I want my $235 – American – ticket for tomorrow's game in Calgary. My plane leaves at eight A.M. Easter Sunday, see, and the courier doesn't deliver to the boonies on a holiday weekend, but the guy figured it was important and called this morning to say he'd do a special thing and meet me in town at his drop-off.

Back in the car, right now, and I take along a dozen coop-fresh eggs and hide a ten-dollar bill inside the carton. The young courier – shiny-headed and bulked up, wraparound shades to keep out the Easter sun, his skillet-skulled pit bull upright and eyeing me from the passenger seat of his van – is huge with delight: "Fresh eggs! Wow! I knew this was important!" He shows them to his dog. "Look what we got!"

THE WAR STARTS at playoff time. Hockey builds tough athletes, but by the end of the season, their bodies have exploded: for how many rounds will this tendon hold, how many wrist shots can I snap from a crumbling elbow, how many hits in the corner before the shoulder separates – again? "Warriors," gush the hockey gurus. In 2003, then Vancouver Canucks GM and former history scholar, Brian Burke, orated on television about Lord Nelson, soldiers fighting minus an arm or an eye, battling for the honour of the platoon. He said of the ageing Trevor Linden, game seven versus the nasty St. Louis Blues, "He was a warrior. He was like Braveheart out there." In war, the rink music is no longer the pumpy, campy Queen's *We Will, We Will, Rock You.* For key faceoffs deep in the defensive zone late in a playoff game, it's irony-free heraldic trumpets, gladiator power chords, John Williams movie scores off a Hollywood battlefield.

This remix of sport and war isn't new; many sports hatched as military or paramilitary training, and the two arenas have for centuries borrowed lingo – not to mention rituals, strategies and the economic fruits of partisanship – from one another. Some date hockey's birth in Canada to 1855 when it was played by English troops stationed in Halifax and Kingston. Phil Jackson, once and future coach of the LA Lakers, used warrior principles to rally a Chicago Bulls team of stars and bad boys. "A basketball team is like a band of warriors," Jackson believed, "a secret society with rites of initiation, a strict code of honour, and a sacred quest – the drive for the championship trophy." Jackson decided to school his team on certain principles of the Lakota Sioux, whose "warriors had a deep reverence for the mysteries of life" and who didn't consider the self to be separate from the tribe. For Lakota warriors, "life was a fascinating game. They would trek across half of Montana, enduring untold hardships, for the thrill of sneaking into an enemy camp and making off with a string of ponies. It wasn't the ponies per se that mattered so much," Jackson told his Bulls, "but the experience of pulling off something difficult together as a team."

At playoff time, though, the rhetoric gets ridiculous. Broadcasters and players – who reportedly watch war films and listen to Winston Churchill to stoke for key games – take what should be a metaphor (in other words, a figurative comparison of two *un*like things to enlarge the meanings of both) and treat it like a simple comparison: a hockey player is *just like* a warrior; a team is *just like* a squadron; losing a game is *just like* losing a battle. Same stakes, same heroes. That's the first cliché of hockey that needs a good shake.

Here's the second. Right before puck drop, *Hockey Night in Canada*'s self-styled poet laureate, Ron MacLean – quoting bad Eagles' lyrics like Richard Burton doing *Hamlet* – goes wistful and chokes out Canadian hockey's season-ending über-cliché: We all dream about playing in the NHL, we all dream about playing in the Stanley Cup finals.

We do not. Ron is over-acting about a certain brand of boy raised in cold places where ice happens every year, everywhere. Do we all dream Ron's dream? Most little girls don't (Shaunavon redheads notwithstanding) and really not girls raised more rain forest than ice-covered pond. The NHL engine – media pistons pumping and spewing – is fuelled ineptly by such mythomania. It distorts our national identification with the game and lies about those who love it. And it excludes a population of fans willing to commit, to stay loyal, to spend money.

Conventional sports wisdom has it that fans are fans because they identify with players and the game because they've played it – or imagined themselves as star players out on the frozen pond come winter – in childhood. So the wisdom has it, then, that women who didn't play hockey – or men who grew up to be poets on balmy Vancouver Island or fishers in the waters off Haida Gwaii – are not the fans real men are, burly men from smelter towns in Ontario, grain farms in Saskatchewan, or pulp mills in northern Quebec. In 1972's *The Death of Hockey*, Bruce Kidd and John Macfarlane gush, "Like the ball games of the Mayan Indians of Mexico, worshipped because the arc of the kicked ball was thought to imitate the flight of the sun and moon across the heavens, hockey captures the essence of the Canadian experience in the New World. In a land so inescapably and inhospitably cold, hockey is the dance of life, an affirmation that despite the deathly chill of winter we are alive." Yikes, really? What of primroses in January?

The NHL machine ignores people like me, women who abhor the easy cliché, the hypermasculine rhetoric. Okay, they build arenas that resemble shopping malls for us. Oh, and kudos, boys, for the ridiculous girlie replica jerseys with the figure-flattering cut and raglan sleeves so we can pretend to have boobs like Shania Twain. I don't want to be Markus Näslund and I don't want to shop.

I grew up watching Habs vs. Big Bad Bruins on Saturday night, sprawled on the living room carpet while my dad colonized the recliner with a big hunk of cheddar cheese in one hand and a Labatt's Blue in the other. His heart attacks were still to come, sure, but that's how it was in Vancouver in the seventies. Dad took Jean Béliveau, daughter took Bobby Orr. The Vancouver Canucks entered the league in 1970; I was fourteen. Over the next few years my father and I went to games at the Pacific Coliseum. By that time, though, Bobby Clarke and Dave "The Hammer" Schultz were cracking faces and winning via intimidation. Throughout the league, fists fired and blood spewed. By the late seventies, for a Vancouver girl travelling inward, even Gretzky had Dave Semenko and that made The Great One less great. The game was too rough and I looked away for a long time. My dad stopped looking when the WHA paid players millions to be mediocre.

Pacifism was an easy bottle to guzzle in the seventies and so I also looked away from my father. Post Vietnam, bra-less anti-war gauze-wearers appealed more to a teenager like me than did the suits and their power and democracy and capitalism. Besides, there was that new folk music and the chords were easy to learn and Joan Baez had great hair and male musicians wanted her. Who could be lonely in that music scene: Joan had Bob, Carly had Sweet Baby James, Simon had Garfunkel, the Mamas had the Papas.

I was a smart but sad teenager. I was smart but made very dumb by grief, and so the pairing of war bad, peace good allowed me to assume that my father's participation in World War II was shameful. I remember being in that same den, maybe even watching hockey's parallel violence together, and feeling outraged that my father had gone to war, let alone killed people from the cockpit of a Lancaster bomber. If you're not part of the solution you're part of the problem, man, and that's how I saw it. It didn't help that he wouldn't speak of war, or flying, or Germany, or the prison camp he lived in for eighteen months as a twenty-four-year-old except to chuckle through the occasional anecdote: one night he'd watched a slow and sleepy German guard patrol his Stalag #1 barracks in Barth and saw the guard's unleashed Alsatian go on ahead, lap him, and attack from behind, thinking the guard an escaping Kriegie. My father loved that bit of slapstick, but the guard story was about all I heard regarding his time in a POW camp. Maybe it's a newer grief making me dumb again, but I would sacrifice Tom's dachshund, Mrs. Greta Kreigie, to be in that den in Vancouver with my father, watching *Hogan's Heroes* and listening for which parts made my father laugh.

DURING WORLD WAR II, Johnny Canuck was pictured as a caped strongman who protected Canadians from the Nazis; Canuck began as a nickname for Canadian soldiers, a term of military valour. Easter Sunday, April 11, Trevor Linden's birthday and the first 2004 playoff game played in Calgary – Flames versus Canucks. My father's been dead for twelve years. History is huge and vague when you're looking for a person in it. My resources are few. I have *A Wartime Log: A Remembrance from Home Through the Canadian Y.M.C.A.* This is my father's journal kept in West Compound, Stalag-Luft I, Barth, Pomerania, Germany, Room 9, Block 8. The hardcover is dirty beige cloth with a lovely retro red maple leaf on the cover. The binding's a mess and held with three wide pieces of retro Scotch tape. The handwriting inside is my father's. I expected to find ghostly details of his trauma, suffering, mind and heart as a young man in jail in war in Europe. I'm a schooled reader. I read for pattern, implication and ambiguity. I know that real history is small: it resides in the list of books my father read while in camp, in the flat descriptions of camp routine – the plays, the films, the showers – *The average was one hot shower per week and any amount of cold showers in the washroom. For washing hands and faces cold water was used.* But this small history relies too heavily on my imagination. I have to fill in his physical and emotional experiences. He does not divulge.

The book contains pictures drawn and painted by other men and a water-colour signed by my father, titled "Day Dreams," that depicts a young man in blue pants too short, a boy's cap, hands stuffed in his pockets, strolling in the shadow of an observation tower and high barbed wire. Above his head, a dream cloud puffs with two bathing beauties at the beach – one in a polka dotted two-piece, the other in orange, a discreet mark of penciled cleavage on both, a blonde and a redhead. Lists of household articles, rations, a menu from mess dinner Xmas, 1944 at Stalag-Luft I; the contents of an American Red Cross POW Xmas Parcel; rhymey poems; a reproduction of the Postkartes sent to my mother at home in New Westminster and to his father and mother in Victoria. At the centre are twenty pages of heavy grey paper, intended for photographs or mementos.

The book's too cheerful for the kind of history I'm looking for. It's like the POWs were given a workshop on scrapbooking by some over-schnitzelled Fräulein and told to throw in lists and data and dull details but no commentary.

Each time I read this book, I'm frustrated: most pages are blank. My father couldn't keep a better record? What was he doing with his time, that rotten kid? And I'm irked, too, that this isn't the sort of journal we expect from war literature: full of poignant and heart-wrenching moments of personal triumphs and pains, a portal into the tortured soul of a prisoner who would grow up to be my calm and funny father, the Habs fan, the tennis ace, the congenial auctioneer. I missed my chance to talk to him about this. I didn't ask the questions. The least he could do is hint about what he was feeling, seeing, wanting.

But there is magic in this book. A few days ago, I discovered an ink drawing I hadn't seen before, trapped in a section of blank pages, signed by my father: a farm in a snow-covered valley, smoke from the chimney, fenced paddocks with fresh stumps from a recent clearing. The barn is larger than the house; a coop leans next to the barn. If this was my father's other sort of daydream – a small farm in a safe valley – he never realized it, but the landscape and setting are remarkably like my own small farm in Metchosin.

And this morning, flipping awkwardly through those twenty stiff and mostly blank pages as I'd done countless times, I found a painting by "Chuck" showing a menacing Lancaster bomber – the now familiar blackness and gloom of its body – yellow bombs drop around it, searchlight cones cross the sky from below. The bomber has been hit behind the cockpit, and my father's initials are written in red on the side of the plane, below the dome of the rear gunner turret.

Pastoral and idealized bliss on one page, wartime terror – also idealized – on the next. Each image is improved by the other; my father is more complex because his book contains both.

I have friends who travel by air badly, who medicate and meditate and still panic, who do extreme Buddhism at take-off and landing, whose body odour changes and skin goes papery as they prepare for take-off, domestic or continental. Some of my favourite icons are bad flyers: Wayne Gretzky is a not-so-great one, as is his literary counterpart, Alice Munro. Tom wanted to be a pilot and took lessons: nausea.

I love to fly and thrill at take-off and landing, smile hugely to no one, sit by the window and watch the flaps and bolts and rivets on the wing, watch the angles and the incline and suspension and try to keep breathing. On that early morning plane from Victoria to Calgary, rising, in my customary seat over the wing, I deliberately thought of my dad and his own final rising in his plane the night of March 24/25 1944, from Lincolnshire to Berlin – *There was still a doubt about the weather. Frontal cloud was moving eastwards and this might not clear Berlin before the raid –* and thought my chest's fire would melt me. I went maudlin and wished we were on our way to this game together; that he was playing tennis with Lily and watching the Bruins and Habs try to regain what they had, seeing our lambs born and patting Max's Labrador head where it rests at his knees. "Oh god," I wrote in my own journal, "I might be starting to grieve, so late and long." He was born in March – the Ides of March – he was shot down in March, and he died in March, when I was thirty-seven and busy with a two-year-old and living like a Jackson Pollock painting looks.

Another pack of clues: *Royal Canadian Air Force Pilot's Flying Log Book*. At twenty years old, in December 1941, my dad was flying Tiger Moths from Edmonton; by mid-January he could write: "Certified that I fully understand petrol system, endurance data, engine lubrication and function of the auxiliary controls of the Tiger Moth aircrafts." April 1942 he was posted at Saskatoon and flew a Crane. There are many signatures from officers, and each time I see one, I get pissed off. In my father's "Summary of Flying and Assessments for Year Ending July 17, 1942," some asshole, one L.A. Harling, Squadron Leader, under "Any points in flying or airmanship which should be watched" has typed, "Does not look around enough in the air."

My father flies a Cornell at Vulcan, Alberta, and in October, 1942, gets a bone of encouragement: "An average pilot with no special instructional faults. Should make a good instructor." What's that supposed to mean? Average. And is the nice bit about teaching supposed to suggest he'd make a better teacher than a flyer? Those who can, do, those who can't, teach, is that it? No, the course was an instructor's course. Relax.

In Claresholm, Alberta, it's an Anson. And again: "An average instructor in all aspects. Should study AP129-Chap III." I hate these guys, their snippy tone. He's a kid, get real. Still, in Claresholm my father's disciplined for the time he "Landed undercarriage retracted-Night," an accident deemed caused by "Carelessness mitigated by inexperience and inefficient undercarriage warning devices." Maybe it smartened him up, this wee mishap, pushed him into better performance. August 1943, he's training at Hixon, Staffordshire and flying a Wellington. And in "A Summary of Flying and Assessments for Course commencing July 21, 1943," with a grand total of 823.45 hours of flying – night and day – he is assessed as "Above Average" with "Nil" points to be watched.

Off to training in an Oxford in Yorkshire, then a Halifax. January 1944, "Certified that F/O Jackson has completed 16 crash landing and dinghy drills and 8 parachute drills during the course of his conversion with No. 1656 Conversion Unit." His summary on January 16, 1944 as a "Heavy Bomber Pilot," again, "Above Average." January 22 he's into a Lancaster at No. 1 Lancaster Finishing School: Above Average. Then, finally – Wait. Wait. So soon? – to Lincolnshire.

The neat columns, his meticulous record-keeping end on March 26: "**Pilot, or 1st Pilot**: Self; **2nd Pilot, Pupil or Passenger**: Crew; **Duty (including Results and Remarks)**: (Berlin) Operations as Ordered.

Twenty-eight months to train my father from shiny-face neophyte in a sluggish linen-covered biplane, to a tough veteran willing and able to kill people from the complex cockpit of a matte black bomber.

It must have tortured my father when I was in my own early twenties, rambling and confused, marrying and divorcing, quitting university, playing country music in shitty bars, dating jackasses and bringing them home for Christmas dinner. But he never compared my aimlessness with the life he had; he never tried to enforce the sort of discipline he'd known on my chaos. This is the first time I've had any interest in coming so close to my father's past, to touching the cold metal of his last flight as a pilot at war. It has to do with why I've also turned back to hockey.

Revelling in the game for the past two years, pumped full of delight in sport and lust and optimism – having what's known in certain cultures as fun – I am offended, still, by hockey's rhetoric. I've learned nothing but cynicism from the "hockey players are just like warriors" schtick that the NHL and its media clingons spew at this time of the season. But there's something: maybe my father was just like a hockey player when he signed up and joined the air force, trained to do miraculous things with his body and brain. He put on a uniform, got handsome, and then played a really big game, a game like five Stanley cups at once for the Habs, a game he lost – one last rush up the gut, time winding down, stopped cold at the blue line by an impenetrable and heavily armed defence.

Hockey players are not just like my dad, but he was a lot like them.

OFF THE PLANE at ten in the morning, an unexpectedly clear and warm day in Calgary, I rent a car and drive south on the hillfree and curveless Deerfoot Trail to the Lancaster Museum in Nanton, Alberta. The gutless rattling tin can of a car – why call it Focus? – is puny in the big dirt parking lot. I know the Lancaster is in the hangar out back, but I want to go slowly. In the cluttery front rooms, there is a swastika-ed armband for a German guard given to a first officer when a prisoner at Stalag-Luft I. I admire a pale-coloured poster – *Exhibition Hockey Match Sunday 3:30* – showing men with sticks and sweaters and smiles. Over in Stalag-Luft III, Barry Davidson wrote, "There was another fellow in camp who knew Conn Smythe and I knew Don MacKay in Calgary. And we [decided to] see if they could send equipment to make up two pretty good hockey teams. We had guys there who had played with some of the top pro teams, so we had some real good hockey games. The Germans loved to watch."

It's quiet here, except for the burble of a perpetual videotape playing in the hangar. The mothball smell of conservation is comforting. The details, the lists, the stats, are available on walls, in glass cases, in pamphlets: *Strike Hard Strike Sure*. Over 10,000 Canadians died serving in Bomber Command. For every 100 aircrew in Bomber Command, fifty-one were killed on operations, nine killed in crashes in England, three were seriously injured, twelve became prisoners of war, one evaded capture, and twenty-four survived unharmed.

The odds were against my father, against me.

The pamphlet says, "With speed, ceiling and lifting power that no other aircraft could match, the Avro Lancaster was the most successful bomber used by Bomber Command during World War II. Generally flying under the cover of darkness, air gunners manned the rear and mid-upper gun turrets but the Lancaster had virtually no defensive armour." I'm the only visitor to the museum this morning and walking into the hangar and toward the plane is like taking off: a thrill. I circumnavigate it twice, touch the black metal and look up into the compartments where bombs were held. Black underneath, so sinister and yet ludicrous that such an aircraft could be hit from below at night in 1944. Many planes came back from raids intact but with the rear gunner dead, too exposed in his happy-looking bubble so far from the pilot.

Inside the plane finally, it's cold and creaking and narrow. Hard hats are required and even still, at five foot four, I bash my head on the low ceiling. If I bend forward and extend my arms, I can touch both side walls of the plane. The crew sat here, held on to dangling loops like city commuters in bullet-proof vests, close enough to touch knees, but not close enough to hear voices, too dark in here to see one another's eyes. I sit under the plexiglass mid-upper gun turret, my big green carcoat buttoned to the neck and wrapped around my knees, and look back to the rear turret.

The noise must have been staggering. Death would be cold and cramped.

I have the handwritten copy of a letter from my father to author Martin Middlebrook in response to Middlebrook's call for info for his book, *The Berlin Raids: R.A.F. Bomber Command Winter 1943-44*. Middlebrook was a Lincolnshire poultry farmer who was so moved by the military cemeteries erected on the battlefields of World War I that he wrote ten books about major turning points in the two world wars. In his May 1985 note to my father, Middlebrook writes too breezily for my taste: "I would naturally be particularly interested in a full description of your being shot down on the 24th March 1944 – known, I believe, as 'the night of the big wind'." Naturally.

My father wrote to him, but it's hardly the "full description" Middlebrook dreamed of:

> "The night of the big wind" is a good description. I heard later that many crews found themselves over the Ruhr Valley, and all those defences, on the way home.
>
> *Berlin's flak and searchlight defences.* They were both heavy and concentrated, but, as with other targets, we had to ignore them and fly through the searchlight cone on a steady bombing run.
>
> We were shot down on the March 24th trip to Berlin. As part of the Path finder Support group we arrived over the target first, and when the marker flares went down they were behind us. I decided to go around again and make another bombing run, a mistake. We were shot down east of Berlin, by what we believed to be a night fighter which maneuvered beneath us and strafed us from a top mounted gun, for the length of our Lancaster. The plane caught fire and I ordered the crew to abandon the aircraft. After determining that five of the crew had been killed in the attack, my engineer and I bailed out. The plane appeared to blow up about 1½ minutes after this. Because of the high winds we landed about 30 miles southeast of Berlin. I met up with my engineer about an hour after landing, and we commenced to walk to try to get medical help for him as he had been wounded in the legs, although not badly. Being after midnight by this time, no one would have anything to do with the "terror fliegers." We moved around for the rest of the night until a forestry official finally took us in and while he went to the nearest town on his bicycle to get police, his wife gave us breakfast. The rest is quite routine, off to a fighter base where we both received of medical help, my engineer staying in hospital. I was shipped off by truck and train to Berlin, where I was kept overnight at Templehof. By train the next day with other aircrew to Frankfurt and the interrogation centre nearby.

Middlebrook has inscribed my father's copy of the book, "For W.R. Jackson, who flew 2 raids to Berlin as a Lancaster pilot of 166 Squadron, but was shot down on the night of 24/25th March 1944." On p. 248, titled "Night of 30/31 January 1944," my father has penciled in, "First Trip," and my mother has added "Rex to Berlin." On p. 276, "Night of 24/25 March 1944," my mother's written "disaster." A few pages later, my mother has testily crossed out "Bill" and written "Rex" where Middlebrook has got my dad's name wrong and published a few lines of his letter. I'm more choked that he changed the lovely poetic, calm comma before the words "a mistake" in my father's original letter and made it, instead, a more melodramatic dash.

I have to leave the plane for awhile.

A Tiger Moth: how did a twenty-year-old learn anything in such a child's toy, let alone how to fly in war? Among the installations, one honours the women of war, nurses in particular. The nice sweater-vested man from the front desk pops his head in, smiles at me and disappears.

And then I'm back and inside the bomber and sitting, again, hands up my sleeves, at the doorway where my father would have stood to be sure his crew were dead. The cockpit is closed today for restoration and I can only stand straight up in the upper-mid turret and look into the plexiglass window and see where a pilot would have worked. I'd like to sit in that seat and see what he saw, but maybe this is best. It's such a long way back to where he would have had to check on his crew, the flak stinging his own arms and legs. A long, cold, loud and dark journey to find them gone and his plane coming apart.

This second time, my knee is stiff with the cold and I have to hold on to the stair railing to return my hard hat. A mannequin at the bottom of the stairs seriously startles me. The blue/green eyes – my father's colour. The handsome head has been turned by a clever docent to watch me deplane. The parachute he's wearing is flat, like nothing, and he's got that air force blue jacket I remember from the closet in our basement in Vancouver. He's not smiling. He looks like an athlete: fit, intense, arrogant, game face on and in charge of everything at such a young age, with so much to lose.

Hours have passed and there's a woman, now, at the front desk. She looks like a parole officer but acts like a tough and tired nurse while she rings through my Lancaster tie tack and the boxed model I've bought for Tom.

"Derek tells me your father flew a Lanc."

I give her the few details I have and she understands the sketchiness, looks hard at my face which is trying not to cry.

"Did your dad ever talk about the war?" she asks.

"Nope."

"Mine neither. None of them did."

I take the chicken sandwich I packed at home and a bottle of grapefruit juice, a few red grapes, and sit outside in the sun at a picnic table. It's a good place to think.

THE SAME NIGHT, I cab to the Saddledome. I've worn red by accident and I have a moment of ticket-scam panic when my pricey internet score won't scan at the entrance, but then I'm in and no one comes to take my seat when the game gets going. Outside, this is like Vancouver, the sun bright and warm, fans happy and optimistic in their jerseys: Fleury, Drury, ghosts of squads past. Inside, though, things are different. The arena is old and a not so slick return to the frontier times of hockey. Everything's too small. The seats are hard and close, and there are no roll bars to keep us in our seats. It's a ride at a portable carnival, set up on a hot August day to break some hearts, impregnate some teenagers, and leave a certain stickiness across the landscape. At GM Place, I'd be in a comfy seat next to a Harry Potter six-year-old boy in glasses, the one who shares a birthday with his fallen hero Todd Bertuzzi, and Harry would be licking a strawberry yogurt cone with his tidy dad. Here, I squeeze into the uproar of the Calgary Saddledome, into a hard seat at one end of the rink, high behind the net, Lancaster tie tack poked into my coat collar, surrounded by aggressive and drunken lads in their uniform of red, who shout racist taunts at the row of Indo-Canadian boys who also came from Vancouver to cheer their team, to watch rich wonderboys play a fast game and be called warriors.

PERHAPS IT SOUNDS as if I'm done with the game, that it's too violent again, that things happened – bad hockey things – over two years that have sent me into a reverie of hero-worship for my dear departed father and will cause me to belittle the game and its knuckleheaded, ego-burdened players. Not so. I should be clear. A week after Todd Bertuzzi lost it, lost everything and the world grimaced out loud, a lovely fibre specialist who keeps a flock of Icelandic sheep down the road ran into Tom at a fleece-throwing seminar and asked about me.

"She's away a lot, working on the hockey thing."

"Hockey?!"

"Right."

"I *have* to talk to her. I have to talk to her about this whole business." I like this woman, and I'd heard her outrage before: the evil public school system, she believes, handcuffs kids into rows and makes them think as one; border collies don't herd sheep, they terrorize them. It's hard not to appreciate those passionate about good. She's not saying let's increase the wolf cull, or let's ban safe injection sites. She's compassionate. She wants things to be good and fair and pleasant and she punctuates her sentences for effect. "Tell her: we should talk. About: *hockey*."

"She likes hockey," Tom warned.

"Oh but not this hockey."

"She doesn't mind the violence. She's pretty pissed at the media right now, but I don't think she's mad at hockey."

I wasn't; I'm not. I was a pacifist at sixteen, but I've outgrown the privilege of ideology since then. I adore the game again, but I want it to adore me back, to prove it can handle a woman like me. For two years, I've been watching hockey watch itself, and watching myself watch hockey and others watching it, and others watching me watch it. Despite the game's back and forth, the win or lose, the simple lines and enclosed space of the rink, the ugly violence bad/pretty goals good, it is not a simple game.

Bardic Ron MacLean may be partly right: men want to inhabit hockey players, to be them, and to experience the world on metaphorical skates, flying fast and smooth while crowds go nuts. What do women see when they look at hockey players? And what do they see now that they didn't see in other eras? My fibre friend might say professional hockey expresses a macho world – built on aggression, intimidation, and win-at-all-costs, obsessed with stats and records, reliant on an idealized masculinity that likens players to warriors, one that doesn't want women anywhere near. Why, then, do women watch and cheer?

Look at old photos of games at the Montreal Forum and check out who's in the crowd. Women have always been expert and knowledgeable fans, schooled in the game's strategies and details. Though the idea seems ridiculous and radical and even counter-cultural, I want to look at the game through a woman's eyes and heart without apologizing for not skating fast and hard on an outdoor rink growing up. I want to ask questions about what hockey does to women like me. Literary journalist, Lawrence Scanlan, in *Grace Under Fire: The State of Our Sweet and Savage Game*, says, "Creative writers don't necessarily have *the* answers, but more often than not they have *interesting* answers." (He's not including Mordecai Richler, we hope, who wrote, "Gretzky, his immense skills undeniable, has to be one of the most boring men I ever met, inclined to talk about himself in the third person.") If one of the questions is: what would a woman get from a sport like hockey, my answer would go on for years. But it would start out this way: through sport – and a fully inhabited body – we can recover from loss: of family, of youth, of self.

Writer David Adams Richards, in trying to explain how hockey "is more than a game," has written that it is "the non-intellectual impulse for life." He doesn't speak for me. Maybe it is the ultimate integration of body and brain, impulsive *and* intellectual. Doug Beardsley explained it this way: "The randomness or creative disorder of a hockey game is one of its greatest attractions. Almost nothing is predictable, anything can happen. The game appeals to the more irrational side of our behaviour."

Vancouver won the playoff game in Calgary that night, 2-1. I watched Brad May trip and his face hit the goalpost below me, the blood and mess. I saw him writhe on the ice and saw him uncharacteristically traumatized. Flame Rhett Warrener – he who did the tripping – broke a playoff code by standing nearby and waiting for May to be okay. May had said after the morning skate, "There isn't a player on that team who can push me around." Maybe not. He gave the puck away early in the second for Calgary's goal. Brian Burke would later say, sure, Brad's face is a mess (twelve stitches) but "You should've seen the goalpost!" Hardy-har.

Also, Cloutier. The rink is so hot I have to take off my coat and the sweater I wore thinking these old rinks must freeze. Jason Hartley, Director of Engineering at GM Place told me about ice last year: "The guys are getting bigger. The whole sport has evolved and the equipment has become a lot more sophisticated than it was in the days of Bobby Orr. Some players have the trainers put a very aggressive radius into their skate blades which in effect hollows out the middle of the bottom edge of the blade. The skate blade acts as two razor sharp knife edges, as opposed to the old smooth blade I skated on as a kid. Strap this skate on a guy weighing 240 pounds and let him rip it up and, oh yeah, he can wreak havoc on the ice conditions." At every rink, engineers have to ensure that the ice is as hard and fast as it can be before, Hartley says, "it hits a critical threshold of becoming too cold and brittle, which is when it starts to break away in chips. This occurs over a range of half a degree. Add a building loaded with 20,000 people all releasing heat at a rate dependent upon their level of interest in the game and you have a variable climate that needs to be controlled at optimum conditions for ice performance."

There are 20,000 people here, too, and huge furnaces in the ceiling that blast fire and incredible heat every time something good happens, like when the game starts. I'm hot. I'm thirsty. The ice must be total shit late in the first period of a goalless game. Cloutier comes out of his crease to handle a shot by Oleg Saprykin, his skate catches a groove. He tries to coast back into the crease but buckles, falls, and that's it. Johan Hedberg finishes the game – right down to the *Braveheart* faceoff war music in his zone with seconds to play in his one-goal game – and takes out Craig Conroy's face with his goalie stick, too.

The sports news back in my hotel room predicts: knee ligaments, it's the knee, oh no, not the knee. Undisclosed lower body injury. One crack reporter gets the scoop. This just in, "Cloutier was seen leaving the rink on crutches. The injury-prone goalie has been hampered by a knee injury before." But will he be okay to play tomorrow night?

My plane the next day won't leave until three, but I like the brightness of the Calgary Airport and go out early to read, surrounded by planes at rest, planes departing, arriving. At noon, I have a smart-coffee and a *Globe and Mail*, and I'm reading about Kathleen Kenna, the forty-eight-year-old *Toronto Star* reporter wounded by a grenade tossed into her jeep. It landed under her seat and blew up in March 2002 in Afghanistan. She is unconscious inside the transport plane that could take her to hospital, has lost almost two-thirds of her blood, and the plane's stuck in the sand on an airstrip with two hundred Taliban soldiers a kilometre away at the other end of the runway: "Major Wright could see springs from the jeep's seat, straw matting, shrapnel, glass and metal embedded deep in her muscles and torn flesh. He could see her right hip bone and exposed tendons, muscles and other bones." Her husband sits nearby. There is much more to the story: about prayer, the end of Kenna's heartbeat and her revival, the U.S. Chinook helicopters coming to help, bearing her stretcher through ankle-deep sand at 7000 feet above sea level with land mines, they found out later, planted everywhere either side of the runway. The story is long and it's too much for me. I'm glad no one looks at people in airports, because my face is stupid with tears and my hands are shaking like a soap opera. It's as though the description I need of my father's last flight – details and anguish – have been provided for me in this account of a woman my age, a reporter, trying to go on living and working in war.

"Ya, he's here at the airport. He's right over there. Ya. He has a cast on his ankle. No: ankle." The voice is big and bright and one of the Indo-Canadian dudes from my section last night relays the latest news through the wee cellphone snuggled in his huge hand to a buddy back in Vancouver.

He's right. There's Dan Cloutier, wearing the usual sweet smile and congeniality and a swanky blue and red track suit, his black hair glossy, chatting and laughing with a couple of oldtimers. He's lugging the foot cast – clearly an ankle injury – and sitting twenty feet away, his chaperone – a ringer for the courier guy who delivered my ticket – reads *The Atlantic* several seats over. Dan's got a fat hardcover, an athlete biography, but he doesn't get to read it: he has his picture taken with kids ("Mind if I stay seated?" he says with a grin); he's pleasant to the asshole who asks about the injury while Dan's on the phone; he's hunky with the deep brown eye contact to the teenage girl who asks him to sign her math textbook; he rolls up the rim to win and gets up to put the empty cup in the appropriate bin. His heart must be broken. He's wearing only one hi-tech shiny shoe; on the right is the ankle walking cast and his toes are showing.

I fold the paper into my backpack and settle into my coffee. A fiction writer takes notes like these, alert to detail and expression and dialogue. A real journalist would be over there in a flash, notebook out, chummy handshake pumping. But what to ask: How does it feel? What happened out there? What now? I already know the answers and don't wish to ask him to relive the trauma. Hockey players, says Brendan Shanahan, have traditionally been conservative when it comes to talking about the game. But maybe their reticence is more like the soldier's reluctance to relive battles lost, the indignities, the sad and wasteful endings. To ask my father to talk about his time in Barth would have been selfish; to ask Cloutier how it feels to be done for the season would be rude. He's a public man in a public place enduring a gut-shredding private emotion. Why intrude? A real journalist would know the answer and get to work.

Have I compared one handsome and bewildered walking wounded goalie – the weight of the team on his shoulders – to the downed fighter pilot?

FOR GAME 5, Ron MacLean and Kelly Hrudey are a couple of Alberta boys, know-it-alls delighted by Calgary's success, beseeching on behalf of such deserving fans. But they forget Vancouver's fans, as if we moneyed urbanites, we roller-blading, protein bingers with the great haircuts don't deserve to be happy and proud.

Jovo's getting to me. His boyishness, his laughter and black Lab-ness and now his determination: "We will adjust," he says, suddenly a leader, an officer. Näslund we've seen tormented, but Jovo I don't want to see saddened by his own inadequacies. I want faces bright again.

Helium-filled and fat-lipped Craig Conroy says the Flames are like soldiers, and they win and lose as a team. In another series, CBC's Glenn Healy tries to say Detroit are like soldiers: in WWI, in 1940, they didn't know how to fight and in 1945 they did. Huh? The analogy – even the history and its logic – is fucked. Even the war metaphors have gone goofy and Calgary wins 2-1.

Game 6. First shift is awesome technically and Vancouver is playing their own gorgeous game. Also clear is that Brad May wants to score. His play is urgent and just this side of manic and he does score, in the second, and too suddenly it's 4-0 Vancouver with nowhere to go.

The Calgary goals seem like accidents, but there are no accidents in playoff hockey. One goes in off a high stick, the next gets to the net via a hand pass, the next two are ugly deflections. Each finds Alex Auld's five-hole and so appears strategic. Brad May's cut has opened up again.

Kiprusoff tilts his mask back from his broad and smooth face. He looks like a calm, huge, wide-eyed seal.

The Dalai Lama's in town and speaks of the playoffs: "Winning is all right, but more is learned from losing." Duh.

Jovo takes a stick over the top of his head and can't rise. At the bench he's trying to get the top of his skull to pop back out of his face, out of his cheekbones. No call. And MacLean finds this funny, claiming Jovo is known for overacting. What news of the stick to the head of a star player?

In overtime Hrudey and MacLean pick Sanderson and Mike Keane to score, but they're idiots: Crawford's shortened the bench and neither player's taking shifts. I pick Morrison, the only one who could possibly do it. And he does and falls to his knees and lets out his howler monkey whoop.

The broadcasters – a coupla numbskulls – sound like rotten parents, nagging and hectoring the child – Vancouver – not living up to potential, not scoring As and scholarships, and over-praising the child who shows determination – Calgary – fawning over the one who learned to tie his shoes against the odds. Former goalie Greg Millen is a know-it-all parent with the keys to the car, the allowance to withhold, the love is full of conditions.

I feel myself going more private, less public, alone like adolescence inside my head, pretending boyfriends and optimism and big changes for the better. It's too soon to end this series. Game 7 will come, and I will write about what it brings, but the thrill of Game 6 deserves to last, to behave like its own ultimate moment.

FANS LIKE ME don't watch hockey, we read it. The hockey nexus – the league, owners, teams, players, media and advertisers – under-reads hockey and overlooks those parts of the game women respond to, like scruffish players in sharp suits saying hi to Mom back home in Cranbrook. It's possible to ignore winning versus losing. What matters is the narrative of a team's journey, players as characters – complex, flawed, heroic, unpredictable – and the game is more when we can identify with players' values or at least understand their motivations. I'm pushed away by much of hockey's hype. I don't rise to the rhetoric of militarism. I don't need the words of Winston Churchill or the soundtrack from *Braveheart* to get charged for a playoff game; I don't need to imagine hockey players as war heroes in order to cheer. I want the game to be different from other arenas of aggression and conquest. It *is* different.

Vancouver in 2003 was a great place to come back to hockey, where players gradually became the tragically flawed definitions of complex, heroic, unpredictable. And every night the narrative grew more surprising and exhilarating. It was also a time and place to come back to parts of myself I'd looked away from, starting back when I thought my father was a killer and sporting events had become, in George Orwell's terms, "orgies of hatred."

CHAPTER TWO

BORN AGAIN

The goal of life is not to feel nothing.
— Germaine Greer, *The Change*

*He had noticed how many women were among the spectators, and for just
a moment he thought that perhaps this was why — that here actual male
blood could flow, not from the crude impact of a heavier fist but from the
rapid and delicate stroke of weapons, which like the European rapier or
the Frontier pistol, reduced mere size and brawn to its proper perspective
to the passion and the will. But only for a moment because he, the innocent, didn't like that idea either. It was the excitement of speed and grace,
with the puck for catalyst, to give it reason, meaning.*
— William Faulkner, "An Innocent at Rinkside," 1955

Athletes aren't born; they are built by conditions that dare the heart to
ossify. Professional basketball has crack-addict mothers and convict
fathers (when there are fathers) and players who grew up on morbid streets
with grannies and coaches subbed-in for parents. Hockey's families may be
more traditional, the social landscape gentler (I want to argue against myself here and call Jordin Tootoo and Jarome Iginla and Brian "Spinner"
Spencer and Jonathan Cheechoo as evidence), but the ranks that Canadian
hockey players must climb through — from post-toddler to pre-teen to
draft-man — challenge even the most gifted and muscled. How many times
a day did college-smart small boys like Brendan Morrison or Martin St.
Louis hear — implied or expressed — that they'd never be who they wanted
to be? Imagine saying that, even once, to the average adolescent. And,
okay, imagine being Spencer growing (screwed) up in Fort St. James (he
once said "Hockey is a reckless abandon game. You've got to be aware of
360 degrees at all times. Only a fighter pilot in the sky has more dimensions to worry about." *Does not look around enough in the air . . .*). And
Tootoo in Nunavut: the violence, the intoxicants, the pressure and

depression, the ice deep on top of everything. Iginla's mom in Alberta: single.

My mother met my skinny father at the train station, tanned and gorgeous in her white sharkskin suit, once the Russians had freed him and he'd arrived back from Europe in 1945. Their hands' first touch. The look into each other's eyes. His uniform. They married soon after and soon after that settled in Vancouver.

My father was thirty-five when I was born and they already had two other daughters, ages six and eight. In Vancouver, he was an auctioneer for Maynard and Sons, and we moved into a neighbourhood that boasted good schools and lovely homes and neighbours who were old and young, artists and doctors, politicians and lumber barons. Maple trees, laurel hedges, rhododendrons. A springer spaniel and a big yard with fruit trees and a back lane, BC Lions games at the stadium and my crush on Willie Fleming. I spent Saturdays with my father downtown, polishing silver for the auction, or vacuuming Oriental rugs, or deciding which Royal Doulton dog figurine I wanted for my room, on my own among beautiful objects that people valued. My father led me to fine art as daily life.

If the influence of place can be measured in surviving details after forty years, then Maynard's was my primary influence. It was a huge warehouse with many rooms – or time has made it huge and me less small – and I know where the best places are, up and down, back and front: where I plugged in the radio to hear The Monkees on 1410 CFUN and where to find the key to the pop machine to get a stubby bottle of Coke if my dad said yes; where the most important paintings hung, the Emily Carr and Group of Seven; how the huge silk turquoise Indian carpets that lined the walls were dangled from far above. I can smell the rot in the green bathroom behind the office, the camphor of the black teak chests shipped from China, the smoke on the brocades and velvets from the Chelsea Shop's fire sale.

I was seven or eight when my sister, the middle one, was diagnosed with Hodgkin's disease as a teenager, and the silences fell. In the early sixties, treatments and care for cancer were few. For such an old disease, the medicine was new and there was a pervasive fear that cancer – its symptoms and bad luck and aftermath – might be catching. My parents didn't speak about their ordeal. Cobalt, periwinkle: these words came into my childhood as possible solutions to my sister's doom. My mother began her idealization of the medical profession. My sister's vomit burned a hole in the bottom of the plastic wash basin she used in the room next to mine after chemotherapy. I only know a constructed mythology: doctors believed my sister could live only two years and yet kept her alive for a miraculous and tortured seven. She died a month before her twenty-first birthday.

On an autumn afternoon in 1968 – I'm twelve and my sister's eighteen – my father doesn't come home from work. It's just after Remembrance Day, and my mother gets a phone call from him to say he'll be home soon. He doesn't come home. Someone – I am twelve and details seem useless – finds a suicide note in his Pontiac Parisienne under the Burrard Street bridge. His wallet is in the water. The lyrics to a couple of songs – *If it takes forever, I will wait for you* – are written out in my dad's handwriting and left on the front seat.

Out of character. My father was not complicated or melodramatic. I remember him expressing anger to me only twice in my life. Though he was a fine athlete – tennis champ and golf natural and one of three Jackson basketball brothers on Vancouver Island – he was not manly. His joke was that he had the right tools to be a handyman, but he never bothered to get the tools. He was a gentleman, but also sixties sexist: he expressed appreciation for Peggy Lee's ankles and only when I was in my thirties did I catch on that "ankle" was probably a euphemism for a more cleavaged body part, he was that subtle. He resembled Perry Como in his smooth singing and cardigan sweaters. *Would you like to swing on a star*, he'd croon expertly and his eyes, like Perry's, would twinkle. He loved to laugh. He loved the sports news at eleven o'clock. He hated crass and rude and foul. He loved lunch hour cribbage with his pals over a glass of beer at the Vancouver Lawn Tennis Club and I can see him there: neck tie loosened and suit jacket swept over the back of his chair, white hair high and wavy and missing the Brylcream of past decades, hanging out and swapping puns with sporty types, young taut women in flippy tennis skirts scooting past. I have the perfect crib hand he drew and my mother framed from January 23, 1962. He liked watching sports on television with me, sometimes all day Sunday.

For these and other reasons, my mother didn't buy for a minute that he'd killed himself: work pressures, too much stress, a bad deal for a corrupt client, pressure from the boss, these were the culprits, she theorized, and he was running away. She remembered a trip to Sparwood, BC to appraise logging equipment and a crane that hit his head and knocked him to the ground. She remembered the scar over his eye from the night his plane was shot down. She wondered about head injuries. Then my mother got angry and the world searched for my father. Over the next months, the phone might ring – I picked it up once – and there would be groaning on the other end, an anguished groan. My grandmother in New Westminster would get the same call the same night. The police put a tracer on our line, a howler, they called it. I don't remember how it worked, but it felt like we were on television.

By whatever logic, I've always considered this to be a story that belongs to my parents. I've resisted asking questions and opening wounds; maybe my mother designed it that way and there are details to hide. Call me a shitty journalist, but I think those details belong to my parents, as my father's time in Barth belongs to him. I have bits of truths and bits of drama, handwriting. I'll never have the whole story of my father's times away – either one – and so I reconstruct.

Early in January that year, I turned thirteen and an unsigned birthday card came in the mail. At that time, I felt alone. The world was full of drama and none of it was about me. My sister was ill, my father was gone, my mother was distraught and tense: I wanted attention and thought that if something bad would happen to me, they'd notice. With a teenager now, I know where such narcissism comes from and why.

We had snow and ice that year in Vancouver. After school one cold and white afternoon, I ran in the streets with boys throwing snowballs and fell and slid into the curb with my right knee. My friends knew it was bad – I couldn't walk and I was known as an athlete, not a griper. They fetched the vice-principal who drove me home in his lush sedan. My mother lay on the gold velvet loveseat in the living room, resting, I realize these days, from the hormones and stupid fatigue of a woman's mid-forties: "What have you done now?" she asked. What she must have meant was, "What have you – my family who I have to care for but I'm too tired – done now?"

Cracked kneecap: it swelled huge and within a couple of hours I couldn't stand and spent the night alone in the den on the couch. The next morning, my mother phoned a friend with a station wagon to take me to the doctor. Then a specialist. Then into hospital, the knee was drained, set, and a plaster cast from the top of my thigh to my ankle that would waste my quadriceps muscle while the other leg continued a growth spurt. That night, my sick sister and her friends sneaked into the ward with daffodils and a chocolate milkshake and sat beside my bed making jokes. My mother had sent them after she'd received another mystery call – this time it was my father saying he'd be home right after work, see you soon. My mother was fed up. She told my father she couldn't talk because I'd broken my leg. She lost it, my wily mother, chewed him out and hung up.

I was home the next day, or a couple of days later. From the dining room window, my sister saw my father drive by the house in an unfamiliar car. I was told to stay away from the window so he might think I was bed-ridden. The strategy, apparently, worked, although the story didn't get simpler. A few days later, a hotel manager in Nanaimo on Vancouver Island called a doctor to treat a guest suffering from a bad flu. The doctor recognized my father. He was suffering from amnesia, had dyed his hair back to his boyhood black and secured a new name and driver's license. "Drowned Man Found Alive!" the morning paper said. He stayed in the psychiatric unit at the hospital at the University of British Columbia for awhile and then he was home with us.

I WAITED TWENTY YEARS to go back into that story. I was studying James Joyce at university, *Ulysses*, and writing short stories with Jack Hodgins, who as a master teacher had convinced us to write about what matters, what mystifies us, what needs telling and sorting out. The search for the father, mythomania, the daughter who left the home of Molly and Leopold Bloom: these sparked me and I spent days in the basement of the library, trying to find my father in archived newspapers. I had suffered my own breakdown in my early twenties – there was a knee surgery to keep the now slipping cap on track, a stupid short marriage, my own time in a psychiatric unit, inept rehab for the knee, a lovely long screw to hold tendon to bone. Drinking through my twenties. Now, sober in my thirties and back to school, information was missing from my memory bank. Certain dates were gone. What year did my father leave? There had been lots about it in the newspapers, but did both dailies run the stories, or did only the morning paper carry such scandal?

As naïve wanderers on epic journeys do, I discovered the unexpected key to an old puzzle. The papers of the late sixties printed not only reports and articles about the conflict in Vietnam, but also staggering images of violence, pain, and brutality, of wrecked soldiers, their faces plain with grief and terror, their bodies shredded. It was the week before Remembrance Day, 1968, and the papers were making the most of the heightened emotion. My father saw this when he came home from work each evening, poured his beer, got his cheddar cheese, and settled into the big brown recliner in the den with the newspaper and his sports scores. And then – I scrolled the pages on the dark little screen and finally found the stories about my dad – his brain broke. It must have been a version, twenty years after his own war had released him, of post-traumatic stress.

I grew up believing, as a teenager should, that my broken knee had cured him and released him from prison, like the Russians.

IN APRIL 2004, after the Canucks had won the first playoff game against Calgary, *Vancouver Sun* columnist Shelley Fralic looked forward to baseball season. "I don't do hockey," she bragged, "Don't get hockey . . . I actually don't like hockey." Fair enough: I don't get why the newspaper's travel section's so big in such a temperate city. I don't do travel, don't know why people read about it instead of doing it; I actually don't like travel writing. But Fralic has a theory about why she never warmed to the game growing up in 1950s Vancouver: "I am not from a place of white weather." She goes on. "I was born and raised right here, the only place in our country where snow is rare, where ice is even rarer, but for the odd gin and tonic, and where there are no little frozen backyard ponds in winter that fathers can smooth over so little skates don't catch on the bumps." She believes fans in Vancouver landed here from elsewhere and brought their "blind devotions" along.

Sure, it was hard to get passionate about the Canucks for the first twenty years, but that was a team problem, a skill problem, not an ideological one. It's the game Fralic objects to, and she believes others like her – "girls mostly" – can't get worked up. "It's just such a cold game, played in cold arenas, on cold surfaces, and by players bundled up against cold, hard contact in layer upon layer of insulation, to the point of lost recognition." At playoff time she looks forward to her boys of summer, to bratwurst and beer, A-Rod's smile and the back of Derek Jeter's neck browning in the sun. I, too, look forward to Ichiro's stretches – a photo of his yogic sleeve-tug/bat-point salute to the pitcher graces my desk – but I don't buy her logic. Her resistance to hockey probably has more to do with pace: for some, hockey is too fast. William Faulkner, in 1955 and fresh off his Nobel-Prize-winning season, saw his first game this way for *Sports Illustrated*: "the figure-darted glare of ice, the concentric tiers rising . . . upward into the pall of tobacco smoke trapped by the roof – the roof which stopped and trapped all that intent and tense watching, and concentrated it downward upon the glare of ice frantic and frenetic with motion; until the by-product of the speed and the motion – their violence – had no chance to exhaust itself upward into space and so leave on the ice only the swift glittering changing pattern." That ain't Safeco field, nosirree.

As for Fralic's contention that "girls" don't like the game, I'm not sure what gender proves about anything, let alone a preference for languor over speed. At first, Faulkner thought women were the whole point of the game, he saw so many there. Did Fralic and I inhabit the same city?

Watching fast hockey with a teenaged daughter is a good way to heal a muddled brain. My father's Habs (he was born on Vancouver Island), led by gentleman Jean Béliveau, and my Bruins, led by the wonky-kneed Bobby Orr, were exciting to watch. In the 1969-70 season, during my father's recovery, four years into the league, Orr won the scoring title – 120 points – he won the Hart Trophy, the Conn Smythe, and his team won the Stanley Cup. He scored the winning goal in overtime. My father and I watched that game, in May 1970, thirteen months before my sister's death. She would spend her nineteenth summer in Paris at the Sorbonne and die in St. Paul's hospital in Vancouver – pneumonia – the following June, after Béliveau and the Canadiens beat the Bruins in seven games. But the world of my father and me in the den in 1970, that world was still capable of ice and sports and naughty long-haired heroes like Derek Sanderson and Orr. Just before the Cup-winning goal Orr scored in overtime – the trick and planned pass from Sanderson – I said to my father, "This is it," and the puck came around and found Orr.

The next year – spring 1971 – my father – still recovering from amnesia, from his time missing – stressed to me that Béliveau was the sort of player – the sort of man – we should admire. A handsome gentleman, no naughty elbows, the home game sweater, the *bleu-blanc-rouge*, a little grey at the temples of his shot. Béliveau's last season and that year my father fell for Ken Dryden, too, his attitude, how he knew everything, could stop anything. The McGill law degree, the clean face, the wiseman posture: chin on glove on stick. A tender. I took the Bruins, I took Orr and the black shirts and Sanderson's urges. My father in the big chair, feet up, rubbing the shrapnel starting to surface in his forearm, the game helping him back to the present. Me on the loveseat with my long legs crossed, a springer spaniel's head at my knee. My sister upstairs purging chemo. The Canadiens took the Cup.

SALT LAKE CITY, February 2002. I was nearing the halfway mark, as they say in sports, of my twentieth semester of teaching. A victim of a self-imposed rat race, my days conformed: drive forty minutes into the city, teach, read, mark, drive, write, read, mark, sleep. No exercise, no recreation. My back was wrecked – ribs popped if I pulled buttercups in the garden; sacrum locked with the legacy of late-life childbirth; left shoulder rode high and tight from constant worry. My neck slipped out of alignment if I slept an extra half hour Saturday morning. Headaches. My right knee could barely support my weight, the quadriceps muscle long since atrophied, an ugly pothole left behind. That leg was shorter than the other, and my back endured several twists where my body tried to cope with the structural consequences of asymmetry. I looked like a Picasso – cubist and mixed up – but not avant-garde. Sometimes the pain, or the worry of that – made me cry like a lonely crone. Wait: I was a lonely crone.

Television abducts children to service a capitalist and filthy dirty culture. This is its only purpose. In February 2002, the lonely crone hadn't watched for six years, except for Gulf War coverage in 1991, days one through three of a protracted childbirth. I didn't miss television. I hadn't watched hockey since the seventies, when my father and I still got a charge from each other.

I don't remember why I watched that first game, but in 2002 it was Canada vs. Sweden at the Olympics – a humiliating 5-2 loss for Canada, bye-bye goat-horned Curtis Joseph for the tourny – and there were Markus Näslund and Ed Jovanovski skating miles on big ice in their bright jerseys, their sticks busy. These were Vancouver Canucks? No one seemed angry, no one got their teeth punched out. Everybody's handsome and super-skilled. I watched all the televised Olympic games. Near the end of the tournament, Canada vs. Belarus (never heard of it), Tom and Lily and I rode the train up island to Qualicum Beach. We bought sticky Chinese food and watched games from comfy seaside beds and kept an eye on Lily out the sliding glass door: on the beach, she is more Pacific ocean than child of the hyped-up nineties.

I fell for the Slovaks, too – Ziggy Palffy's quick everything and Marian Hossa's mighty legs – and for other blond Swedes – Sundin and Alfredsson and Lidström. And especially the Canadians. It's hard to imagine that I knew nothing about those players (coach Quinn, of course, was familiar from his gig in Vancouver, as the 1970 recipient, in fact, of the Canucks' first fighting major), had never seen their faces or watched them shift gears and change the game's speed. Today, I'd know them without numbers and names, by skating and wrist shots and muscle in front of the net, their voices, the inflections of a northern Swedish accent versus a southern one, scars along the jawline.

By the time they'd won Canada's first men's hockey gold in fifty years (the women won gold a couple of days before) – Jovo setting up the game winner and Lower Mainland boys Joe Sakic with two goals and two assists, Paul Kariya's opener – I knew the North American game had changed from the seventies version: now there were systems, strategies, a defensive zone I didn't recognize from when Orr scooted through it and onto the freeway between the blue lines. Some black Alberta kid – Jarome Iginla – scored twice.

The victorious, happy and glorious Canadians revelled on ice. I expected a Phil Esposito Canada Cup debauchery, a Caligulaic celebration where bleeding boys hug, gap-mouthed warriors oiled and lubed for the post-game strip joint and the broads.

In Salt Lake City, though, babies. Veteran Joe Niewendyck took to the ice gleefully, his tot in a tiny red and white striped sweater, probably knitted by a hip granny, tucked in the crook of Papa Joe's arm. Other players – the grittier than thou Michael Peca – lifted wee ones from the stands and onto the ice. Some guys, like weepmeister Ryan Smyth, were crying and singing as "O Canada" trumpeted olympically. High above, the team's GM, Wayne Gretzky, embraced his lovely, teary, oft-preggers wife. Hulky defenceman, Chris Pronger, told a reporter, "We took a lot of inspiration from how the women's team played."

Hockey players?

Anne Kingston, writing in the *National Post* and sounding like the wickedest stepmother, thought not:

> That solemn moment intended to capture the dignified sportsmanship that is Olympic tradition was utterly cluttered with banal domestic detritus – children squirming in their fathers' arms at centre ice, Steve Yzerman holding Owen Nolan's video camera and filming Nolan receiving his gold medal, network television lingering on images of Janet Gretzky grabbing her husband in manic glee. There were those charmed, no doubt, by Joe Nieuwendyk holding his little daughter and Mike Peca holding his son, even though Peca's child looked far too old to have a soother jammed in his mouth. But . . . there is a time and a place for everything . . . [T]he Olympics are no longer only about excellence; they are also about the theatrics of overwrought sentimentality . . . And few things up the schmaultz quotient faster than a babe in arms.

Guilty: I was charmed. The Olympics are not "only about excellence," at least when hockey is concerned. They are also about national pride and identity, corporate sponsors, profit for the host, an inability to accept defeat, separating winners from losers. These, in part, caused the American women's team to reportedly stomp on the Canadian flag before their gold-medal match. They also feared televised national shame and humiliation at the hands of a wussy leaf-wearing nation like Canada. The televised Olympics have always been about theatrics, too, and whether you call it "overwrought sentimentality" or pity, fear and catharsis, the experience for spectators is a complex one. The men's gold-medal game had been intensely hyped; the game itself was great and played by the game's most brilliant – and roughest – players, led by that loveable old tractor, and Hodgkin's disease survivor, Mario Lemieux. For me, seeing the game for the first time in years, seeing it fresh, the real catharsis didn't come with the final buzzer and victory. My satisfaction – and amazement – came when Wayne hugged Janet and the cameras cared, when Joe hugged tiny Tyra and the cameras cared again, and when the men's faces were so willing to share their happiness with their own children. The repeat came on at ten; Tom and I watched every minute for a second time. Contrary to Kingston's reading – that what happened was staged and cynical bullshit – the post-game I saw looked more like a bunch of regular guys behaving normally: fathers share with their children these days, they are not ashamed to be fathers and husbands. The beers and the profits can wait.

I watched the Canucks from then on. The first game – who knew you could get so many on TV? – they blew a tie in the last second – uh-oh, this again – but there was Todd Bertuzzi being more and more his high-scoring and hard-hitting snarly self into the final month of the season, and then suddenly they were grinding like a garage band into the playoffs and beating the Rolling Stones – Detroit's wrinkly Red Wings – games one and two.

And then I fell hard in an unexpected way. Markus Näslund, posed in the newspaper, magical in the sharpest double-breasted Armani suit, his face chiselled and hair curly-slick: *My children have shown me the power of sheer innocent joy. They always have a bright outlook on life and it forces me to be positive.* He shares a birthday with my dead sister. He wears steel in his leg to repair a shattered fibia and tibia. He became my pretend boyfriend.

And when Detroit won the Stanley Cup that year, grenade-kneed captain Steve Yzerman – hey, from the Olympics! – lifted the cup high with his brown-eyed girl, Isabella, at his side, her arms up, too, a grrrl-power parody of her tough and happy dad.

This new hockey was a barn full of jubilant line dancers and they grabbed my arm – me, slouching against hay bales in the darkest corner, worried about my weak knee, that I might pop a rib or want a cold beer or twelve, that I wouldn't know the steps and was dressed all wrong, that I was too fucking old – and dragged me onto the floor and joined me up to the long and twisting line. "Dance," said the game.

"I WANT TO USE MY KNEE." My family doctor understood, ordered X-rays and sent me to a physiotherapist specializing in athletes, Olympic athletes.

The physio resembled the hippie clog-wearing car dealer who sold me my Mazda in 1987, hippie gone high end with taupe linen and soft leather and infrequent hair above a shiny forehead, glasses but rimless. He made a reference to classical music I didn't understand and pointed to the nothing patch of arthritis the x-ray showed, then yarded and steam-rolled and ratcheted my right knee, made me crouch and scamper like a circus chimp in blue terrycloth sport-shorts across his office floor. Scamper suggests many steps: more like two.

"You'll never have full use."

I want to play tennis with my hotshot daughter.

"You'll never be a tennis player." He thought a nice cycling club would feed my competitive side – "You can even do some racing with the right group" – and then wrote a prescription for a high-end knee brace, suggested trekking poles to get cardio on the beach, and wrote a list of strengthening exercises for knee and core. Find what you like to do, he said, and keep doing it. Come back in eight weeks, he said, but I didn't know what for.

My family doctor was pissed. "You need Silken Laumann's physio," he snorted. "Or: a PT." He grinned like he was really in the groove now, flashing the lingo and getting me pumped for Olympic trials.

"A what?"

"Personal. Trainer."

He offered to find me another physio and I told him, no, I need to do what the first guy told me first. But trekking poles? Why not Tilley hats and Lee Valley garden shorts and orthotic walking shoes and a good sturdy underwire bra? Why not just delete me from the Still Sexed Up database?

I also asked my doctor this: say I've got a character in a story I'm working on, and say she finds herself attracted to hockey players late in life. Could there be a physiological reason? He told me of a study. Take three public bathroom stalls; spray male sweat on the walls of one. Women will choose that stall over the others. We are built to like the smell of male sweat.

"But my character gets worked up watching them on television."

"Well, there's the disinhibition caused by the screen. Plus when she sees the sweat, she's having a Pavlovian thrill to the times she's been near sweat. The body remembers."

"Hormones?"

"Well, given her age, there could be a precipitous rise in testosterone as the estrogen diminishes."

Next stop, a kinesiologist at the rec centre on the highway into the city. This is November, early December. A close friend had died on November 11, Remembrance Day, a muscles on muscles guy, dead at forty-two of a heart attack while walking the Galloping Goose with his wife and two kids. The kind of death that makes you think of the word 'pluck' or a cork coming out of a bottle of great wine. I'd been teaching an extra class. I was wrecked and tired and the PT was a tall, smooth-faced triathlete with sinewy legs who mistook me for a younger woman and so set the bike tension too tight. For an hour in the pumping and grooving weight room he showed me hamstring machines and pin weights and optimum reps and digital heart rates and wrote it on a tidy blue card so that in a couple of days I could do it again, by myself.

In two days I couldn't remember what anything did. I feared sticking the pin in the wrong hole or mistakenly clipping the tricep rope carabineer onto the lat pulldown bar. I felt deep shame and sadness. Ball crunches seemed a stupid thing to even try: what if I slid off and hurt myself? I didn't go back.

For a few minutes on New Years Eve 2003, my first full season with the team, the Canucks led the whole league. And by then we'd been to a game in Vancouver versus Calgary. We missed the first period because the ferry couldn't sail until the southeaster blowing out of Puget Sound calmed down, but we got overtime. Trevor Linden took teammate Trent Klatt's stick in the eye, shook off his gloves, vaulted the boards and ran to the room. Play went on. Ohlund fled the game, too, his knee a twisted mess along the boards. Injured, sure. But they'd be back.

* * *

I like a swinging chick who really knows what's happening, who grooves on life. One who's kind of warm, wet and wild . . . I know somewhere there's one person who can do that for me and who will put up with all my idiosyncrasies like

digging pork chops and French fries and great Chinese food. And she'd understand my dislikes, such as mustard, queers, dying, phonies and drunks. She'd understand my thoughts about drinking. When I drink, my lips get numb. And when my lips get numb, I relax. Now if I'm relaxed I close my eyes when I'm kissing, and if I close my eyes when I'm drunk I get sick and my head starts spinning. So I stay sober. Sex is more important than drinking, so I don't drink.
  – Derek Sanderson, *I've Got To Be Me*, 1970

IN 1970, I was fourteen and in love with Derek Sanderson. Yes, Bobby Orr was the ultimate; I wasn't stupid and the thrills came every shift with him. But Orr was way better when he skated with Sanderson. It wasn't only the persona – Sanderson's dark counter-culture hairiness, the white skates, the face both menacing and comic, the skating well and fighting and dressing like an Edwardian outlaw, like sex. The crew-cutted miracle boy Orr got more beautiful with Sanderson's dirtiness nearby. Their incongruity worked, but then, as now, the game's less obvious details drew me, ones that required a keen and obsessive eye. The game's meaning didn't reside only in the obvious on ice and what appeared on the sports news at eleven and in the stats in the next day's paper.

I read the game for little things: Sanderson could win faceoffs better than Esposito (he credited a photographic memory); the sweeping poke check he'd practised with his dad was a contortion of coordination, will and strength; and he had the wiliness to lead the league in short-handed goals. Sideburns, sure. But he was a special kind of intelligent and did things no one else could. Orr seemed delighted by him. (Sanderson wrote about one shopping trip, "It's a joke to watch Bobby get fitted for a pair of bell-bottoms" because he's "got a big can, too big for his body.") The mythic overtime Cup-winning goal, Orr levitating and stretched horizontal above the ice and celebrating and smiling and falling at the same time, improves if it's preceded by the stop in play before the goal is scored. Sanderson calls Orr over to huddle and tells him what to do, settles him down, and then there's Sanderson behind the net, slip-passing out front to the crossing Orr, tricking Glenn Hall, the way they'd planned. The image improves. Orr finally drops out of the air and Sanderson slides along the ice into the picture and wraps his arms around his buddy, embraces him like he's found the swinging chick of his dreams. The complicated and layered relationship between Orr and Sanderson makes the image – that goal – so great.

Orr lost millions, lost knees. But after the string of singles bars in Boston named for F. Scott Fitzgerald characters, after the mansion in Philadelphia that belonged to Edgar Allen Poe's estate, Sanderson turned up famously destitute and drunken living under a bridge, addicted and depressed and unwell. I was compelled by that kind of hockey player as a teenager, but not now. There's too much to lose by padding those players – and the kids watching them – with a kind of unquestioned worship that implies an "anything goes on and off the ice" code of conduct is the entertainment we're looking for.

My first year back in hockey, I wanted to watch Linden looking Christ-like with the kiddies at Camp Goodtimes; I wanted to see Bertuzzi chat it up with the Midget riding the bus on Hockey Day in Canada; I liked the players on their stationary bikes, post-game television, the whole pack of them Tour de Francing and de-calcifying, riding together, but getting nowhere. Getta look at those quads. Where, now, the Sandersons?

Calgary journalist Eric Duhatschek – twenty years on the Flames beat and newsy Hockey Hall of Famer – says the NHL lifestyle has adjusted to the times, but also to the needs – and metastisizing egos – of young men. "The motivation for being clean and sober varies from player to player," Duhatschek says, "some do it because they've adopted 'my-body-is-a-temple' as a way of life. I know of at least two NHLers who quit drinking beer because they were on a high-protein, low-carb diet. Others pick and choose when they go out on binges."

Earlier in the season, I'd watched a short TV piece on Maple Leaf Gary Roberts. He'd rehabbed after neck surgery in 1996 only to have operations on both shoulders after the 2002 playoffs (Don Cherry quipped Roberts had carried the team on those shoulders, hence the need for reconstruction). Everything for Roberts was about core strength – that über-metaphor for survivors of the twentieth century. He balanced on Swiss balls and twirled free weights like a scarred up, determined and demented California sea lion. It would be easier to go to the gym, my band of black knee brace keeping cap in line, remembering the look on Roberts' face doing ball push-ups on his brand new joints. He now runs his own so-called elite gym in downtown Toronto: halogen mood lights, mandatory post-workout protein shakes, memberships starting at $800 per month. Imagine going *there*.

Roberts is old. Born in 1966, he's one of a few greybeards alive while I was still at Maple Grove Elementary school. But veterans aren't the only ones trimming the fat from their moneyed lives. Duhatschek says the twenty-two-and-unders in today's NHL are "a completely different species." A lot of interested parties have a lot to gain from the right product. "They are groomed, by agents and parents, from their mid-teens to say all the right things and do all the right things for 95 per cent of the time. They understand that the money is so big, the rewards so great and the competition so acute that if they want to make it to the NHL there isn't the margin for error there once was – or the capacity to forgive."

A guy like Sanderson might survive today because he'd be placed in the NHL's substance abuse and behavioural health program, but those with his appetites and ghosts have a hard time finding tolerant teams. A compassionate Wayne Gretzky phoned Theo Fleury – "an enigma wrapped around a stick of dynamite" – in his rehab hospital to ask him to play for Team Canada at the Olympics. Fleury had a huge tournament, full of a small guy's heart and flash and skill; he took a key Czech crosscheck that ignited Gretzky and the team. Fleury, though, revisited rehab. Duhatschek says, "clean and sober," Fleury could have played for any NHL team. But a number of GMs have told the writer that under no circumstance would they ever bring a player like Fleury to their team because of the potential effect on young players "who could be led astray by a quote-unquote 'old school' type like Theo. Why, they ask, run the risk of having a Fleury or a Phil Housley drag their top young players to a strip club in Columbus and have their names and faces plastered all over the newspaper?" Fleury couldn't possibly do enough on the ice to excuse the damage he might do off it.

WHEN I'M CYNICAL about that slimy web of interested parties who profit from sport and control its image, I see the good deeds that teams like the Canucks do as self-serving and strategic: show fans the benevolent acts, the charity events, the good dad smooches, the donated jerseys, and we'll be willing sign-me-up narcissists, eager to identify with the team and not gripe at having to work eight hours to afford a ticket to a two-and a half-hour game (brew, burger and yogurt cone not included). The team's main charity is Canuck Place Children's Hospice, a residential facility where terminally ill children (over two hundred a year) and their families receive care and comfort. A cynic sees the obligatory shots of the all-forehead Sedin twins carving pumpkins there with bald and all-forehead sick kids as heart-tug PR. Or when Brian Burke brags during the team's spring telethon that many mornings, players' cars are already out front of what was once a lumber baron's fancy mansion when Burke pops around on business, a cynic smells exaggeration.

The year Gary Roberts was born, I was ten and living near where Canuck Place is now, and my sister was sixteen and already into the third year of a seven-year death by Hodgkin's disease. In Vancouver, in the sixties, cancer wasn't a box-office affliction. No one knew it or knew to fear its melodrama. Privacy was still a big deal for families in crisis – the movie-of-the-week was a fledgling genre – and trauma was a private matter for a family to endure, however heroically. And my parents were heroes, strategizing about how they could raise two healthy daughters in a healthy way, while another haloed kid disintegrated. My mother soothed me with books: I read Hemingway and Steinbeck and Daphne duMaurier before I knew a boy's kiss. Saturday night: hockey watching with Dad while I skunked him at cribbage. I was allowed music played at all hours and all volumes, regardless of whether it was The Monkees or Harry Belafonte or James Taylor folk-schmaultz. *Two* spaniels.

But to admit she might die would be to give in to a malevolent power that listens for doubt in nice families, and my parents never did. I still get anxious when I hear the word 'terminal' because it's a word we never used. Likewise, 'die'. Once, I cried when my sister came home from more chemo and I could hear her through the heating vent that connected our rooms, throwing up; I'd had enough of stoicism and agony. I angered my mother that day. And when my sister died when I was fifteen, my volleyball coach – who had seeded in me a love of little-guy politics, bluegrass and the well-executed forearm pass – was hurt to tears that no one alerted him I'd been living in a family full of pain.

I didn't understand my sister's death – didn't discuss it with those trained to prune grief's tendrils – until I was thirty. Before then, death talked to me many times. I flirted with it, and even kissed it hard on the mouth. Pro sport's greedy capitalism may enrage the cynic, but look at Markus Näslund in the website shot: reading to the sister of a dying kid, her head resting against his big bicep, his face calm and smooth. His voice is Swedish and lilty and he's droppin' his gs because the language – and the world – is softer that way. *Would you like to swing on a star?* he croons.

BEFORE THE PLAYOFFS in 2003 (the year before the Calgary series), for the last game of the regular season, I went to Vancouver. On the morning ferry, tidy pensioners in matching fleece vests and matching sneakers hog window seats; he holds her coffee until it cools while she knits and he gazes out at the roiling waters of Active Pass. She's working on a cotton-candy pink squeaky Sayelle something.

"Bertuzzi," she says, head up at the end of a row. "Who's he play for?"

"Dunno."

"Must be Vancouver."

"Dunno."

"You're the man," she giggles. She's flirting with her own husband. "You're supposed to know."

Hockey is winter? Not today. Hockey is a fast run through a flat Active Pass, low cloud threatening rain, green and mild and misted. A dozen bald eagles soar dinosaur big out the wide windows. I take a boat to see hockey. Here, you can miss the first period because the prevailing winds kick up and blow so strong a ferry can't dock. The ship is full of jerseys, the predictable Näslund and Bertuzzi wannabes but also imposters: MACINTYRE, who's he play for? Straight-haired blonde babes swim in home jersey white but also, tidy men, Linden lookalikes *avec* goatee and skinny bowed legs; the scrappers and a Sopel clone in headphones; fans in wheelchairs – huge people wrecked but waving flags, men in the *bleu et rouge* road jersey, their girlfriends skinny, pale and their eyes plumped with make-up. Lily's Jovo jersey is in my bag, and I'm not sure why I don't put it on and be one of the group. Instant insider, team spirit, be a joiner. This is the last game of the season and for once it's an afternoon game so we can motor across the Strait of Georgia this morning and motor back at dusk. The guy wearing Näslund's jersey is too confident, superior: you're not him, buddy.

There's a headache coming, and I'm wearing old-style Levis, retro high at the waist, tight and soft and close at the ankle, a red T-shirt and a black barncoat, the underwear is silk, my hair is washed like this is the Monkees at the Agridome with my dad and I'm twelve. I even have a pimple.

I'm way early and stand behind the players' bench, waiting for the warm-up skate. Goalpost thin blondes with beers pose behind me, earrings a-dangle, and clearly want me to move. The music gets big, the rink is one huge pulse, and then it's almost too much to see the players so close – No helmets! The hair! – and not touch them or make eye contact. It's like a big rec room and we're here together. Bertuzzi passes not a metre from me.

Then I'm in a seat high above the visitors' bench. During the American national anthem, dozens of Viagra signs flip and light around the rink. There's Palffy, and Linden is the best player on the ice, ripping it up with Artem

Chubarov and Jovo, going for the division title. What with Colorado where they are in the standings, the Canucks only need a tie against this struggling team to come out first. Näslund is at the top of the scoring, along with Colorado's Peter Forsberg, and needs points today to beat his boyhood chum. We've been told by experts to care about such hierarchies.

The game takes, what, fifteen minutes? The woman beside me missed the first period and when she and her date finally get settled and the second period's going, she applies scented lipstick (my head!), talks about what time she got out of bed, about who said what to whom at work and DOES NOT PAY ATTENTION. It's her fault they lose and Näslund doesn't score. My back has seized. Shut out. One real goal and LA scored it. The boys are on the ice for the end-of-season jersey exchange and they look like shit. Näslund takes the microphone and leans on the boards like Sinatra after too many rye and sevens. "As you can tell," he says to those few still here, "we're pretty upset. We had a chance to win our division and we choked."

A dozen eagles at dusk in fir trees above Active Pass, their white heads fluorescent in this diminishing light. I must endure the inevitable ferry analysis swirling like a demon tide rip, surly boys coming down from their fancy hockey beers: they don't have it, they didn't want it, the team's too focussed on feeding fucking Näslund the puck, every time I think 'maybe this year' and then they blow it; LA came here with golf bags on their backs, fer fucksakes, and Vancouver still couldn't get it done.

My analysis: LA was phenomenal defensively, didn't take penalties, played disciplined. Vancouver seemed flu-ish, tight and scattery. Näslund is recovering, we are told, from bad shrimp at a team dinner, whatever that means. But no one needs to be sorry for that game. The boys will meet St. Louis in the first round.

ATHLETES REACH a peak of fitness that is so exhilarating they want to keep reaching it. Most people recovering from injury will rehab until they get strength back; they could go further, but they stop, satisfied to reach the point they were at before injury. My osteopath, Gail, says I'll need six weeks of strength training to reach a point of enthusiasm where change – the feeling of increased power – is noticeable. I stepped over a dead shrew on her deck when I came in, and we talk about deer fences as she prods my bones into temporary alignment. She, too, thinks I should cycle, but says, "What do you want to do?"

I say "run" but that's not true. I mean to be strong enough to run, to be in control, to swim a long time, forget this knee, this stupid sign of weakness. I want to be strong and stronger. I'm horizontal, four feet off the ground, the air full of rosemary, the wind blowing rain off the ocean and onto the window. She stands beside me, touches a finger to my forehead and asks, "Why haven't you done anything until now?"

I book three appointments with a PT named Jeanie at the rec centre. Whenever I say her name at home, Lily crosses her arms in front of her straight torso, bobs her head and blinks: magic. At seven A.M., the weight room is bright and cool and I love us all. Every woman tattooed. Women older than I am – older and way bigger and more confident – lift weights decked out in Jane Fonda ass-cracker leotards that expose the dragons circling their ankles. Bodies slow-motion on the recumbent bikes – good for? – that seem implausibly injured and challenged. Jeanie stays close, watching my moves on the spongy floor, especially when my shoulders come up to take any burden from the rest of my body, or when she sees my ankles collapse inward because my arches have gone south. On the hamstring machine, I feel a pinch of pain behind my knee and panic, drive a mile down This Ain't Gonna Work Road before Jeanie adjusts the weight.

She smiles. "How was that?"

"Good."

"Everything's good with you." She smiles again. So I'm the machine, wearing a pale grey #44 Bertuzzi T-shirt. Its dark line crosses above my chest and I can watch the line in the mirrored wall to make sure my left shoulder has not crept up. I'm tough in this T-shirt. I wish for a tattoo.

Doing measly 7.5-pound bicep curls, my arms look Popeye good, but my eyes – no make-up unlike those around me; likewise, no earrings regardless of dress code – are pouched, lined and sagging. So's my neck. My middle seems rolled on itself and compressed into my grandmother's abdomen. I exaggerate?

The night before, Tom had asked, "Why do you want to do this?" and I went through the reasons I'd given Gail but added that I wanted to enter menopause strong and active so I won't need drugs and to – I confessed some vanity – look better, to not resemble other fifty-year-olds when I get there in a couple of years. He was asleep by that time, rankled by the word 'menopause,' rudimentary in his attention to my body, but not interested in a chick who's whined about a bum knee for ten years and still can't take out the compost.

Jeanie says we'll meet in a couple of weeks. No, I say, I'll try this twice on my own and then you can check my form. No problem, she chirps, same time next week.

The change room air is freighted with secondhand chlorine and my eyes are red when I'm done. Is there euphoria? Yes, but also doubt and sadness from what I saw in the mirror. "Do you wear orthotics?" Jeanie had asked, inspecting my feet as I pulled a mint green surgical band across my chest. Orthotic is a word like dentures, and there's something about the weight room that feels like a clinic, like *Cuckoo's Nest*. We are unwell or obsessed with unwellness and come here to come here, so we're at least somewhere doing something. Getta loada the outcasts, the weirdos, the Dr. Seuss bodies and goofy expectations. Jeanie might be a tolerant nurse who'll mock me at the bar after work.

I stop in for playoff groceries on my way home. The checkout girl is playing adult today. She can't remember the code for snap peas. A produce boy will come to our rescue but meantime, "I'm nineteen," she confesses, "and I'm waiting for my first GST cheque. Some of my friends already have theirs and I'm wondering when I'll get mine. It's only fifty dollars but that makes a difference right now. My boyfriend and I are really broke right now, and if I get that cheque I can get a nice fish for my little niece's birthday. Ya. I'm thinking about a fish. She's five. I think a fish is pretty easy to take care of and she'll learn a little bit of responsibility."

"And how it feels when something you love dies." I mean it in a good way.

She looks shocked, like the thought hadn't crossed her mind. "Well, I'm thinking of a Chinese Fighting fish? And they're tough."

JOYCE CAROL OATES calls boxing a story without words but doesn't mean it has "no language, or that it is somehow 'brute,' 'primitive,' 'inarticulate,' only that the text is improvised in action." And, she says, that action is a "dialogue between the boxers" that responds to "the mysterious will of the audience which is always that the fight be a worthy one."

Likewise, hockey. Hockey is a story without words and its language is found in the movement of players against and with each other. They move in response to the will of the crowd. But because we get the added dimension of character development in hockey's story – we understand players' motivations, the struggles to make the team, and we enjoy, thanks to non-stop media attention, the incongruities of a brain bruiser also being a good father, and because the protective visor keeps them handsome longer – we can watch an awful game, an unworthy one, and still give the game a place in the story of the season.

In 2003, the Canucks lose Game 1 against St. Louis 6-0. From the opening minute, awful. They seem confused, suddenly, by the rink's dimensions. They try to play dump and chase, but instead play dump, chase, forfeit. The penalty kill stinks. St. Louis scores on the first power play, a stupid penalty Bertuzzi took and deserved more for, an elbow to a head along the boards. Näslund gets nailed for a trip on Tyson Nash that is more cosmetic than real, but welcome to playoff officiating, early rounds. St. Louis looks like a pack of grown-ups, the Canucks like slow-skating and insolent teenagers pissed off because Dad's watching sports and they're missing their favourite *Mod Squad* rerun.

Näslund looks bothered and bewildered. Bad shrimp still? Bert can't make shots and falls. Morrison flits like a tropical fish, delirious with positional possibilities, so many angles to anticipate: *I'll be here. No, here. How 'bout here? Here I am.* Jovo and Linden are solid, consistent, great and experienced players. The Sedins, though, skate in Bergman slow motion. Spirits are low, resolve missing. If I wasn't afraid of sounding like one of those ferry boo-birds, I'd say it looks psychological. They seem mortified – the crowd waved white towels to start and left booing – and I don't know how they recover from this public embarrassment. Pride: can it cope under these circumstances?

We're told teams are judged by the post-season, that the eighty-two regular games are played only to determine home ice advantage. But the rising action of regular season – complications, goals met and missed, small victories, setbacks – these are the best parts of the story wherein characters are developed and revealed, stakes raised and themes explored. Yes, we read for the climax – playoffs are one long, brutal climax – and to find out what happens at the end, but the journey is the most interesting, crucial if a reader is going to return next year. It's useless, of course, to argue against the prevailing culture of competition and hockey. My opinion is ridiculous and out of step. But I now have regrets, worries, serious doubts about a team that has so caught and fed my imagination. As if the rest of the story – the men and their kids and their good deeds and heavy hearts – was false. Or irrelevant. Smarten up: it's a great story with great characters. Layered, complex, scarred, diligent, persistent, nasty, kind, benevolent, over-sexed, over-paid, under-educated, small-town, vulnerable, loyal, handsome, and not handsome enough. Individuals.

After the game, it's 10:30 and past my bedtime and my rotator cuffs tingle darkly with this morning's routine. Dogs bark in the pollen-heavy night and I worry for the spring lambs. Tom has not committed to this team and merely tolerates my new obsession. He has other things on his mind and keeps his distance from allegiances. Still, I can trust him to keep what is said in this room in this room. I make a terrible pillow-top confession: "I think they're done," I whisper. "I love them still, but they've had it."

CHAPTER THREE

HOCKEY OWL

The first man was small and quick, dark of face, with restless eyes and sharp, strong features. Every part of him was defined: small, strong hands, slender arms, a thin and bony nose. Behind him walked his opposite, a huge man, shapeless of face with large, pale eyes, with wide sloping shoulders; and he walked heavily, dragging his feet a little, the way a bear drags his paws. His arms did not swing at his sides, but hung loosely.
    – John Steinbeck, *Of Mice and Men*

Then it was filled with motion, speed. To the innocent, who had never seen it before, it seemed discorded and inconsequent, bizarre and paradoxical like the frantic darting of the weightless bugs which run on the surface of stagnant pools. Then it would break, coalesce through a kind of kaleidoscopic whirl like a child's toy, into a pattern, a design almost beautiful, as if an inspired choreographer had drilled a willing and patient and hard-working troupe of dancers – a pattern, design which was trying to tell him something, say something to him urgent and important and true in that second before, already bulging with the motion and the speed, it began to disintegrate and dissolve.
    – William Faulkner, "An Innocent at Rinkside," 1955

What we see as aboutness the artist sees as just another pattern, infinitely plastic and malleable . . . the artist sees the pattern and feels the mystery that looms beyond the pattern . . . But great art is pattern over mystery, it is juggling words over whirlpools of silence.
    – Douglas Glover, "The Novel as a Poem"

St. Louis has nine players with the flu but they're good to go. I'm trying to recover from loss with numbers. I don't understand the formula I've used, but I've decided that nine players on St. Louis have a total of ninety-eight years in the NHL and that the equivalent Vancouver players have only fifty-three.

Detroit, which is eliminated in the first round, has 122 years. Näslund only has eyes for me, and I touch the scar on his chin and say, "We can't. This is not the time to break your concentration." Daniel Alfredsson is interviewed after Ottawa's OT win – no shirt, bare skin – but does nothing for me. Swede, sure. But he resembles so closely our ewe #11 that I see only ovine and multiple births. He's handsome, but not Näslund's version. Alfredsson's skin is white as Dorset fleece and his arms look skinny. Näslund is more god than ewe. A troubled and inconsistent god, burdened with powers he can't control or figure out. An earthly god: asked what he would do the night before Game 7, Nazzie says he'd play with his kids, put them to bed, eat pasta, watch the tube, and go to bed.

To switch to Anaheim vs. Detroit on TV was to go from storm to tranquility. The hits were soft, the passes deft, the defensive strategy of Detroit inept but allowed for lovely passes. Stanislav Chistov is nineteen and already a player. We say his name and mock angry hockey players: Cheezt-off, Peezt-off, and the Finn, Teekt-off. Tom says playoffs are like high school love and you notice everything: "I touched her locker, she must love me" or "Oh no, she didn't smile, it's love, she hates me." In playoffs, everything you do or notice means something good, or that it's over.

Apricot Beauty tulips on the table: I love them more when they're shot and blown open with insides exposed, a less rich colour but more true to nature. The morning is wet. Finch song but also starlings feeding on lawn grubs and spinning into the air with long twigs and straw from the lambing shed. Yesterday, I couldn't remember the name of lavender, but I dug the herb garden with Tom and spread chicken shit dark and crumbly, reeking of ammonia and hot enough to warm my hands through heavy garden gloves.

Behind my knee, problem hamstring. My left calf is sore. Last night my right arch fell even further as I did telephone book step lifts while watching Toronto @ Dallas. Every muscle has been stimulated. Even small ones under my collarbone. Patience: a word Linden, my Reserve Pretend Boyfriend, used for playing a tight game and waiting, waiting, waiting.

Bert has played in front of the net all year, but against St. Louis he's beat up, double-teamed, paralyzed and Nazzie can't get room. So for Game 4 they brought him out to the blue line for the PP, sent Jovo and Sopel to the net, and space opened everywhere. Nazzie got a happy stick and the whole team rejoiced.

Klatt scores on a tip from a Salo shot; Bert hits Al MacInnis and Big Al leaves the game; Jovo scores from Bert and Nazzie; a late goal on the PP ruins

Cloutier's shutout, but they have played so well, so hard. Chubarov skates stronger every shift. Ohlund returns after knee surgery, a quad needing serious rehab. Quads: most fickle of muscles. "We should've stuck a fork in 'em when we had the chance," Al MacInnis regrets.

In bed last night, I call Markus telepathically. "Are you there?" and his face comes in, but he won't make eye contact and his voice fades out like a bad connection. "I'm here," he says but fades again. I tell him anyway, "What your father did, making you walk home from the rink? That was bad parenting. That's not what made you great." I tell him not to feel shame, the burden. "Have a happy stick, Markus," I tell him, "you are great." I see his gorgeous body walking back to Sweden, across continents, all the way back, alone. His father's wrong. He is a sensitive boy and should be carried home, a hero.

I won't shave my legs until after the playoffs.

Driving to the gym, I've got Lucinda Williams cranked and here's the daydream: I'm at a swanky dinner in honour of the team, seated at a white-clothed round table, surrounded by the boys. Apparently, I've been using an office at GM Place to write a book and I've won their trust by asking Trent Klatt if he's related to Billy Klatt, another Minneapolis-born player who spent time, I believe, in the WHA when the league was hungry for Americans. Anyway, the guys like me because they've let me use their workout room to do leg presses and one of the trainers digs my attitude and is helping build my quads. Later that morning, Näslund brings a couple of lattés to my office and we chat about education in Sweden, about Arthur Erickson's Vancouver. At the swanky dinner, I'm at the table with the boys and they're in nice suits. A rich boy I went to school with is at our table, too, but he's paid porno cash to a charity to be here and is acting like, as Derek Sanderson once put it, a kid whose father's bought him a toy. He makes stupid remarks and the table gets quiet. Jovo, especially, gets tense in the jaw.

I say, "They don't need you to be an asshole. They don't deserve that."

Rich boy says, so they can hear – he's beery in tone and execution and doesn't realize he's much shorter than everyone else – "They get paid too much anyway."

"At least they didn't inherit theirs," I snap.

He says nasty things about me and high school, and a couple of players stand up big. I feel so aggressive, mouthy. I feel strong, like one of them, or like Lucinda singing *I have been so fuckin' alone since those three days.*

On the way back from the gym, I detour past my favourite hayfield near Thetis Lake to visit poet Carla Funk in hospital where they've removed an ovarian cyst the size of a grapefruit. The doctor tried to go in through her belly button, but had a good look around in there, said no way, and cut in across her stomach. The cyst had attached itself to her lower intestine; an ovary was removed and also a fallopian tube. She's not yet thirty. "The best thing?" she says, day three after surgery, a couple of Mennonite types around her, the white blonde hair tied back so as not to drape too melodramatically across the pillow. "On the morphine drip, I'm lying in my hospital bed and a construction worker manifests himself out of the oxygen console across the room. He walks by in a hard hat, says nothing. Then, Todd Bertuzzi walks by in a short-sleeved red and blue plaid dress shirt, stops at the foot of my bed, gives me a nod. My primary thought is 'wow, Todd Bertuzzi came to see me in the hospital; I always knew he was a kind man.' There's no dialogue, just a sort of recognition from me that he is Todd Bertuzzi. From him, I get a sense that even though he's this huge burly hockey player, he's still a man of compassion and thoughtfulness."

I'M NOT THE FIRST to notice that a hockey game – or a year in hockey – comes in three parts, as does the most simple story structure – beginning/pre-season (conflict is introduced), middle/regular season (conflict is developed), end/playoffs (conflict resolved). Other aspects of the narrative arts – reversal of fortune, rising action, catharsis, tragic flaw, anti-hero – also find tidy counterparts in a game of hockey. Sport in general has also been seen as "tragic drama" and here's how one academic described sport's key ritual elements, the ways a sport event can be "a tragic ritual *agon*, a dramatization of the struggle of human beings with nature or of the struggle of good people against antisocial people": one performer, no matter how great, will lose. A tragic flaw – everybody has one – may undo even the best player. A spectacular reversal of game momentum may snatch defeat from the jaws of victory. In each event, a player faces the revelation of his ultimate strengths – limitations as an athlete – and as a person. A tragic loser turns the defeat into a spiritual victory by playing hard to the end. Through pity, fear and empathy, voilá, the spectator is cleansed.

We watch sport for the same reasons we watch drama, and it's not hard to see why both excite us in similar ways. We are hard-wired to enjoy those elements. We expect them in our entertainments. Another writer adds more

elements: not only is the sport-drama likely to be part of "a regularly repeated pattern" (like other celebrations and rituals), the game is ritualized –
national anthems, coin toss, matching unis – so everybody gets worked up as
a community, as a group, and so the individual is transcended. The athletes
are transformed into superhuman creatures who can't slack off and be like us
or the drama won't convince us. The importance of this drama is that it *symbolizes* everyday power struggles, and the simplicity, the orderliness, of the
game contrasts with the chaos of the real world where it's often hard to figure out who won, who lost.

Others have noted, too, that much of this narrative structure is supplied –
or stressed – by sports commentators, "people with a magnificent grasp of the
obvious." We're told what to think and feel by media contracted to construct
the best story for the most spectators. So before (and throughout) a particular
game, we're told via statistics and history and player interview and
play-by-play and puck-sniffing cameras, that our team must win this game to
overtake the first-place Avalanche and therefore secure first spot in the division, something they/we totally want. Or we understand that our fave
defenceman is back tonight from a career-threatening eye injury: How will he
perform? How will the crowd respond? Or our two all-star forwards are battling for first place in league scoring, they're one goal apart and may even
reach the coveted fifty-goal mark. Will it be tonight? Who passes, who shoots?

Broadcasters feed us everything we should know and understand. There's
no need to be anything but passive. They know everything. They have stats.
They have the inside scoop. They have cultivated sources. They actually talk
to the players – come on – and they know what's brewing behind the scenes.

A comparison: say I visit the library looking for literature – a work of art
made beautiful by the author's attention to subtext, detail, irony, image, texture, form, language, paradox, subtlety and complexity of character – and
the librarian scoots me over to the Harlequin Romance racks. I've been mis-
led. Still, I may also find that reading such a book is kinda nice cause I don't
have to work hard. I know what to expect – especially after snorting a few –
and know I'll experience certain forms of arousal on a regular basis. I could
read while chug-a-lugging margaritas and still follow the thread. The librarian's job is also simplified: he doesn't have to read that egg-headed literature
in order to do his job. He can know that Harlequins are fiction and keep
suggesting readers go for the simple, predictable pleasures. I'll read a few,
sure, then be so bored I could skin the cat for kicks and find another library,

or another way to spend my time. Or I'll write my own book instead of passively slurping.

Lots is missed if we read the game simply, or let strangers interpret the game for us or assume all fans read or experience the game identically. When media simplify a game's narrative, they deny more creative relationships between game and fan, fan and player, the role of the fan in creating the game and influencing its meaning. When a fan like me takes to a team – or when I grain the sheep, or plant a double row of broad beans, or housebreak the dachshund because my husband never got around to it, or imagine planting rhododendrons (not too deep, lots of peat) with Markus Näslund on our first date – I am on an artistic journey.

Marilyn Bowering is a novelist, poet and playwright. She is a lovely woman – sensitive and gorgeous; willowy and silk-voiced. On the few occasions we've shared a stage or living room couch, I feel like the rough-edged country bumpkin next to her stylish and smart sophisticate. We were both on the bill at an author reading in Victoria in the early summer of 2004, waiting to check the microphones and sitting on comfy seats in the darkened back of the hall. I overheard her say, "I just want Bert back" and, though surprised by her confession, knew immediately who and what she was talking about.

I wrote to her later and asked about the appropriateness of the "hockey as drama" metaphor. She was born in Winnipeg and although her family left for Victoria before she turned four, she remembers skating on the neighbourhood outdoor rink with her father. "I wouldn't stay with my mother," she says, "pulled away from her hand to try and join the game. In Victoria we watched hockey with the rest of Canada every Saturday night. It was definitely part of feeling close to my father – I was a Leafs fan, knew all the players etc. My own daughter did the same with the Canucks: she met them, in fact . . . and I'm sure it was a father/daughter thing there too. There's the special language, the shared joys and sorrows – hockey is a bonding experience. Who cares about the dishes?"

For Marilyn, "drama is meant, of course, to give the spectator the feeling of observing real life in real time (the unities of time, place, and action.) There's no doubt we're watching something 'real' as compared to imagined or faked when we watch hockey: the outcome feels unpredictable and demands that the players engage with (ideally) heroic levels of physical effort, intelligence and intuition. We watch players for hubris, and consult the stars on their behalf – I understand that NHLers are notoriously superstitious. Then there's catharsis (I disagree that the spectator is passive): in fact to conceive of hockey as our national theatre seems right on track to me.

"The conflict has ritual elements – maybe more so in the past than now (e.g. between Montreal Canadiens and the Toronto Maple Leafs.) The east/west thing – with the Canucks being very much the west has picked some of this up again. The importance of characters in hockey is inarguable: not just the heroes, but the prevalence of telling details by which we recognize them – from tantrums to hair styles – and not so much off-the-ice stuff as one might expect. We don't seem to care what the players get up to in nightclubs – it's the on-ice dramas, the themes carried from game to game, series to series, country to country . . . (yeah, I like the idea)."

Marilyn's is a convincing version of why we feel so affected by a game, and she does allude to how the canvas of hockey includes more than the realistic depiction of tonight's game. Still, I do care what the players get up to in the nightclubs, although not in order to judge; I want details, surprising ones that contradict the heroic, that set up the ultimate pleasure of incongruity: the shy, goal-scoring Scandinavian climbs the table and drops his pants with a stripper; the rookie small forward off to play a season in Czechoslovakia reads Hemingway; the surly power forward kisses his little boy with daunting affection. The form of drama is too limited for the version of art I have in mind. All the world's a stage – okay okay – but the stage isn't all the world.

What bothers me about "hockey as drama" – even though it lends hockey a certain grace – is that "drama" suggests a split between actor/producer/director and spectator. The audience is to a great extent passive, except in their assigned role. I think the experience of hockey is more participatory than that, and the narrative we follow through a season (or a game) is not linear as suggested by the term "drama" and its beg/mid/end. Also, there's more to reading hockey. Form, colour, texture – things that are not intrinsically conflict-laden.

Carla Funk grew up in Vanderhoof in northern BC. She is a sylph with butt-length straight blonde hair. She resembles a more religious, clever, humble and sarcastic Anna Kournikova. Her poetry is intense, dark, and also playful in its treatment of the tangled world of Mennonite towns and the toll they take on a creative spirit. In 2006, she was chosen Victoria's first Poet Laureate. I would never have pegged her as a hockey chick. But she says she loves "the not-knowingness of the game . . . I love that it's not a movie, that there's no scripted ending waiting for me at the end . . . that it's freeform, liquid, undetermined. I love the energy and the sweat, the intensity enacted on ice that translates to crowd roar. There's a strange communion, too, watching hockey with a group of people. The audience becomes an extension of the on-ice team for which they're rooting."

Carla, too, watches the game with her daughter. "She'll grow up and phone home from wherever she is in the world and we'll mention last night's game. It's a communion thing, again. I think of 'story as community' . . . perhaps that's one of the big draws; hockey is a shared narrative, a story that unfolds and then becomes something in common. Hockey as story as community?"

During the 2002/03 season, she became entranced by Todd Bertuzzi and told me then – sure, we're a couple of English majors – she considered him to be "everyman."

"Everyman? Really." I thought her comparison might be a tad naïve. She seemed new to the game, and I wondered if she might have under-read Bertuzzi's style of play. "How so?"

"He's a good father, a good player, a hard worker. Everyman."

"Everyman" comes from Medieval literature, first found in a Flemish play in the 15th century in which *Everyman* is an allegorical figure of the human race, summoned by the allegorical figure of death. He discovers that his buddies *Fellowship, Kindred, Cousin,* and *Goods* won't go with him. It's *Good Deeds* (or *Virtue*), whom he previously neglected, who finally supports him and who offers to justify him before the throne of God. Okay. Maybe Bert is Everyman and Nazzie's Mr. Virtue. Fair enough.

In literature and drama, the term "everyman" has come to mean an ordinary individual, with whom the audience or reader can identify, and who's often placed in extraordinary circumstances. With the character of Todd, Carla suggests a nice fit for the hockey as drama metaphor.

"'Drama' doesn't ring as true for me as 'art' – somehow it assumes the players have a script handed to them and they need to abide by the 'dialogue,' set narrative action. I like the structural parallels, but the heart of it seems off-kilter. With hockey as art, though, I see more room for the various styles of play, each team's aesthetics. I think about collaborative artistic movements or 'groups' from the past and the present – the Bloomsbury group, the Group of Seven, even the Tish poets. These artists came together within a more fluid realm of purpose. I also think about the act of creation and how that same fuse that gets lit in the creative imagination is like the fuse lit on ice once the game begins. It's almost orchestral, symphonic: a group of musicians practise their parts, put them together and sparks fly. The game plays out more loosely than a symphony though, more jazz and blues, I'd say, with some rock and roll.

"Can I read hockey like a poem?" Carla asks. "It would be a Purdy poem – loose, swaggering, fists and beer. It would be devoid of pretension when the game is at its best. If I strip away the associations I bring to the game depending on which teams are skating, then I'd say that hockey is like a poem for its attention to detail. A poem demands the eye focus in on the very syllables of words. The game, too, demands that attention to the second, to this tiny puck flying across ice. Also, a good poem surprises the reader, as does a good game of hockey. The power of the startle is common ground."

Award-winning playwright Joan MacLeod grew up in Vancouver about the time I did. She's the author of such celebrated plays as *Amigo's Blue Guitar*, *The Hope Slide* and most recently, *The Shape of a Girl*, a monologue grounded in the 1997 killing of Victoria schoolgirl Reena Virk by a gang of teenagers. "My dad took me to my first Canuck game for my sixteenth birthday," Joan tells me. "It was the Canucks' first season. They played Chicago. We went early to watch the warm-up. I believe it was Bobby Hull's last season with them. My dad told me that Bobby Hull was a gentleman (pre-wife-beating days). I remember Bobby Hull standing at the boards and signing autographs for ten minutes before going to the dressing room for pre-game stuff. We lost the game but I had a great time. Although I wouldn't admit it at the time (I was often a sulky thing) I loved spending time just with my dad. I know he enjoyed the fact that I was enjoying hockey. How did that happen? Certainly I was avoiding doing school work. I really got hooked watching Ken Dryden in net for the Canadiens. Maybe that was the start of it, all my dreams come true – a smart hockey player. I was crazy for Dale Tallon that first year of the Canucks. I remember listening to their games on the radio. During that first season, even though they didn't do very well, they never got shut out. I believe they were the only team that year to never be shut out. To this day I hold onto stats like that; I search them out."

Joan agrees that a game is pleasurable because of the whole experience of the game, "the dramatic tension of not knowing what's going to happen next (but desperately wanting to find out)" but that's only part of it. "When I walk into GM Place," she says, "I love the buzz that starts before leaving Georgia Street. Even the scalpers seem endearing and authentic. I love sitting with thousands of people and sharing an experience with them. Like theatre, it isn't just the conflict. It's the spectacle. I also love screaming with thousands of people. When else do I get to do that? Ultimately, like good art, it's the emotion of the experience that stays with me. And it's a sensual experience – the sound of blades on ice, slapping pucks, grunting, skulls cracked, the way the air smells cold."

AFTER MY FATHER recovered from his impromptu stress leave, the need to support his family flooded in around him. He was hired – this is way before Antiques Roadshow was a glimmer in some capitalist's eye – by a downtown appraisal firm as a Fine Arts Appraiser. No more fast-talk auctioneering, no more Caterpillar tractors in Sparwood, no more weekends table-polishing for me. For him, it meant a nice office, better suits, an embossed business card, trips across the country to lend his expertise as to the value of sterling silver tureens, pewter steins, Lawren Harris spooky landscapes, Chippendale chairs and Georgian double pedestal desks. He knew everything.

For me, his new job meant Sotheby's and Christie's auction catalogues. These came to him from London with a list of prices attained at auction for each item; my job was to transfer each price to the white space under the lot's description. For the years we had together, before I left home at eighteen, my father would bring home a stack of catalogues on a Friday night and I'd spend the weekends reading, marvelling at the colour plates, getting paid a dime for thin ones, a quarter for fatsos. I still remember the Arts and Crafts catalogue from an important sale in Chicago. Gustav Stickley's clean lines, the possibilities of oak, form married to function. Sure, I learned the gruelling rote work of the underpaid secretary, but it was also an education in history and beauty, about how art is everyday, how beauty is not perfect or clean or even shiny but found in a wood's flaws and twists: the birds-eye of maple, the brush's slip on hand-painted porcelain, the corner where the Haida basket doesn't angle right and so we know a human's hand was there.

After several catalogues devoted only to them, I became obsessed with Japanese netsuke. These are miniature sculptures that served both functional and aesthetic purposes. Kimonos didn't have pockets in the 17th century, and men suspended their tobacco pouches, pipes, purses, or writing gear on a silk cord from their kimono sash. To stop the cord from slipping through the sash, a toggle – a netsuke (rhymes with Gretzky) – was attached. The netsuke was often decorated with elaborate carving, lacquer work, or inlays of rare and exotic materials. For my sixteenth birthday, along with a springer spaniel puppy I'd begged for (my first birthday without my sister), my father gave me an ivory netsuke, an egg – not even two inches long – with an even smaller carved baby bird, beak up and open, emerging from the top. It is ingeniously made: the bird moves and could only have been born there, since no one can figure out how it was inserted. I've tried to get it out, but the baby bird won't fly. It was an apt symbol of birth, of fledging, of a girl about to fly from her family's troubled and emptying nest.

For awhile I collected cobalt blue bottles and he'd surprise me with a milk of magnesia or a pale blue glass insulator he'd found in his travels. When I left home for university, my father visited his favourite antique shop and found the perfect Early Canadian ash table for my kitchen and four rod-back chairs to match, chipped and wobbly, beautiful and with me still.

It's inane to behave as though things matter more than people. When Lily was toddling, I refused to move valuables from low shelves. She was told to be gentle but allowed to touch, to hold, as I was. It's impossible for me to ignore, though, the importance of things – artful, crafted, lovely – in my life. I wonder, looking at his drawings in the prison camp journal, whether he fancied himself an artist, too. Art is everywhere.

LET'S AGREE THAT in the last thirty years, postmodernism allowed television commercials to act like art. When we view ads now, we don't see only product information and persuasion to purchase, wasp-waisted ladies in fat-skirted dresses holding a bottle of bleach like their Stanley Cup. Now we see parody, intertext, irony, aural and visual texture and representation, a questioning and broadening of what is entertainment, culture and commerce. Sure, it's all capitalism, and it's gross to pretend commerce can be better when art is attached, but still. The industry standard for "ad as art" might be set by Nike. One ad in particular helps to explain how I read hockey and demonstrates the "power of the startle."

I've watched this ad fifty times, on television and on my computer. I could watch it fifty more. Each time, I'm dragged into an arena and onto the ice through the end boards by the throbbing bass line – ten bars of rising, single-note crescendo – of New York garage band, The Mooney Suzuki, playing "Don't Fence Me In" while the Swede Markus Näslund and the Russian Ilya Kovalchuk play keepaway. It's a mock-up, an imitation of a professional game – one team wears Canucks jerseys, the coach is clearly interested in the action – and yet the two players don't seem able to dance with the whole team:

they're too good and too stoked by each other. *Oh, give me land, lots of land under starry skies above, don't fence me in.*

Then, in a surprising parody of a breakaway, the two players follow the puck out those kicked open end boards and onto the streets of New York, in and out of hotels, restaurants, cabs, alleyways *Let me ride through the wide open country that I love, don't fence me in* and finally back onto the ice as their teams and fans await their return. No sooner have they joined the play *Let me be by myself in the evenin' breeze, and listen to the murmur of the cottonwood trees* than Kovalchuk bears down on an uncharacteristically defensive Näslund, his shot rings off the crossbar, and the two players watch it soar, once again out of the arena. "Let's go," they gesture, and we leave them dangling from the glass, trying to escape the confines of the rink – *Send me off forever but I ask you please, don't fence me in* – back at the beginning.

The version of the song is infectious: the singer is out of control with emotion – brash, crass, pumped and optimistic; he can barely catch his breath and his voice whines with passion and irony and sexual excitement. This is New York, after all, and the song is anti-urban irony versus the pastoral and laconic lyrics. In an interview in *Splendid*, an online music magazine that reviews mostly indies, The Mooney Suzuki's Sammy James explains how the ad came about:

"Nike commissioned us to do our interpretation of an amazing Cole Porter song. And we were very excited to do that because I love the song and when we read the treatment of the commercial, it was this great celebration of New York City, and the spirit of New York, and we were really psyched and inspired to be involved in that." Not surprisingly, James is asked whether cutting a commercial for Nike would damage the street cred of the indie band. Not surprisingly, a guy who got paid Nike bucks has a justification for his commercial enterprise: "It's not like the dark specter of sacrificing your artistic integrity visited us one night with a sickle in its hand and a bag of money in the other," James replies. "There was this really cool group of creative people coming up with this great idea for a commercial, and they were inspired about it . . . Like a Nike ad isn't a commercial. It's in the genre of pop art."

I'm not sure who you have to be to see the ad as a celebration of New York; it's clearly a sixty-second ejaculation in response to hockey, and neither team wears the now-embarrassing Rangers logo, that symbol of excess and greed and arrogance and cellar-dwelling. And I don't care who says it was the brainstorm of edgy hypertext wiseguy adboys: Al Purdy did it first, thirty years ago, in the poem "Hockey Players" which coins the famous definition of hockey: "this combination of ballet and murder." Part of the ad's power and pleasure, what helps it stroll into the arena of artistic appeal, is how it refers to Purdy's poem visually and in terms of plot:

> We sit up there in the blues
> bored and sleepy and suddenly three men
> break down the ice in roaring feverish speed and
> we stand up in our seats with such a rapid pouring
> of delight exploding out of self to join them why
> theirs and our orgasm is the rocket stipend
> for skating thru the smoky end boards out
> of sight and climbing up the Appalachian highlands
> and racing breast to breast across laurentian barrens
> over hudson's diamond bay and down the treeless
> tundra where
> auroras are tubercular and awesome and
> stopping isn't feasible or possible or lawful

Given that stanza, you might think Purdy's poem is a reverie on the Canadian game, played out east, for the purpose of uniting a country steeped in an incomplete history, an over-simplified and idealized blah-blah on hockey players and their sporting culture. That it's the cultural opposite of the Nike ad. No. The poem veers into a commentary on the game's essence and the body and soul of the player who plays for the hockey nexus, one that includes the likes of Nike, even though it was written decades ago:

> And what's the essence of a game like this
> which takes a ten year fragment of a man's life
> replaced with love that lodges in his brain
> And takes the place of reason?
> Besides the fear of injuries
> Is it the difficulty of ever really overtaking
> A hard black rubber disc?
> Is it the impatient coach who insists on winning?
> Sportswriters friendly but sometimes treacherous?
> – And the worrying wives wanting you to quit and

83

your aching body stretched on the rubbing table
thinking of money in owner's pocket that might be in yours

And Purdy doesn't let up on the real reasons the sport exists, now that it has been taken out of the natural landscape and placed in an arena where profit is the motive for most involved. Retroactively, he doesn't allow that Nike ad to stand as a lovely representation of the freedom and open-endedness of the game and its players. Grow up people: it's about profit and power. And yet the ad gets more beautiful when read in the context of Purdy's foresight and wisdom:

Out on the ice can all these things be forgotten
in swift and skilled delight of speed?
– roaring out the endboards out the city
streets and high up where laconic winds
whisper litanies for a fevered hockey player –
Or racing breast to breast and never stopping
over rooftops of the world and all together
sing the song of winning all together
sing the song of money all together . . .

Part of why I keep looking at that ad is because it's a poem and I get excited at the way it communicates with Purdy and vice versa. I get a charge out of the meeting of minds, the overlap, and of course from the surprise of those bodies leaving the rink because they have to. And then there's the music.

Back in Stalag-Luft I, my father writes in his journal – or is this book a graphic novel? A poem? A butler's pantry? A log sort? – "There were quite good assortments of records on the camp, both modern dance records and classical records. A lot were private and the others were communal. Communal records with communal gramophones were sent to blocks through an American officer and private records and private gramophones could usually be borrowed at any time. As a result, the 'Kriegies' could have a jam session, or a quiet evening of the heavier classical music, quite frequently." Back at home, in New Westminster, my mother and her twenty-year-old university girlfriends were listening to the surprise hit that hooked up the laconic winds of Bing Crosby with the sleepy and smoky harmonies of the Andrews Sisters, for the sexy, legato and swinging 1940s version of Cole Porter's "Don't Fence Me In."

Buried deep in his next Red Cross package, my father finds the record carefully packed by his sweetheart at home, and the song becomes an anthem for the men within the barbed wire, an inside joke, the POW's equivalent of the stretch pass, the breakaway. *I want to ride to the ridge where the west commences/ And gaze at the moon till I lose my senses/ And I can't look at hovels and I can't stand fences/ Don't fence me in.* Imagine the physical and emotional torment the song caused those men. Take your pick – The Mooney Suzuki or The Andrews sisters and android Bing – the song is sexy as only Cole Porter can be. Desire is always at the heart of the bass line's throb.

The "power of the startle" came the second time I watched the ad and couldn't pull myself away from Näslund's face, the quick sticks and familiar jerseys, the joke of the game and its resemblance to Purdy's poem, which I encountered in even that first viewing. Second time around, I could place that sixty seconds into the context of the whole song, to align the whole spectacle with the memory of my father and mother, with their love affair – even during war and across the troubled water – through music. It's a complicated minute.

THEY GET BY ST. LOUIS and for the second round series against the Minnesota Wild, it appears Näslund has bleached, straightened and cut his hair and is wearing a gold chain deal at his clavicle. Does he not know I loathe bling? Lily watched a bio of Jovo and it's like she's had a first date. She knows his parents' names, that they came from Eastern Europe, and that he's a good dad to his little girls. She resents his pretty wife. Bert looks stronger, smarter and more arrogant all the time. It's hard to hate the Wild when five come from B.C.

It's been two weeks in the weight room and Jeanie reminds me to focus on small steps of improvement, this after I can't stop looking at a woman whose body is strong, long and perfect. Her leg press weights were huge discs, like tires on a logging truck. I want calibrations, stats to quantify muscle development. Why need numbers now? But I don't have knee pain, no joint pain. My leg muscles burn but not a dangerous pain. My ribs pop out at the back, and my neck feels unstable, but I've worked through it via door hangs and patience. No headache again this month, but I'm having insomnia and if I lie awake, I worry. So I imagine myself with hockey players, as a part of the story, and I'm asleep in a minute, sometimes two.

One reverie that lets me go to sleep: I'm in Toronto because I've been nominated for the Giller Prize. I'm there by myself, out in the lobby of the Four Seasons, wearing red floral but funky and my arms are miraculously toned, the Canucks – spiffy suits and damp hair – shoulder through the doors and greet me, wish me luck with the book, which they loved apparently.

The last time this kind of obsession happened, it was the wee Mancunian, Davy Jones of the Monkees, "Daydream Believer" blaring on the radio at Maynard's Auctioneers, my dad taking me to see the "band" live at the Agridome, and then a personal signed letter from Davy – "You don't have to be a bird to feel the way you want to feel" (I'd told him in a letter I aspired to be a seagull); I knew he drove a Jaguar XKE, knew his likes and dislikes via *Tiger Beat* mag. A school chum dropped by the summer of 2003 and Tom waved his arm across the hunky pics adorning our fridge – Markus, Steve Nash doing a hamstring stretch, Bert holding his kid, Brent Sopel hiding behind hair. "Look what I have to put up with now!" he appealed for sympathy. My friend strolled past him to have a look at my latest knitting project. "She's always been like that," she said dryly.

She's right. But till that moment I hadn't recognized the similarities: as I grind the gears up the offramp of fertility, I'm becoming more like that twelve-year-old teeny-bopper in love with a five-foot-four big-eyed pop singer.

Some nights at the Gillers, Markus becomes my platonic date for the awards and he's proud to be with a smart, talented babe like me. It's good to feel this awful crush, to remember how powerful and powerless lust can be. I'm pleased for my body, sure, and also sad – deeply – that I will never entice a man like him again. This psychological fixation, though, this default consciousness that goes to Näslund, can come off pathetic. I imagine a couple of hip blondes watching me from afar and smirking and vowing never to be old like me. Did my mother feel this for Frank Sinatra? Is it interesting? I don't know, but if it isn't, that's even more sad.

That's the reverie, but on Saturday, my friend Bill Gaston – who wrote the hockey novel *The Good Body* and played pro in France – goes to Vancouver in real life because he's up for a B.C. Book Prize really. In Bill's book, hockey has-been and now grad student, Bobby Bonaduce, remarks that body-people (hockey players, models) are exotic to head-people (academics). Bonaduce – the whole novel – constantly underlines a separation between mind and body and yet idealizes the special kind of hockey genius that is a perfect overlay of body on mind. Although the subtleties of communication were shared as a team in the room, on the bus, behind the cameras when Bonaduce played, "on ice is where it really happened. The brilliance of some. All senses sparking, working at the widest periphery, aflame with danger and hope both, seeing the whole picture, the lightning-fast flux of friends and enemies, the blending of opportunity and threat. Words didn't stand a chance here." In real life, Bill arrives at the awards at the Bayshore Inn and a bus pulls up and young men in spiffy suits and damp hair get off. "Hey!" he says to his wife, "There's Cliff Ronning!" And it's the Minnesota Wild, post practice, in town for Game 2 the next night. "They all looked really small," Bill tells me, "and their faces surprisingly uncut."

Gail asks if I'm using the gym at night. I say no, too embarrassing with those twenty-year-old males pausing long to graze between sets. "Don't worry," she says kindly, "you've fallen off their radar." She asks me to press my knees back into the table and is cheered by the "something there" – a muscle beginning to flex. She is amazed by the human body, by how years and years of nothing won't kill a muscle. How, even at eighty, a muscle will begin – very quickly – to regenerate.

The series is getting tougher physically. A fan in Minnesota behind the penalty bench tells Bert to shave his back. Responding to reporters who ask about the hits he's taking in front of the net, he says, "I appreciate your concern for my well-being, but I'm a big boy and I can look after myself." Linden wore his lucky suit to the airport. He calls it his "go-to suit" and says he's wearing his "go-to tie, too." The reporter calls it an impeccably tailored, single-breasted three-button job. He is Adonic in clothes. The NBA playoffs are on, too, and it's odd to go from Tracy McGrady's smooth skin and smirk and his diamond earrings, to Keith Primeau's scars and open wounds. *Macleans* magazine's James Deacon says, "the Canucks also have the league's goofiest tough guy – no one is safe from Todd Bertuzzi's practical jokes and wise-cracks." He calls Näslund "the league's most earnest and honest captain" but spells his name wrong. "Team Happy" he names them.

Game 6 and the headline in the *Vancouver Sun* says "Remain Calm." I take this as a bit of communication. Fifteen years ago, I tried to find peace via kindergarten meditation. I had to breathe for a long time in an interesting way and shut out the clatter and clutter of voices in my head, clear a space for an all-knowing spiritual guide. It took a few tries, but I made contact. The guy seemed suspiciously Jesus-like and it's possible I'd gotten in touch with everybody's collective cliché, but then I was supposed to shut up and listen, hear the words that were to be my lesson from the spirit I'd conjured. Today, a million jokes come to mind, cynical one-liners to excuse my foray into mysticism.

Then, though, I was desperate for a trick that would – at thirty and starting from scratch – fool my brain into believing the future was bright, or manageable, even hopeful. "Remain calm," he said and I've used that mantra ever since, when too much is on the line and I might come, once again, undone.

So I take that headline – *Remain Calm* – to be a touch base from my go-to guru. But by nine o'clock, it's over and they lose 5-1. I thought coach Jacques Lemaire didn't allow that kind of offence. What happened to the "shut-em down and win by one" strategy? How embarrassing. I am remaining calm, wondering if they can endure such shame, such a blast to hubris. The last game between them is tomorrow night. I am irritable, bothered by the stench of a chocolate cake box mix Tom has made. The house smells of bad sugar and edible chemicals. In early interviews, they said one more round was their goal for this year and that became my goal, too. They've done that, be happy. No.

They haven't lost three in a row all season.

They love their fans.

They know how to travel.

They have more to lose.

They have home ice, last change.

They own the ice.

Tonight's game, says Näslund, will "show what we're made of" but I disagree. It shows, certainly, aspects of determination, will, intelligence under pressure, excellence of coaching, fitness, ability to concentrate. It shows how well two teams can prepare for a game given only about twelve hours – after a quick flight, sleep, a meal or two – to prepare. But what they're made of has been demonstrated over the course of the season. A poor game – or a good one with a loss – can't erase the good games and brilliant plays. A good game – a win – does not erase the last two boners, or others that showed the team still has flaws, gaps, character. The Wild claims Vancouver was too cocky.

When Burke says "character" he means it only in the positive sense. But character, to me, means complexity and the ability to shapeshift, and that means winning and losing and growing from both, wherein growing is the aim, the journey most important, the ceremony most meaningful, not the outcome statistically. Renegade fan, that's me.

Swallows are back for the playoffs, scouting the perfect roof pitch. This is the longest day. I am irritable, anxious and distracted, fed up with the dull parts of the world and hooked on drama; only the lives of those twenty young men seem important and worthy today. It's everybody's game seven.

AN AWFUL LOSS, shameful. This game is so hard on body and head. To see Bert finally score a brilliant one, to believe it will be the game winner, to feel such relief and glee. And then to watch the Wild score three goals, two off chaotic bounces, for Bert to be penalized late and then the Wild score with no time left, a pattern that will repeat next year Game 7 versus Calgary. And then to see him bent over and pained at the bench, unable to raise his head, hands shaking, fingers pinching the bridge of his nose; grieving the passing of a golden opportunity, of his heroic moment, his heroic self.

"How does it feel?" Bert is asked within minutes of losing. He is on the locker room bench, trying to cope. What kind of question? It's a counsellor's question: get the talking cure started, son, articulate the pain, get it off and running, say it. No. It's an asshole's question: spill the blood, let us watch your pain grow and spill over, you owe it to us to say it out loud. "It sucks," says Big Bert and he can't go on, has to get up and leave the scrum, a pattern Näslund will repeat after the Game 7 loss to Calgary. Tonight, Näslund says he feels empty. Former Vancouver GM Bud Poile who joined the army after his rookie season, was said to be so "conditioned to winning" that he was "volcanically allergic to the humiliation of defeat." So, too, Team Happy's brilliant wingers.

They've played two games in twenty-four hours and there's much to learn from watching these men swallow defeat in their own style. In minutes, Morrison has shaved his playoff beard, end of ritual. He is composed, yet repeats the outrage of two goals off bad bounces, Cloutier, Cooke, and Morrison are honourable and calm in defeat. Cloutier is even logical. But not Bert and Nazzie. Bert swears and blames and comes apart. Näslund is unable to speak.

SUNDAY MORNING, the yearling ewe with ear tag number 19, kept despite her bow legs and whom I know as Nazzie, births a big ram. Wednesday: at eleven I go out to check the remaining three ewes. The day is sunny, an ideal lambing day. Number 11, ringer for Daniel Alfredsson – the too-long and wide tangled hair, the low centre of gravity – is nickering beyond the coops and under the blackberries. She's passing a water bag, goes down, and then up. I can see a nose coming out; two more down-and-ups and there's most of a bony head. Alfie's agitated and doesn't want horizontal. Tom's due back around noon, and at noon the head's been out for half an hour. The nostrils are flickering, but I don't know how long this can last. Every year, a new scenario to figure out. Clearly, the lamb's legs haven't come out first as they should. They're probably bent back and blocking the shoulders' exit. I'm not strong enough to get her into the stall and besides, it'll be easier with Tom. I watch and wait. He's back. We get her into the stall, ease her down onto her side – I hold her front legs and press on her neck – and Tom's up to his elbows in the ewe, trying to find and figure out and get a grip on all those legs. He pulls hard. We wait for another contraction – my hand on her belly can tell it's coming – and out slides the lamb, looking good, alive and kicking. Another few minutes and Alfie stands. A few contractions – she's looking at both of us, her hairdo's a mess – another lamb falls easily onto the straw, enclosed in a tight placenta. Tom rips it open (wondering: alive?) we clean the nose and mouth and face – and it's up and kicking: two gorgeous, alert and strong lambs. After hauling the bucket of molasses water and a feed of grain, we leave them to get the suckling started in private.

At 3:30 I brew tea and go out to gloat and peer through the cedar boards and into the shadows. What looks like a placenta dangles from Alfie, not quite passed, and above that, a lamb's foot, sharp and white, sticking out.

Again, Tom is elsewhere but close. It's a long fifteen minutes: Alfie up and down and distressed; the two lambs bleating now, hungry and loud. It's been more than four hours since she started labour. The lamb's dead, I figure, but we don't want to lose this ewe; she's never had a single, always twins and last year, triplets. Swedes.

He's back. Tom washes his hands again and when he climbs into the stall, he says, "Well, here it is." "No, that's just placenta," I say but when we cut it away, it's a tiny lamb still encased, not fully developed. That's three.

The foot is still sticking out. We lift the loud lambs into the next stall and get Alfie down, same routine, but this time my face is pressed into her neck, close to her face; I don't want her to die and I'm sorry her lamb is going to be dead, that we didn't check for others. Never triplets two years in a row, and never a Dorset with four.

This one's easier. Alfie's contractions are weak, but Tom can feel the other foot, pulls it close and out comes the lamb. "It's alive," he says, but his tone says, "not for long." I wipe the nose; the mouth is gaping and frantic like a bird's. The body is so limp, the heart fast and terrible; the breaths aren't working.

"Think I should swing it?" and he does, to clear mucus lodged in the windpipe. I don't watch. He brings it back and Alfie goes to work: licking and nickering and pawing.

"I have to go out again. I'll be back at five. If she hasn't improved by then, we'll stomach feed her." He means the last lamb.

He's back at 5:30 and the lamb still isn't up. It's been ninety minutes and that's way too long, given her trauma just to get here. Tom milks out Alfie and down the throat goes the tube and an ounce of thick yellow colostrum straight into the lamb's stomach. Another hour, Tom checks and she's hypothermic. We fill the deep sink in the mud room and in she goes. I thaw a jam jar of milk – kept from this year's first births – and as we dry her with a towel, we feed her stomach again. An hour later, Tom goes out to the shed – we're going to use the hairdryer if she's still shaking – but she's up on her big front knees trying to feed. I go out an hour later – between periods two and three, who knows who's playing – and she's curled warm and calm into a snug and thick-strawed corner. She gets up, wobbly but determined and heads straight for the first available teat, a forager already.

That was a long and full day in this complicated place: wisdom, cooperation, trust, intensity, wonder, details – that leg dangling; that fleece at my cheek – fear, mistakes, regret and panic. I would change nothing, not even the fourth lamb, to make it easier or more pleasing. It is what living means.

A month or so later, mid-May, while I sat upstairs one morning at the computer researching stats on female fans and the NHL, turkey vulture shadows fell across the windows. *Cathartes aura*: first part of the name deriving from the Greek "katharsis" meaning to purify or to cleanse. The second part derives from Greek "aura" meaning breeze. Turkey vulture: purifying breeze. It was going to be a hot, still day and the shadows blocked an already bright sun. This happens when you live on a hayfield that runs for several acres next to a riparian zone of old growth forest and Lennox Creek – creatures die, small and large, and turkey vultures tidy up – but I went outside to look anyway. The birds had landed a field over where our flock was controlling a neighbour's grass; several hung in the drooping branches of a Douglas fir, another stood huge and hunched on a fence post. I got close before they stuttered away, flying and twirling low in the air and then landing lazy and greedy in a cedar. Our calm sheep flocked across a narrow ditch and tore up the sweet grass from under a willow. To get to the base of the vultures' tree, I had to drop into a wide, dry swale and worried about so little water again this time of year.

Literature allows, even prefers, melodrama at this point in the story. I could make you cry with the right length of sentence, the stirring image, the most skillful repetition of key words and emotions. Maybe an analogy from fiercer struggles, a battle waged long ago on a field like this one, a bomber shot down and soldiers killed, two young men wandering wounded through the German night. An analogy would make you think, connect, and so feel more deeply. Or I could turn your stomach. Put you off nature. Enough details – the smell of morning on new wounds, the colour of the flesh in the stomach hole the birds had started, the sun's heat on my hands, the mother ewe's nonchalance – and I could make you cry. And you'd cry because the dead lamb – likely attacked by a small dog left too long off-leash on the Goose Trail and allowed to tear out the anus of our lamb – is the last of that day's four, the one we thought was dead and helped to live, that warmed in our sink, the one that struggled so hard to be alive. Ear-tagged #7, her eyes were still intact so death was recent. You'll feel worse because it was that lamb and not the first, or the easy second, because that's how stories work. The reversal of fortune, the twist of fate, the incongruities of nature, will make your catharsis more powerful, more pity more fear, a better story. But the ewe – Alfie – won't distinguish between her three lambs. The flock is not sorrowful. They've moved on across the ditch to the sweet grass under the willow. It's only me and you building the story of the lamb's life and death, and now the story can't be whole without both the optimism of birth and the disappointment of death.

LATE IN THE SUMMER I wake up at night to let the cat out and I'm coming out of a dream about hockey. These are ice dreams, players skating and there is chaos and cold, the sweaty smell of bodies close. Because I'm with them, see? I'm either on the ice with them, or I'm on the bench waiting to play, but there's no glass in front of me. When I sleep perchance to rest, I'm going fast and hard. No wonder I'm tired. I've been up all night with the team. Or I've turned into a television camera. Last night, Steve Thomas is there on the ice with me, because I know he'd be nice to me, make the right sort of joke.

Because I didn't exercise during our camping trip, or because I've dropped my water intake and haven't been eating enough. Or because I am ageing after all. The last few days seem to be the beginning of bad times. Yes, my body looks different, but I don't feel much stronger. I must be; the weights have increased, but I feel like a phony. Real muscles, I suppose, take years to form. These are girly muscles. What does power feel like? Does it feel like hockey along the boards?

Heart palpitations are wild, eyesight is weird, moods are irrational. Crankiness like I haven't felt for a long time. There is a musty blanket on my motivations; I have to push hard to do anything. And there's so much to do. How can I have gone from pleasant and fun-loving to cranky and beyond pleasure so quickly?

Is my knee less strong and less sure than even a month ago? I can't do even a few telephone book squats without pain and odd movement in the joint. And of course tonight this is significant, an undermining I don't deserve. The rest of me feels and looks stronger. But that one spot – that whopping big symbol – is still vulnerable, unstable, about to hurt and give out. Tonight, it seems ridiculous and the work of being calm, patient, pleasant and a kind mother is unfathomable. I feel ill and inept. I feel like a fucked up knee.

At the same time, I'm a wimp, a loser considering the end of an exercise program too soon, because it hurts. I watch a Lions game and players limp off the field and I think of athletes who are enduring more profound illness and injury than I am. The spirit of Steve Yzerman and his bionic knee visits me; his bobblehead on my desk bobbles with derision; he sneers at my weakness, at my own head a-bobbling. Is it a case of courage, or will, or do they endure because they're doing the one thing they always wanted to do? Is it a case – this pain tolerance and working through an injury – of caring enough to endure?

What did I think? That this would be a simple, methodical, systematic and quick rise to physical superiority?

Tom is calling me Sporty Spouse. Other times, he's calling me Surly Spouse. He's right both ways. It's like being in an overrated girl group when I'd rather be playing with the boys, the real players, those who know the right chords, who can improvise, they're that good.

I run into a former student leaving the gym, one who was a competitive swimmer when I met him a few years ago. It is a brief "hello" as we meet – he recognizes me and I see him as taller – and I'm drawn to him – Christ, he's possibly twenty-two – in a sexually attracted kind of way. This has to do with his body, although I notice nothing about it, couldn't say which muscles look best or what he wore. It's the sense of him as an athlete. There's a charge, an electricity. So he's not my student, or a boy, but a man who has focussed and pushed his body, has competed and won.

But also, he has lost. He's experienced profound disappointment, loss of esteem and self-worth, he knows others were counting on him and that he let them down. And so, emotionally, he is a god, a hero, one who has the capacity to empathize and yet who knows that we have to get over loss, get over shame, and start training again. A character. Any game is not about us. The game is more important than we are as individuals. It's the game that needs feeding and we mustn't wallow in our own disappointments or the game suffers. And so part of the charge is what I learn from him, the standard he sets for my own attitudes to self. Am I making him exotic?

I'm drawn to a photo of Näslund, mid-slump last year, dark circles under his eyes – is that the pain of concealed injury? Deep anguish at letting us down? That photo suggests he would understand my own failures and yet turn his broad back unless I got my shit together and moved on. A trauma coach. With huge thighs and strong knees. But it isn't only trauma and bewilderment.

I ask my mother if she knows the final score of the football game, Lions vs. Winnipeg. I'd watched the first half – trash talk, bad calls and too many almost-caughts by Geroy Simon, screaming arm-waving and head shaking by a frustrated qb Dave Dickinson.

"Are you reliving your childhood?" she asks, and chuckles. This isn't her usual disparagement. She is amused and pleased.

"I guess." And it isn't a return to the hard parts of childhood; it's more a return to the easy, fun parts, not exactly carefree, but the growing up in a great and clean city, falling leaves in autumn, boats on the water, mountains over there, cabins by the beach, Davy Jones pics on my wall. Outdoors and games. Attractions.

Do I have it right? At twelve, I broke my kneecap while my father was missing and my sister was getting all the attention. The two things – fracture and bewildered sense of abandonment – became one. I have not healed either hurt.

"You're wondering why you waited twenty years," says Gail. Well, it's thirty-five, but yes. And wondering what it has to do with my dad. The loss of him for awhile at twelve – Lily's age now – must have been painful, and then his return, my mother's claiming of him and the attendant pain, her denial of me and my own. Is this about hockey? It is. About the den, the television, Jean Béliveau. My competition with my dad, his easy attention, his kindnesses, and shrapnel surfacing in his arm. Is this about finally getting around to grief, coming to it though a weird tunnel or side door, or breaking through the end boards and into the world of play? It is.

THE SUMMER LINGERS, cleanses, and when it's over, as I've said, I aspire to live games. Gaston's username in the pool is FUKT and he's made me join, for twenty bucks, a dead simple, point for goal, point for assist, no goalies, no plus/minus contest. Sure, it's fall 2003, the season's only a week old, and only about six points separates top from bottom, but this morning I am apparently "pool leader" and my photo – okay, it's a photo of James Joyce, owly spectacles and angled fedora – graces the pool's webpage. I have chosen Ziggy Palffy – one of only two pool members to do so – over Todd Bertuzzi and am cleaning up.

This morning, FUKT and I will board a plane and head east to read at a toney writers' festival. As my companion's flying drugs kick in, as he does the Buddhist mind game he must to avoid the strangulating panic of flight and sees a cone of safety envelop us, we take off and there's the surge of life and glee – the suspension of disbelief. Bert's eyes glare out at me from the seat back pocket. "The Great Canadian Male" *Enroute* magazine calls him – a very close close-up in black and white that accentuates his scars, the grim violence of his eyes, the edge of malice around his mouth, and also the mocking of violence that is always around the corners of his eyes. He is an asymmetrical God. He is also a shy man who loves to laugh, but the photo attempts to conceal these qualities. Bert is the character in my story now – Nazzie's sidekick, the burly brash Italian to Nazzie's golden Nord, the red-haired naughty brother, as he once called himself, Steinbeck's Lennie – *I'd pet 'em, and pretty soon they bit my fingers and I pinched their heads a little and then they was dead – because they was so little.* – where Nazzie is George – *Guys like us . . . are the loneliest guys in the world.* I covet Bert's texture. The photo is gorgeous.

And it bears an uncanny resemblance to a painting by Jack Shadbolt, "Hockey Owl." Though Shadbolt became associated with the Group of Seven and other eastern artists, his work is considered regional; his psychic and natural landscapes are found here, where the west commences.

Art critic Scott Watson – once a kindly TA in my Intro to Visual Experience class at UBC in the seventies – interprets Shadbolt's Hockey Owl series as part of the artist's ongoing exploration of ritual and fetish forms which he did, this time, by transforming the owl into a hockey player with jersey numbers painted on like overlapping bird feathers. Shadbolt intended the series to be comic, but there's also a dark side to these images where the figures "disintegrate into fields of destabilizing energy."

Enroute Todd mirrors the Hockey Owl. In each, both dark and brooding eyes are slightly hooded, one eye more than the other. The sharpened beak takes the same angle to the left; no discernable neck. Part of Shadbolt's ironic flair is achieved through endowing the owl – a bird associated with wisdom and intellect, the head – with the trappings, the jersey numbers, of an animal renowned for the body's genius. At the same time, Shadbolt allows us to view Todd not as a thug or a neckless predator, but as a thinking man trapped in a bird suit.

The *Enroute* story is subtitled "The King of the Mooks." Philip Preville fallaciously suggests there are only two types of hockey player – those who come with incredible talent and don't need to work hard, and those like Bertuzzi, who must embrace hard work in order to survive, the mooks. He then borrows from Mary Shelley to elaborate – "If Don Cherry were Dr. Frankenstein, he'd have built Todd Bertuzzi to be his hockey monster" – and then describes the player: "looks like he was born on the wrong side of the bed. He is ruggedly handsome, which is another way of saying that brute strength and athletic prowess really can change public perceptions of beauty. He wears a natural scowl even when he is perfectly relaxed . . . He might as well have bolts sticking out of his neck. Other than that, he's a regular guy."

Preville then offers an explanation – a touch snide – as to why the Canucks were unable to beat Minnesota in the second round of the playoffs. See, Todd's favourite film is *Braveheart*, "the story of a Scottish mook who became a warrior, put his people first, spent his life drawing and shedding blood for the cause of victory, and became a legend." The writer suggests, for one thing, this might be why Todd is always last man out on the ice, that "by going last every time, he elevates himself within the group. He becomes Braveheart." "I just like coming last," Bertuzzi counters, a disingenuous act of self-elevation. But Preville maintains he over-identifies with Braveheart. "If the rink starts to resemble the battlefield of 14th century Scotland," he cautions, "you're probably taking things too seriously." The Canucks lost because they tried too hard to be warriors in a boy's game, Bert especially. No mention of the artistry of Bert's drop pass, incongruous in such a fast game, musical, syncopated magic.

In a 2002 article, ESPN's Eric Adelson captured Bertuzzi in a more complex way. Drafted in the first round in 1993 by the Islanders, Bertuzzi was disappointing. Not enough grit, according to coach Mike Milbury, and so the megagritted Clark Gillies was invited to have a word with Todd. "If you're built like a freight train," Gillies told him, "don't drive around like a Volkswagen." The analogy bombed and Bert's game got worse. Four years later, in Vancouver, the complete game gelled.

Bertuzzi was born in Sudbury, site of the mysterious geologic feature known as the Sudbury Structure. Some believe the huge crater was caused from within, by a mass of magma that rose and solidified before violently breaking through Earth's surface. Others believe it came from the sky, the result of the impact of a huge meteor. Bertuzzi's father, Albert, is a working class tough guy, mythically strong and boastful about the family's aggressiveness. "Todd got a snowmobile for his seventh birthday," according to Adelson. "The next day, he plowed it into the side of the family garage. By age 15, he stood 6'2", 195." His father says Todd doesn't respond to criticism: "he has to be stroked" instead. By the time he came to Vancouver to play under the usually ego-busting Mike Keenan, the ego was already mangled and Keenan had to stroke. "He had dealt with a certain level of rejection," Keenan said. "There were unrealistic expectations, and he put a great deal of pressure on his own game. I tried to get him to understand it wasn't going to happen overnight."

Though Adelson depicts a player with a sense of humour, with a past, with a wife and kids who help put the game into context, he also refers to Todd's difficulties over the years – and still in 2002 – with his "smoldering anger." Golf helps; also, a workout routine that includes running drills, football receiver out-patterns and badminton; longer minutes; Markus Näslund.

Put that Braveheart photo alongside Hockey Owl, though, and Todd Bertuzzi is made complex once again, not the man of the easy analogy, the persistent cliché, the belittling analogy or the simple story. He's the Sudbury Structure. He's as textured as feathers, as interesting as night, as genius as a neck that turns all ways.

SPORTS HISTORIAN Allen Guttman believes hyperbolically, "If the runner's stride (and agonized grimace), the gymnast's vault (and forced smile), and the goalie's save (and muddled brow) are not forms of art, they certainly arouse in us emotions related to those we experience when we listen to one of Bach's cantatas or contemplate a still life by Chardin. Unquestionably, there are physical performances that live in the memory like the lines of a poem." A 2004 year-end compilation DVD sent out to Canucks season ticket holders includes bits of interviews first broadcast for pay-per-view subscribers before games. The style is grainy documentary, odd camera angles, a wash of blue, and deliberate focus faux pas. It is some marketing student's A-plus project: seduce the chicks, man, but let them think it's art.

The best interviews feature Bert and Nazzie. In one, we see only Näslund's chiseled face and bright eyes being interviewed; he looks away suddenly to his right and whines like a teenager, "Hey, do you mind?"

"I wanna watch you," comes Bert's off-stage and crinkly adolescent voice.

"No, you can't," Näslund tries. Bert and Jovo take the seats next to their captain, Jovo between the two rough and tumble puppies. Bertuzzi slouches magnificently. A body fat index of what, negative three?

"Don't worry about my interview, no," Näslund gripes. He is tidy and handsome in a black golf shirt, hatless and clean shaven. All's forgiven in seconds. "You've got the same shirt as I do," he says to Todd. "I have the same shirt but in black."

"Cool," comes the reply. Todd is one huge slouch, ball cap pulled low, tattoos to the pits and arms propped behind his head, or one hand is wrapped across the side of his face, holding up his huge head, holding back the laugh.

Näslund tells the interviewer how he and Todd are more similar than people think. "He's a little bit bigger and louder and better looking." He's delighted with this repartee, full of twinkle, looking over at Todd to see what sort of reaction he's getting. Jovo looks like the pre-verbal brother, toggling his silly head between two hero brothers, unable to keep up, but glad to be included.

The interviewer asks Näslund, "Is Bert as grumpy as everybody says he is?"

You can smell something burning as Nazzie's brain does a quick risk analysis. "Around the rink, yes," says Näslund, trying to say that his friend is complex, not limited to how fans and media see him, and also trying to taunt the big asshole who crashed his interview. There is a long pause as the camera watches Todd avoid a reaction.

Then Todd speaks directly to Markus. Both men are delighted with themselves: "Keep riding the fairytale this city has about me being grumpy, buddy. I'm a character here in this city. Nothing more than a character. I go to the rink and I put on my costume, and then I go home, buddy."

"The big S?" Näslund ribs, "They force you to put on the big S?" Todd's laughing now, but it's a joke between the two all-stars. The performance is meant for each other; their faces are full of glee.

"I just heard him laugh," the interviewer says to Näslund.

"Yeah, he does."

"You got no clue, buddy," says Todd Bertuzzi. "No one has a clue."

CHAPTER FOUR

IN THE ROOM

Sport is our way of preparing young males to act as physical enforcers of a vigorously defended economic and gender order grounded in inequality and domination, it is not fun and games.
— Varda Burstyn, *The Rites of Men*

"You slimy fucking cunt! . . . You fucking well stay away from my god-damn friends! I didn't give you permission to talk to them! I'm sick of you bunch of cocksuckers! You write lies about me and I'll have lawyers crawl-ing all over you. I don't forget people who try to fuck me!"
— Alan Eagleson to Alison Griffiths

Hi Lorna,

Friday should be fine, but it's important that I don't let your expectations get away from the reality of these guys, and how they usually do interviews. I would say that you'll probably only have 5-10 mins with each guy max in the dressing room after practice. Media access is for ½ hour after practices by NHL policies. In addition, they don't last very long with interviews due to the high media de-mands they have every day.

Hopefully you'll be able to get the information you need in this time frame.

Take care,

Chris

Early December 2003 and a 4-1 loss to Calgary. Näslund left the game with that groin. Things might go better for me today since it's unlikely he'll be practising.

My stomach has reached new levels of acid. I'm rattled. Why am I here? How did this happen? Yes: there is courage involved, I'm brave and willing to risk and those are admirable qualities, yes. New situations – mega-stressful ones – so I'm alive, right? And terrified. I'm afraid of humiliation, that I'll embarrass myself and they won't let me back. I'm out of my element and might drown.

ON THE BUS into Vancouver, a nice balding Regina man, my age, asks about kids today. He's worried about the violence and our default setting of aggression. I question how or if things have changed in the last twenty years and characterize the young men I teach: funny, hard-working, determined, compassionate, obsessed with drugs and sex, sure – who isn't? – but also inspiring. He's glad. "I'm reminded of that song by Billy Joel," he croons, looking out at the frosted fields of the Fraser Valley, red-tailed hawks and winter-skinny coyotes checking the dormant rows, herons tall in the ditches. *We didn't start the fire, it's been burning all along.* It's early for shitty pop tunes, but sure, okay.

I've bought a tape recorder, soft-sided satchel, black jeans, ankle boots, notepads, books on sports writing, three days parking at Swartz Bay terminal, a return ticket on the PCL bus, two nights at the funky hotel. I almost bought lipstick. I didn't shave my legs, so it can't be about sex. But it is a first date. Yesterday, I tried to find shoes to make me look sexy while not hurting, in a skirt that hit an inch too far below my knees, in an orange sweater I made myself and love but which is not flattering, and again in the mirror trying on jeans that rode too high on my hips for this decade. I realized: I'm not lovely no more. I am a woman past prime who once could make a thirty-year-old stud-man itch. But not no more. Past a certain age, it's all country twang.

But today isn't about attraction or appeal. It's about a story, about men.

I have long held a fascination – maybe hero-worship – of women who work as foreign correspondents. Ann Medina, Anna Maria Tremonti, and these days Canadian journo-chicks like Kathleen Kenna off to scary places to track risky and complex stories we need to know, taking photos we have to see if it's going to work out for democracy. They risk life, but it's more than that, a mix of up-tempo smarts and the ability to look brainy in perma-press khakis and a blue Oxford shirt. Mary Tyler Moore, semi-ditz reporter, tossed her toque into the cold Minnesota air in the seventies because she was so tickled to be a reporter in a man's world and still have a cute apartment and date handsome guys with chin clefts. In Vancouver in the seventies, it seemed possible to be the flip-haired, A-lined Mary but not the trousered Margaret Bourke-White.

Each summer, say between the NHL Awards and the draft, or between the draft and when the Swedes fly back for camp pre-season, we should read *Net*

Worth, by David Cruise and Alison Griffiths. The history of the business; why players' salaries now resemble social insurance numbers when they used to make less than car salesmen (in fact, some *were* car salesmen in the off-season to feed their kids); why the one-time player profile – under-educated and full of heart farm boys laced up for the love of the game – changed: *Net Worth* exposed the financial and psychological nihilism of icky Alan Eagleson and contributed to his eventual incarceration *vis-à-vis* the disappearing players' pension fund. Griffiths and Cruise were also critical of the "lazy, greedy, infatuated sports writers" who let the testochrats in hockey do whatever, as long as they got their smart beers with the boys and their not-for-print injury scoop. Griffiths endured the egomaniacal Alan Eagleson's foul mouth, his threats, the tomato juice he dumped down the front of her dress, and she still got her quotes. She took a quick boo at Bobby Hull's balls in hospital – *"Gawwwd!" moaned the Golden Jet as Alison introduced herself. "Will you look at these!" He yanked open his baggy sweatpants to reveal the swollen, empurpled orbs of his testicles – it would have been impolite not to look.* – and got on with her questions. Mary Tyler Moore meets Lucinda Williams: let's be her!

In 1990, a sports reporter for the *Boston Herald*, Lisa Olson, was in the locker room of the New England Patriots football team when a player cocked his cock at her and asked, no doubt rhetorically, "Do you want to take a bite out of this?" A team's a team, right? So others dangled and taunted. When Olson complained and the scene became public, the players accused her of being a "looker"; that is, a reporter who lets her eyes wander below the waist of athletes while worshipping in their cathedral, the locker room. A Miami Dolphins wide receiver elaborated and called her a "dick-watching bitch." Even though women sports reporters had a constitutional right of access to interviews with players since a Federal Court ruling said so in 1978, the Olson incident caused a new debate about a female reporter's rights and the sanctity of *the room*.

For my first visit to a professional sport locker room, I read tons. Players – okay, mostly football players in the USA – routinely riff obscenities in the room when women reporters attend, apparently, and they throw jockstraps and dirty socks and wadded up tape at them, too. Reporters who want to keep their jobs, who want to be seen as professionals and not whiners, come to view this as teasing. I became versed – in a neurotic, pathetic sort of Mary-Tyler-Moore-manic, self-doubting way – in some women reporters' self-imposed codes of conduct: looking – or the appearance of looking – is not allowed; stay out of the shower lane so you don't see players naked; carry a big notepad and look at it instead of their body; don't smile because that's flirting; wear pants. In other words, you're an intruder, so watch it and behave yourself. Peter Gzowski recalled the Oilers' locker room in New York in the early eighties; at least five women were writing about hockey regularly for the New York press. The room was full of them. See? There's one in the corner trying to hold eye contact with the heartthrob handsome – and nude – Donnie Murdoch.

I freaked myself out. The locker room did not seem welcoming for women; too many rules, for one. And it seemed governed by a culture that services old-school newspaper beat boys and sports-show gel-hairs and gives them whatever they need – post-game stats, pre-game predictions, insider yuck-yucks – to oil the machine of the team's public persona. But it gives them – or writers not part of the machine like me – little else.

I like the term *hypermasculinity* when applied to the culture of sport. Cultural critic Varda Burstyn uses the term to describe an ideology that proposes "an exaggerated ideal of manhood linked mythically and practically to the role of the warrior." It's a playful, edgy way to suggest that in our appetite for games and their high-priced trappings and ideological simplifications, fans are caught up in something full of energy and also full of risk if they're female or care about females. Professional sport is a bullhorn that blasts, "men are stronger and more interesting than women, they're the ones worth watching, worth spending huge money on, worth emulating." In sport, men dominate women in every way that matters to a species genetically coded to attack, have quick sex, multiply and then attack again. Olson wasn't welcome in the room because as a reporter, a professional with the power to criticize the men's game, she had the ways and means to invert the sports-power hierarchy and screw its sidekick, gender bias. And the only way to take that position away from her, since they weren't allowed to kick her out, was to make her presence in the room all about sex, to suggest she was there for one thing: to cock watch.

As if that's a bad thing. Sport – from its origins in Greece to the Williams sisters on the tennis court and Börje Salming's hot underwear video (I can't take my eyes off the skate cut on his still muscled back) – contains sex and also sets it free. According to Burstyn, "bodies are not merely collections of muscles, bones, and will; they are also animated by sexual drives." Even though sexuality in sports – and everywhere else – has been distorted and devalued or over-played, sport "is a powerfully sexualized arena." Burstyn assumes "that the force of Eros – driven biologically, experienced sensually and organized socially – is an in-built drive that is present and seeking expression, at both individual and social levels, within sport and its culture." The erotic isn't a shameful thing, even when it is a dimension of sport. It's inevitable. "Any practice of intense physical engagement," Burstyn points out, "will by definition have erotic elements or erotic effects, since the body is a sensual and sexual entity, not simply a collection of muscles and reflexes."

When a woman enters a men's locker room and that room is also her workplace, is it sensible, reasonable to insist that the erotics of the situation and setting be ignored? If I happen to be turned on by men's wrists – I am – should I avoid looking at Dan Cloutier's to keep up the mask of professionalism? What if Markus Näslund's collar bone is showing? Do I look at that and let him see me look, or pretend not to? There's that scar on his jaw. And his hair's wet! Forgive me: I'm heating up. What a slut.

I CIRCUMNAVIGATED GM Place twice before asking a kind man at the jersey store where to find gate nine. Of course, it's around the bend, under the overpass that crosses False Creek, at ground level, where the ice is, my dear. The ice on which they practise.

PR guys are known as *flakmen*. Chris Brumwell had said to ask for him at the security desk. A beefy dude makes a cellphone call, scoots back around in his rolling big-armed chair like Rod Steiger's sheriff, and tells me, head up to Section 117.

"Section 117. Section 117." I'm trying to make it mean something.

"Section 117. You're going to the practice, girl!" he condescends. This feels like seventies television. I adjust the satchel on my shoulder, slap on the sticky-backed visitor badge, and enter the elevator. Suddenly, there's a taller, thinner, more tanned uniform beside me smiling patiently and inserting a James Bond security card before punching in a top secret security code – or 117 – and backing out of the elevator. "Take care," he says.

"There is nothing less empty than an empty stadium," wrote Uruguayan philosopher, Eduardo Galeano, in his brilliant meditation on soccer. "There is nothing less mute than the stands bereft of people." GM Place is an empty hall now, like a high school at summer break after the janitors have done their final tidy up; bright Vancouver light broadcasts through the big windows. A gal could curl up in the sun with a Daphne du Maurier mystery and a nice cup of tea, over there beneath the ten-foot Paul Bunyan poster of Todd Bertuzzi, snooze, and never have to force herself to find Section 117 which, it turns out, is behind the players' bench.

I sit ten rows back, watching practice, behind the real reporters and their confident slouching, their obvious ease and familiarity, their jeans and ill-fitting sport coats. They share inane comments and easy analysis about this sport ("Sydney Crosby in Pittsburgh? Gotta love the draft!") and all others; we are in the stands, where clichés are horked, chewed and regurgitated. Jim Hughson, play-by-play for hometown TV and future HNIC game-caller, is handsome and pleased; his confederate Dan Murphy is young and pleased: the TV sports guys have charisma, a little shine on their faces, longer legs or they exercise more than the, let's see, "lazy, greedy, infatuated" writers.

Jovo is showing off. A female has arrived: me. He is the class clown teenager, or a youthful Labrador retriever at play. Brad May is looking, too. No Näslund here, but Bert, Linden. They know I'm here but peer up wearing frowns, not desire, suspicious like dogs who've sniffed menace on the wind, territorial. Or it's all the stupid freak-out reading I've done. It's too dark up here for them to see.

Forwards are down there in pairs; one shoots, the other picks up rebounds and scores. The defence are doing power play stuff, passing and shooting from the point, trying to get it through. The rink is small and close and nothing seems very difficult. Say I was a beat-chick. I'd get bored with drills and mid-ice huddles with the coach I can't overhear, and I'd come to resent my editor for insisting I be here to watch every practice, jumbo coffee clutched and notepad parked. But today, it's like watching the poetry of horses running in a huge paddock: don't stop, don't slow down.

I was late, practice is over. The beat boys – I'm the only woman for miles, except a European's broad-backed mom on the bench – leap the railing down to the tunnel and stroll off to the room. I'm to wait for Brumwell to come and get me. It's a long wait and the rink is warm, or maybe that's the walking I've done. It's peaceful. Mattias Ohlund comes out the other tunnel to reach up for his little boy dangled from above, a dad coming off the morning shift.

Brumwell's dark head pops up out of that tunnel – he's tall and tidy and athlete-calm – and he beckons with a finger. I walk the steep stairs in new boots to where he is, hand him my bag, "hold this," and climb over the railing. "Careful," he says – he's what, thirty-two? – and I'm pissed off already. Can he not tell I have *two* quads now?

There's a security meeting for players at 12:30 (Kidnap prevention?

Avoiding extortion? Groupie tips?) so I'll have to be quick. "I'm going to close this door in case anyone's naked," he says and I do a comic whimper and wish to take it back immediately; test failed. He walks like a basketball star, pumpy and pistoning. And then – presto – I'm in.

The lights are dim, the wood is clean and blonde like their wives, the carpet plush. My eyes adjust to the subtleties of the lighting and the deadened acoustics. It's more bank lobby than cinderblock sweat palace. I expected the brightness of concrete, the stink of wet skates. But I've seen the room a million times on ten o'clock sports, so why didn't I anticipate this? In my panic, I've reverted to cliché. "Stand right here," Brumwell says and places me on the carpet, near the team logo and I'm not sure if there's a penalty – instant banishment or a liniment shower – if the long square toe of my new boot touches the crest. They don't tell you anything here; there should be a handy checklist of rules and regulations for newcomers. Ohlund's kid shoots pucks at the wall and past my ankles.

I am the only woman in this room.

Ruutu is not totally but mostly naked – a chest like asthma – skinny on a bench behind a scrum of beat boys. Morrison, down bench, is thick with his own media brainsuckers. He's wearing hi-tech underpants and I can see his bare toes.

Linden stands over on the wall of fame, the line of honcho stalls – Näslund, Bertuzzi. He's pack leader, watching, making sure. But this isn't about me, right? This isn't about me. The dog metaphor's gone too far. But he knows I'm here, Linden, and appears wary. I'm surrounded by men in towels, tightly wrapped towels and bare chests and bare feet. These men have been in the shower – fuck, I *knew* this would happen – and I'm so trying to keep my head up, my eyes front. This is a huge test: will she or won't she. Am I making this up?

Fiction writers are trained, or predisposed, to look. We see everything and stockpile details including the whitest scars in the most private places, the exact glint of light off a Swede's wet hair, the cubist angles of a man's feet when they've been crammed into skates since five years old – so that the story is true. Details make stories true. A Sedin in a towel. Cloutier over there, so narrow and tight I think it's Tom for a second. How tall *is* he? I'm afraid to look closer, trying to be cool, to break down my own self-consciousness, to push it away and observe everything. There is too much to observe. And there is no eye in team.

And here's Johan Hedberg, back-up goalie for Sweden at the Olympics, how do you do, and he's so close I should smell sweat, but it's like they've sprayed a neutralizing agent in here. Goalies have smooth faces, unscarred. "Can we sit?" I ask and wonder if I've screwed up. "Sure," he says Swedishly, but I'm worried now because we seem to be sitting in Ruutu's space. Brumwell moves away, but he's never far. I could be anybody. Hedberg's wearing black spandex boxers. So close to my thigh, his quads look efficient. Eye contact, they train for that. I have my wee notepad but I can't read *and* make eye contact. For once, I have questions.

I'm wondering how Swedes – since Börje Salming (his near-nude torso still fresh in my mind, the underpants drawn up over ass-crack) was a superstar in the early seventies – may have changed not only the playing of the game – with their flippy passes and superb conditioning – but also the personality of NHL players in general. Salming was beaten up by Philadelphia and The Hammer in his second game for Toronto, and we hear still about chicken Swedes and their unwillingness to fight, but the game, too, is less willing. Maybe Swedish young men are different than North American ones and they bring a certain temperament to what has always been a cocky, arrogant game. Hedberg won't say anything negative about anybody, but he has thought about the difference between an eighteen-year-old Canadian player and the Swedish version:

"What I think that the Canadians do have, when they're fifteen years old they usually go into the Junior leagues, then in the NHL they get drafted and they get traded and they're pretty much on their own. They get the families they're living with, maybe, and they've got their teammates. They've got to take responsibility for their own lives. I grew up in my hometown, I played in my hometown, I lived in my parents' house: eighteen years old. It was a guarded life. I think maybe Canadians are more used to living a grown-up life right away. Takin' care of themselves." He drops his g's like Markus and his eyes are small. I suspect he had a good relationship with his mother.

I've asked Eric Duhatschek about Näslund, about whether we're to buy the clean living, priestly demeanor. I was trying to gauge the captain's influence on contemporary players and whether he defines a new generation, but ones who come with a European set of codes of conduct. Is Näslund really getting off on water sports and hospital visits? "I think he'd be the same, no matter which generation he belonged to," replied Duhatschek in an e-mail. "He reminds me of Håkan Loob, who played a decade in Calgary" – and whom

Näslund names as a boyhood idol – "A finer person, I've never met. I hate to generalize about any group or nation, but in my experience, there are few bad-guy Swedes. Whatever their parents do, they seem to raise well-rounded children."

All this talk of exemplary citizens, the great guys, the wonderful humans, the foreigners and I'm missing Derek Sanderson: the fast lane, the hair, the thirteen times in detox, the cocaine and Valium, hauling hay for his horses in his burgundy Rolls Royce when the tractors and trucks had to be sold, the first beer at seven years old in Niagara Falls, Ontario.

"You can't live like that," says Hedberg. "Because the competition's so high here and everyone knows that if you're not in shape or not taking care of yourself, you're not going to be in the league. There's too much on the line when you're making great money and having a great life." He believes people like me have returned to the game because the game is that much better – with faster, more skilled, and conditioned athletes – than it was twenty years ago. Europeans should get credit for some of that discipline.

We talk about the difference in education in Sweden versus North America, and he seems more keen to talk about what matters – his kids' education, the quality of programs, teacher training and their relationships to students that he admired in Pittsburgh – where he led the Penguins heroically into a Cup semi-final – before coming to Vancouver. The cynic in me resists what must be some business major's graduating thesis/marketing model: give us a bunch of ripped and ready athletes with no closeted skeletons and great smiles, who care about their families and help build a strong presence via charity work and you bet we'll buy tickets, we'll buy for the whole family and feel good about doing it because the team is us, or like us, or like we would be if we were making millions and playing for a living. "This team is a good school, too," Hedberg says and looks at me closely. I want Johan to start more games in goal now because he cares about education and doesn't misbehave.

"We have fun like everybody else," he says. "But now there is high profile everything, and back then guys didn't make as much money and they were working in the summertime. Now this is our job and the only thing we have to focus on. I don't think it's the marketing thing; I think it's the true nature of the guys. We are good people. I look around this room and they're all good people."

I look around the room and freak. Brumwell's facing me now; he's too polite to point at his watch or give me a hook around the neck but I get the message. It's like a male cocktail party in here, without the cocktails. Others in the room are having chats like this but I'm the only one sitting down. "When you're tired of the playing you have all the time in the world to spend with your family," Hedberg finishes. "Now, it's the good life."

"I'll see if Brad's still here," says Brumwell. What's that supposed to mean? I've taken too long? I thought he was in charge of May, making sure I get my man. This joint has too many doors. He doesn't tell me exactly where to be. I stand with my back to the bench, and holy shit wouldn't you know it, I'm in the shower lane. Linden's way over there, on veteran row, trying to look like he's not watching me. And I'm trying not to see anything in the showers, and then my boyfriend Näslund comes out another door – French farce, or what? – and he's in the same room as me and then he's passing through, grinning, grinning at Bert over there with Linden – shouldn't a cranky groin make him limp? – and I do look at his ass in those jeans. Yes, I do. I want to check it against the website version, I think, or I'm in love with him. What's the difference? And then he's gone, out another door. My gaze goes back down Shower Lane and, oh shit, here comes Morrison, one very tight towel around his small forward's waist, another princessed around his shoulders, he's coming right at me, will pass within inches, his Nike sandals squeak (I know he's near; I can hear his feet) and I turn my head slowly away and it's a terrible turning away. The pull is towards him, his face, a quip is called for, given the grin I can corner-eye see on his shiny clean face, and a smart-ass quip is so close to my lips: "Man, those feet are loud" but I don't say it. He's testing me. And Linden's watching to see what I'll do. It feels rude to look away, unnatural, screwed. Sport is always erotic: part war zone, part back seat. I look away and immediately – and now – regret it.

There's another Sedin (I think it's another one), this version in jeans.

No Jovo in here. Maybe he's banned when women visit. The coach is chewing him out in the principal's office or throwing a tennis ball for him down in the parking lot.

May's face is beautiful and big and layered with scar tissue. A new batch of oozy lumps hood his left eye. This face doesn't like women much and there'll be no flirting with a guy like this from a gal like me.

I am the only woman in this room, for miles.

But I do not drown.

Me: "Can we sit there?"

May: "No. Over here."

Me: "So has Chris told you where I'm from and all that?"

May: "No, but I know what you're up to so you can just ask your questions."

I gather wits. He's chummy with the real reporters nearby, first names and nicknames and a wave. It's like sitting next to a bear cub – cute but dangerous, strong and mean. He swats and growls at my version of the new-age hockey player.

"Exposure through the media – three sports channels, twenty-four-hour sports radio–and all that attention. Obviously there's an onus on being 'good,'" May says. "You've gotta be aware of your role in society and also just as an athlete, that you have a code that you should live by. But I think there's more people watching so you see it more often. You covet what you see every day. It's just the way the league is today. If Brad May the hockey player is being criticized or scrutinized on how he is as a father and a role model and all these other issues, then obviously you have a greater responsibility. Should it be that way?"

I tell him I don't know, because I don't, but it was a rhetorical question.

"Should it be that way," he self-meditates. "Clearly, I guess, Joe Public's gotta get their motivation and ethical behaviour from somewhere. So if they need a role model, football player, baseball player, hockey, whatever it is, I guess it makes sense, but I'm one that thinks it starts at home." He's debating these points with himself and I get the feeling he does that a lot. He's a thinker, the singlet-wearing tough guy in the bar who buys a couple rounds and then hogs the conversation so he can tell everybody what he's decided about everything. Still, that makes me the lucky shy chick asking the questions and hanging on his answers. "But not every home is a safe place or has the right values, so if they can get that from an athlete, I think then you have to carry that burden. Maybe it seems unfair at times, but I think you owe it to the game of hockey. The game's been great to all of us. And our league and our membership: you owe it to the rest of us."

What he's describing is a code of honour, then, between players, one that creates a culture in which the culture can thrive. This man is an enforcer or scrapper or role player, described in one hockey bible as "a paradox within a conundrum in a puzzle." He has been suspended for twenty games for swinging a hockey stick, baseball-style, at another player's head. More recently, he pleaded guilty to misdemeanor assault and disorderly conduct charges following a fight in 2002 outside an Arizona bar hours after the Coyotes' last game of the season. He fought the nightclub manager and two sheriff's deputies; the sheriff's office recommended felony charges but May convinced everybody he didn't know they were police officers, that he respects cops and would never strike an officer. He was fined $5000 and given a year of probation and a hundred hours of community service. I remember the awful horizontal of him, concussed by a Mats Sundin check at the end of last season, taken from the ice on a stretcher, out for the playoffs. "Are you able to be yourself," I ask him, "in this role?"

"At times, no. At times, no. But you know what? There's a responsibility placed upon us that when you wear the Canuck jersey there's a real code of ethics and conduct that's expected of you. I think every team's the same, but Vancouver makes a point of getting that out there. So I think it's a good place to be."

May drafted high – fourteenth overall to Buffalo – in 1991. He's been in the league a relatively long time, and the only change in the profile of players he'll concede is the amount of airplay they get. "This has nothing to do with your article," he says, as if he knows everything, "but the war in Iraq. There's been 500 soldiers die, not even. World War II there were thousands, millions of people that died and it was never covered. And it's tragic and everything, but every one of them in Iraq is overplayed – and the violence – and you see it and you see it. Life is different today because the world is such a smaller place."

"I've gotta get these guys upstairs for a security meeting," Brumwell intervenes (Suicide bomber? Sniper spotting? Steering wheel locks?) and escorts me out to the hallway, shows me where to turn left and which door to go through to the small world. As I leave, May's already slapping the back of a veteran writer he obviously likes more than he likes me. I could listen to him – watch that face twitch from bullshit to sincerity – for hours.

"So, do I have to be from *Sports Illustrated* to get a half hour with a player?" I ask. Brumwell turns and glowers. I've over-stepped, but I thought reporters were supposed to be aggressive, that you don't get good stuff unless you get tough and demand it, that lousy manners put the *access* in *media access*. Not true?

FOR THE NEXT night's game vs. Minnesota, I have invited a writer, a former student who once was a model in Paris and is now doing graduate studies, who writes quirky, complex fiction, and whose poet parents will be amused –

or betrayed – when they know I've exposed their first-born angel-face to a culture like this. Clea – she of the blonde hair and hockey-wife-long legs – will join me tonight.

23/11/03

Yeah yeah, let's! You'll have to fill me in on, oh, how the game works, who's hot and who's not beneath all that gear . . . maybe I'll get hooked. Ok, I'll try and watch a few games beforehand to get a handle on some of the rules etc., but I think in order to really care about the game I'll need some bios on the characters, I mean the players, and you can fill me in on all that as they do stuff like fight and fall on the ice. Totally cool.

4/12/03

You mean I can't wear a mini skirt and half top? How are they gonna see me and want to marry me if I'm like all bundled up? Yes, call me when you get in if only to get me more pumped up than I already am. Go Canucks go! Do you have things to wave around like towels or whatever or do we get those there?
Can't wait!
Fan-in-the-making

I get a haircut in the morning but no colour. The new grey meets the old colour job like the clear, bright, and fast Thompson River meets the muddy brown Fraser at Lytton. I shop for clothes so they'll see me and want to marry me. But why would they? I consider a sleek black leather jacket but buy nothing.

It feels like I drank too much last night. My eyes are puffy, the headache, and I have slight shame, like I've done something or said something, and someone's written me off. Maybe I'm deluded as to what happened in *the room* yesterday, but it feels as if I've contravened so many codes – the fiction writer's allegiance to observation, the feminist code of resisting the appetite for the male gaze. Everything Lisa Olson taught us I seem to have messed up. I'm very tired.

The hotel has hand-knotted rugs, the afternoon light is lovely through skylights on the third. The original fir floors creak and shine histrionically. King-sized bed, cotton sheets, satin duvet. I'm drinking bottled water and reading two books at once, a Mark Messier unauthorized bio and a Phil Esposito autobio that is full of bluster.

Messier – star centre for the Gretzky-blessed Oilers and born-again Rangers, dud-centre for the Canucks – was a kid in the sixties who summered in a log cabin on Mount Hood. His dad, Doug, wore number eleven for the Portland Buckaroos while completing a master's degree in education at the U of Portland. Without TV, the family picked flowers, swam in the creek, played cards and, says Doug, "realized the power of conversation and listening."

Esposito – star centre a decade earlier for the Big Bad Bruins, '72 Summit Series warmonger/hero – was a kid in the forties in the all-Italian west end of Sault St. Marie. His grandfather owned a company that recycled slag and was, says Espo, "a mean, sadistic bastard" who once stuck a clothespin on the boy's penis. Espo's father gets credit for his kid's first broken nose.

The bios are as different as those childhoods. Esposito takes credit for every big win and ignores, for example, Sanderson's superior faceoff skills. Anecdotes typically end like this one: "Wayne said, 'Shit, no. She'll throw me out and keep the dildo!'" And it *wasn't* him who dropped the chandelier in Moscow.

The stat-laden Messier book is more reverential and smarmy. The chapter on Messier's flaccid yet dictatorial time in Vancouver – he enraged fans with a *coup d'état* of Trevor Linden and then played awful – only glosses the work of local newsies. It was the most paradoxical stint of Messier's career and warrants better analysis. (Näslund has called Messier his biggest influence; the book doesn't mention that.) But the Vancouver chapter's better than the protracted one about September 11 in New York: Messier cheered everybody up with his awesome leadership skills.

Sex, Mess and little Pavel Bure: that's urban legend, but there's a weird chapter about Mess's appeal to the gay fan base; his private relationship with driver/escort Captan; the transvestite bar; the time he water-skied in a g-string and wig. Sure, the lingerie models, but still. That's a mighty culture shift from Esposito's day, when all the guys were screwing all the babes all the time, especially that panty-grabber Bobby Orr, "the pig."

The Messier book has one key tip for me, though it's beside the point I've been trying to make about the change in the persona of NHL Man: there's a theory out there that a team must endure two shame-making, humiliating reversals before they can win the Cup. Okay, last year vs. Minnesota was one, but has there been another I'm not aware of? Or does this year promise the second reversal?

I TAKE CLEA RINKSIDE FOR THE WARM-UP. "Will they know you now and wave at us?" she asks. She's awestruck by the group groin stretch, Brent Sopel on all fours, crawling like an ugly baby or Neil Young. We scramble through the crowds to our seats and I point at a woman wearing a home white Jovo jersey and ask Clea why women do that. "I dunno," she says, "But I kind of want to do it now, too."

Tucked in our seats, scarf – her first knitting project – over her knees, she says, "I like it when you tell me things about their lives."

The gang behind us are cattle farmers in from the valley for the game. They are down on everything and everybody and down loud. They like to say the players' names and shout to them as if they are inept toddlers in an off-grid trailer park:

"Oh for chrissakes, Malik, *what* are you *doing*?"

"Sopel, what are *you* doing on the fucking power play?"

They want to let each other know how much they know, how much of the game they fully understand. Most of their derision is reserved for Bert. One of them calls him Tard whenever he gets the puck: "Okay, *Tard*, do something." They got 15,000 bales off their fields last summer and are my age or a little older.

"Work and farm, that's all we do. And come to this game."

In the first period, they claim Bert is overpaid, under-productive. In particular, they want more hits from him.

"I wonder what you can buy for eight million?"

"A lot of hookers."

No one laughs, and we feel growing malice at our backs, a sex-charged longing to either be Bert or to see him suffer.

No Nazzie, no bonafide leader, but Bert is fluid and big and everywhere. He's rambling without Markus to pass to; he tries fancy too many times and doesn't get a good look, but he's all bigshot, trying to get it going, regardless, against a top-form goalie. The boys behind us irritate a smart and kind woman like Clea. They use "fucking" a lot and they are negative and blame-y and too predictable for a couple of literary-type writers like us, those who worship the original and timely detail.

"The refs have lost *total* control of this game."

"They never *had* control."

"There's *refs* in this game?" Hardy har.

They amuse themselves with what they think is a depth of knowledge but is only what they've heard from analysts on TV and radio.

"Oh, this is the kind of game Minnie *loves.* A one-nothing game is what they *love.*"

"This is fucking *Jacques Lemaire* hockey."

They learned that from last year's playoffs. They know the same info – we all do. But one guy has *actually played the game* and tries for elevated status.

"Yah, I quit playing a few years ago and used my stick to herd cattle. When I started playing again this summer, I had to take the tape off the stick cause it was covered in cowshit."

They repeat "*cowshit*" like line-dancers.

Things get worse when the ice girls come out. Remarks concerning boobs and butts – "I'm just saying she'd float really well" – abound. There's a woman back there with them – who knew? – and she's mostly inaudible, silenced by that expertise. But the ice chicks get them more worked up.

"Look at the players. They're all looking at them bend over."

They wear white half-tops and spandex low riders. Their cans are huge. Bubble butts, Clea calls them. One of the guys says "lick it clean" as a blonde bends deep from the waist in front of the alliterative Marek Malik, but the woman back there finally has her say: "Sorry," he says, and they're quiet.

They want the players to hit more – "May's not doing what we wanted him to," as if they were in on the signing, gave their views and got the deal done – and they want them to be nasty boys. One of the Sedins is "twinkie." Hedberg comes out almost to the blue line to make a play on a breakaway – successful – and man, they hate that hotdoggery.

These guys don't want what I want. Why do I feel like an outsider? They are wholly themselves always, no affectation, no analysis, no depth. Or do they merely preen for the lovely blonde beside me?

The Canucks are working hard at control. Ruutu and May are dangerous because they're making plays instead of taking themselves out by hitting and pestering. There's always a Minnesota player ready to slurp up a puck loosened by chaos. The Wild are opportunistic, to quote coach Cro from last year's playoffs, and our team is playing needlepoint hockey: tidy stitches, nothing too creative. But lovely, just the same. I am pulling for May; yes, it matters more that Hedberg plays well; I feel anxious for him because we've talked but drawn again by a guy like May, his dark and light, his honesty, his badness, how hard he had to work to stay in a skill-slick league, how mean he has to make himself feel. He's a guy who likes the statistics of war; Hedberg's a guy who sees the team as a school, sliding into metaphor to find meaning.

Regardless of the hot stove analysis behind us, the refs are in control. Penalties are called, some missed, some interpreted. Mick McGeough does a long hands-on-hips stare-down at Morrison who's toppled to the ice, as if to say, "No dives, mister, not on my shift, and wipe that grin off your face, college boy."

Second period, a boy – six or seven – gets a lightly lofted puck in the face right beside the Canucks bench and Clea hands me her twinkly opera glasses. Bert's all over him while play goes on. A trainer hands the dad an ice bag even before a Host comes galloping down the stairs and the kid holds it to his own head. Bert has his face pressed against the glass, watching. Every stop in play – the nurse comes down, the Host is back giving out gifts and writing down info – Bert's watching. A trainer passes the boy a stick and he holds it tight in his free hand. Back to the bench, shift on shift, no Nazzie there to keep him focussed on winning, Bert checks on the injured boy. But the guys behind us are interested in hookers and fat salaries and brutal hits. The obvious and overwhelming heart of a guy like Bert doesn't interest them. If it does, they don't talk it up. We see who we are in players – *self-identification*, the sociologists call it – who we want to be, that's why we make them heroes.

When women dare enter a debate about hockey, it is to be shut down and shut up, ignored or derided, dismissed. Women are only interested in bodies; men, of course, know more, see more, understand more. But those assholes behind me – the ones so mad at Bertuzzi – couldn't see that he was double-shifting and buzzing the red line and also going for the flick in front. They couldn't read the subtleties of his game. They wanted him to hit and destroy and would not want to debate with me the relative risk and wear and tear caused on a superstar's body – not to mention the crucial seconds he will be out of the play and off the puck – when he is hitting, regardless of his size and speed. And they wouldn't like it that he cared more about a kid than about beating the Wild.

"I'm so out of it," says Clea. "Cole and I were having dinner at the Beachhouse this week and Bertuzzi was at the next table and I didn't even know."

"Who was he with?"

"His wife, I guess. Blonde, pretty. Mid-week at around 8:30. No one bothered them." And Clea talks of the water buffalo, how tender that night.

OUT FOR DINNER WITH A DOZEN WRITERS. Some haven't heard of my visit to the locker room and want more anecdotes, others have already heard the post-visit ramble, the talking through of my anxieties and lists of details I'm trying to remember. Between the Moosewood jungly salad and the chanterelle and sour cream pie, I repeat how Morrison appeared to challenge me to look, and it sounds stupid. I'm tired of the whole thing. The writing is now about my ageing libido, its revival, and how comical that is. That's what these friends take from my story. They don't care about the scars above May's eyes or Hedberg's voice. Is it me who's made it all about me and the male body? Tom, across the table, is handsome like Dan Cloutier; his tolerant face flickers behind the candles. He can tell I've run out of steam and don't want to play this silly game. Three guests down to my left sits a friend back from Toronto where he was the dark horse up for a prestigious literary award. Tom says, "Hey John, what about the dressing room at the Gillers. What was Atwood like in the room?"

"Oh, I was careful to look her in the eyes, Tom. I really didn't want to be caught looking down." Hardy har.

The table erupts in a smarty-pants, two-worlds conversation about Atwood and Alice Munro dropping the gloves, the size of their thighs, the style of play, who'd go down first. It's hilarious and ironic and I'm being mocked, but it's better than what came before it.

A few nights later, Lily tapes the game versus Colorado, and I come home at ten and say, "Please don't tell who won the game" and she shouts from her bedroom, "Nobody won the game." Her desire to win – or to beat me – is too strong to let me have the game's outcome. I watch it, though, and probably the only way to fully enjoy it is to know nobody wins. The television camera trains us to obsess for the puck and doesn't let us see the story unfold around it. No wonder I can't understand systems or recognize variations on the trap. I miss the quiet of the live games without the hectoring TV commentary. But it is beautiful hockey – a game with impeccable defence but not defensive. Bert has eight shots on goal; at least half would go in with most goalies but David Aebescher rocks.

Jovo's battling flu – the camera catches him at the bench almost every shift, mopping his face like a shoe – and plays twenty-six minutes. Finally, in the third period, he's tired of the glitzy Colorado team's pretty plays or tired of feeling shitty. He takes the puck behind his own net (Alex Auld bids him adieu, adieu) and Errol Flynns to centre ice, across the enemy blue line, swerves, and at the instant we're waiting for the pretty passing play, the "what would Rob Blake do?" hesitation, he lets go a swift and sure wrister that fools Aebescher who has retreated too deep in the net to cover the angles Jovo's seeing.

Overtime is brilliant and beautiful and it should never end. A 3 on 1 on Bryan Allen and he takes away lanes. He is good at math, according to a newspaper interview, and tonight it shows. The checking line, my favourite line – Linden, Arvedson, Chubarov – allows no goals on eight power plays. Too bad it's not cricket, played for days and days before we have to decide. A tie game is perfect.

ON HIS LAST book tour to Canada, I interviewed writer Richard Ford. He was in a hotel room in Toronto in the early evening; I was snuggled into my office here in the late afternoon, curtains closed, door locked, tape recorder plugged into the phone so I wouldn't lose anything, seat back erect, footstool centred under my desk. When his publicist had asked how long I wanted, I said forty minutes, thinking that didn't seem long. I realize now that it was a huge gift of time. The best interviewers can make even a two-minute scramble between periods or a quick question on the convention floor seem like a conversation between soulmates. Peter Gzowski could do this. However, the affable Ron MacLean is so interested in revealing how much he knows about the game – he's so over-the-top enthusiastic about it – that we get irritated waiting for him to shut up. It's not a conversation with Ron; it's a hot dog pentatonic solo while the band takes a break. Forty minutes with Ford allowed a conversation to develop: polite intros, preamble, nervous laughter from me, a background question to reveal my expertise and qualifications; a little interpretation of his most admirable work to soften him and yet suggest my interest in his work. I could make my voice all dulcet public-broadcaster and not worry about how I looked. And twenty minutes in, everything friendly and chatty and too professional, me smarming about the beauty of his retrospective first person narrator and wondering how I was going to get this guy to drop the literary star persona and do the smooth talking flirtmeister I'd heard about (the book is a collection of stories about infidelity), the maid knocked. Ford's rich southern drawl shouted to her, "I don't need anything, sweetheart, no, I'm lying on it, no, AHM LAH-IN ON IT! Thank-you."

He came back on the line. "The maid," he explained.

"Now, you wouldn't be naked would ya Richard?" I quipped.

"Ha. When Scott told me I'd be talking to you he said 'now when you talk to her you can just lie back on the bed' and I said to him 'she's not going to be here is she?'"

"Ha. Typical," I joked. "Now speaking of infidelity . . ."

We'd had a scene by then, we were characters by then and the rest of the interview is more interesting and revealing because the rhythm and tone changed at that twenty-minute sex-talk mark.

But a sports interview – five or ten minutes in the room – isn't a conversation; it doesn't have stages or moments of intimacy or words to look up afterwards (I did have a quick check of 'covet' to be sure Brad used it right). The maid doesn't come knocking. I don't have time to prove I'm a nice person with a good heart and a fast brain. I don't write for a daily. I can't hold a tape recorder and a notebook at the same time. Ten years from now if I attend every practice and ask, "How important was it to come out strong and get that first goal?" after each game like the other reporters do, if I get sexually harassed by a pot-bellied defenceman from Windsor and don't write about it, if I get more Ron MacLean-CBC-credible and start off with, "Jarkko, when you made that hit on your brother at 2:43 of the second period it reminded me of Phil Esposito going in on his brother Tony – I know your brother isn't a goalie, but still, it's kind of the same so bear with me – and it was game five of the playoffs, Boston had home-ice and the temperature outside was minus 40 and the Boston marathon was in danger of being cancelled and Phil, apparently, had eaten two steaks that night, not his usual one, and Tony had news about Phil's ex-girlfriend back home, but he hadn't told him and here comes Phil, who'd always thought his brother was a bit of a weirdo, and he has the puck and his stomach's killin' 'im, and he's on his own and he goes high glove side and well, that's what I was thinking of when you took Tuumo into the boards and nailed him in the head with your elbow. You really turned the game around. Any thoughts?"

Ten years from now, I might have a real conversation because they'll know I'm the real deal. If it was so bad, though, why am I so pumped about going back?

CHAPTER FIVE

NOT LOVELY NO MORE

Pain, in the proper context, is something other than pain.
— Joyce Carol Oates, *On Boxing*

*[F]orty-eight, the year when things start falling apart . . . It's all very new
and strange, like adolescence in reverse . . . Once women manage the long
curve of menopause, however, they can accelerate down the next straight-
away. But early on, the pavement can run out abruptly with a dive in
mood, or something blowing – a disk, a gallbladder, a rotator cuff.*
— Marni Jackson, *Pain: The Science and Culture of Why We Hurt*

Just before Christmas, 2003, the newspaper posts mug shots – smiling, un-
suspecting – of players not producing. In bold print, their crimes are enu-
merated: BRAD MAY: 0 goals in 28 games. ARTEM CHUBAROV: 0 in 14. The
Sedin twins – their porcelain doll faces – very few in very long. It's a public
shaming. At New Years last year, for one night they led the league. This day,
they are sixth but first in the Northwest Division, five points behind
league-leading Detroit, who have played thirty-five games to their thirty-two.

I'm worried about no goals, okay. But the strategy is different this year:
better defence from great scorers.

Lily and I watch the first minutes of a Colorado/Anaheim game, both of us
under the quilt on the couch. Two hours from now, we'll be shouting and
screaming and accusing in our biggest argument ever, about the computer, of
all things. But now, as the bitter Californians boo turncoat Teemu Selänne, as
handsome Keith Carney takes another puck off his ankle, she says, "You love
Nazzie."

I say, "Oh, I dunno. He's not talking to me any more. He hasn't been com-
municating telepathically. He's moved on, I guess." And it does feel like he's
dumped me for no reason except maybe he's all Nike ego now, a bigshot, or so
focussed there's no room for a woman like me. Lily stays quiet, moved by her
mother's curious admission, however steeped in fantasy. Hard rain hits the

high window above the television. She says, in a girl-at-a-sleepover voice, "Jovo just told me he talks about you all the time."

"He does?"

"Yes, he does."

THEY'RE GETTING BEATEN UP. King, the Sedins. Two weeks ago against Calgary, Näslund without a stick, had batted the puck to the neutral zone, and still took a hard hit on the boards: Iginla came storming in and straight-armed him a punch to the head. Tom thinks this brilliant Canadian strategy and loves Iginla even more – more Olympic gold! – but I think it cowardice and ugly. No one defended or fought back.

Tonight on television, Oilers coach Craig McTavish struts behind the bench looking like the wealthiest Chippendale model locked and loaded into yet another superlative suit. Edmonton has dressed the large and mean Georges Laraque. He reminds me of Queequeeg, the harpooner who becomes Ishmael's friend in *Moby-Dick*, and who, though characterized as a savage, is shown to possess a harmony of mind and body that the Christian white man doesn't have. The official Georges Laraque website calls him "a true professional, adhering to the ethical dimension of being the care-taker on the Oilers team." Not sure what he's adhering to tonight, but he's looking for trouble. Brad May steps up – and has to look way up to fight him: May is 6'1" and Laraque is 6'3" with 30 pounds on him. Laraque seems to back off but it's a sound fight, punches are thrown and connect both ways, and May is cheerful while taking a fighting major, hugging and cajoling with the ref, having a blast. What does pain mean to Brad? "What was I thinking?" he laughed after the game, which they won 3-0. Georges' website tells us this is "not a true reflection of his game" and that he has "a happy, go lucky nature." May puts on the same face for the camera, but I've seen that face up close and there's no "happy, go lucky" about him. In 1991, he scored on his first shot in the NHL; convince me he didn't want that gift to keep giving.

At Christmas dinner – the shrimp cocktail, the roast duck, the pretty candles – instead of saying grace and thanking the wonderful world for everything, my mother says, "I don't think Wayne Gretzky was as good as everyone thinks he was." On this of all days. An old friend who volunteered at a summer charity golf tourney in nearby Colwood has reported Wayne-o golfed the whole eighteen holes with a big fat Cuban cigar bobbing from his mouth. Her friend found this in violation of golf's protocols and was deeply offended, as were other club members. Get those law doggies on his trail!

"A cigar?" I asked at the time. "He was outside, so?"

"He's supposed to be an example for kids. What kind of an example does that set?" For most of my life, my mother smoked two packs a day; I never started. After forty years of smoking, she quit – cold turkey – when she moved next door to us in Metchosin. She wanted to set an example for Lily, she said, but she was also mortified when, during a week-long snow storm and power outage, Tom had to hike a kilometre to the corner store for her pack of smokes.

"So," I countered, trying to keep the temper I used to lose as a teenager when my parents were really talking about class and not courtesy. "So. We thank him for everything he's done for the game, for our nation, for the Olympics, for everything he's sacrificed to be great, for not fighting and showing kids creativity, for having tons of babies and being happy, for loving his father in public, and then we say, 'but sorry, Wayne, we can't forgive a fucking cigar'?"

"He looked like a gangster," said my mother.

"He's an athlete, for chrissakes, not a diplomat!" Of course he's both, but I was building a case.

At the sparkly Christmas table, Tom snuggled under the José Théodore Heritage Classic toque I'd given him.

"History will show he wasn't that good," my mother said. Everybody's an expert. Perhaps she'd been into the wine while thickening gravy.

THE MOUNTAINS IN JANUARY are top-rich with snow, a kind of melodramatic and sentimental purple below I've noticed since watercolour lessons. I don't remember thinking, "these mountains are gorgeous" when growing up here. I went to the water – ocean, river – for my transcendental moments.

I've bought an extra ticket to the Colorado game for Tom so three of us can go. The extra is in the pricey lower bowl, where jackets are thick and clean, haircuts sharp, and the jerseys are signed: "To Brenda, all the best, your friend, M. Näslund 19." During warm-up, helmetless Peter Forsberg is large-headed and princely, hair straight and shiny. His cheeks begin to colour. He is amazingly handsome and becomes more anonymous and brutish when his helmet goes on. He will be the game's first star, in on all the goals. Tom sits in the primo seat for period one, and I have to meet him between one and two for my turn with his ticket. It's distracting knowing he's over there, across the ice. Lily is more interested in catching her father's eye, watching him, than in the game. There are forty men between us, and he looks lonely. He doesn't cheer, I notice, as we do (high five) when Näslund scores.

Ice cream for every meal, or neck massages every morning: too much pleasure. It's hard to watch line changes and keep track of who's checking whom. For awhile, Näslund is on Sakic and that's interesting, but wait, there's Selänne and his matinee idol face and I watch him float for awhile. The Sedin line sometimes gets Cooke and sometimes Ruutu and that's interesting, but there's Tanguay and Hejduk, yikes, and Rob Blake – statuesque – is heading for the point. It's impossible to watch well, to keep track and read the game's beautiful chaos. Colorado will win thanks to a couple of five on three gimmes – Cloutier is hounded in the crease and gets two minutes for being fed up – and also thanks to the return of Forsberg from injury; add the usual game-raising of Joe Sakic when so many family and friends drive in from Burnaby to see him score. Nothing is solved, as they say, in the regular season series between these two teams. Each has won a game and the third ended in a tie. Vancouver is still a couple of games ahead, but the division title will probably once again come down to the last week. Colorado is more confident than ever. Eastern media underplay this rivalry – it's hard for the CBC boys to think there's tension if Toronto's not playing – but we know games against the Avalanche mean everything. As well, the one-on-ones: Näslund and his school chum Forsberg; young Jovo versus veteran d-men Blake and Foote; Burnaby Joe versus Pitt Meadows Mo; mile high versus sea level. The story of these two teams has nuances and patterns. An all-Canadian rivalry would be better, yes, but some of us, hooked on nostalgia, still see the Nordiques logo suggested by the big A on the Avalanche jerseys.

To get to Tom, I had to navigate stairs plugged with men waiting to pee. Or waiting for beer. Or waiting to buy T-shirts. Intoxication rules and it's hard to move. Men are bigger than I am, and I'm swallowed by their horde. The energy in the building is different with this team visiting: the crowd is pumped, aggressive and very intense. Fun is not the point. This game matters. The lower bowl acts more civil and I'm happy for the solitude. But up close, the play is harder to follow. And Mr. Lemme-Coach-Em behind me makes end-to-end pronouncements. Each time Sopel touches the puck: "Oh no!" and each time Cloutier leaves the net for stickhandling: "Oh no!" Shut up, why don't you. "I'd give him an hour every day, just practising his stick work," he orates. An hour's a full game, meathead. You think that would help?

Back safely in the cheap seats with Tom for period three, I can watch Lily across the ice, can see her Jovo jersey's glow. I miss her already, but I'm relieved to have behind me Mr. Lemme-Coach-Em's less pedagogical cousin: "Näslund, you pussy, show up for once."

Say hockey is a short story. If so, women are characters who contribute to the story's unity of effect, its meaning. Without them, there are missing bits of motivation, conflict, point of view problems. Also, if hockey is a short story, then women are readers, too, and readers make meaning. A story isn't intrinsically meaningful. Writers don't decide, "Okay, here's what it's about" and then toss meaning to readers to catch. Meaning comes when each reader takes the words and fits them to prior experience and then decides how life has changed since before the story. Reading pleasure – satisfaction – is equal to the difference between *then* (before the story) and *now* (afterstory). How a story changes us can be what it means, just as much as plot. So women however marginal – outsiders, observers, hungry readers of the game and its men – have a role in a story in which there is no hierarchy of importance – language, structure, characters, detail, metaphor, light, eyes, uniform, work, air, silence, tension, ending, beginning, punctuation, hero, obstacle – there is no order of importance in the way I read this story. My father's here, my sister, and so is Bobby Orr. There is only news and its layers. The league – and its dominant media – forgets that meaning is not fixed, or predictable, or confined to men. I assume those who leave early from a game between Colorado and Vancouver either a) have to catch the last Skytrain to Surrey or b) have already found satisfaction in the story and it doesn't depend on the game's outcome.

It isn't hockey's fault that we don't love art enough to call Brad May an expressionist, or a dirty realist, or percussionist instead of pugilist. Coaches and players – their brains hardwired to their bodies – don't need to think of it as art, although when Bert and Nazzie talk about how the coach allows them to be creative, maybe they do.

Players don't make meaning; spectators do. And we can each make a different meaning without the game losing. The tension I feel when the guy behind me reads Sopel as inept comes because he, by moving his lips and reading out loud, tries to standardize the reading of those around him, to impose his meaning on the rest of us. But, like me, he's just reading, making a story.

On television versus Calgary the next night, Sopel slips in close to the net, knows Ruutu will hold the line, and stays off the right post. He is such a trickster, so out of character and positioned in such a surprising way – not out at the point? Not at the red line making everybody safe? – that no Calgary player notices him. He's a phantom, a puff of smoke. And when Henrik's shot comes, Sopel need not do much – aside from the enchanted hand-eye – to tip it past the young goalie, Jamie McLellan. The story – the long story of this season and last – has changed now that a guy like Sopes can be so unpredictable. It's better, but only if you read for pattern and not aboutness. Read for pattern and you watch for the next time Sopes does a shapeshift and tips a shot from a place he shouldn't be. Read for pattern and tonight's tipped goal is echo and redemption: Remember? That's where he was standing in the playoffs last year versus Minnesota, only in his own end, when the stupid puck bounced off the top of the net, Sopel swung his stick to keep it out but couldn't, so surprised was he – regardless of his perfect position – by the puck's voodoo thang.

There are as many reasons to compare the game to a short story as there are to see it as ritualized and legitimized male violence, as war, demolition, and anti-women, sadomasochistically erotic. The pleasure is great.

THE GAME BORES ME, or not enough's at stake yet, too long till the payoff of playoffs. I've gone egghead. Feminist analysis of sport has me questioning everything. Lily's teacher is baiting her with sexist put-downs and ridicule. As well, he's baiting her with derogatory remarks about hockey players ("Brad May couldn't string two sentences together.") and bad-mouthing *The Old Man and the Sea*. He is anti-intellectual and I'm suddenly outraged at him for getting her to play along. Or is he building her brain to endure the culture she's entering?

I have read now about how professional sports is a nexus that supports an economy of masculine domination, a culture that valorizes warfare and violent domination, winning at all costs, that is obsessed with best via statistics, that is riddled with propaganda that defends team sports as building character, communities, cooperation, self-esteem and fitness. The propaganda disguises how the endeavour does these things to grow capitalism's profits at the expense of women athletes and spectators, of the poor, and of truly healthy lifestyles.

I have read that sport "develops a standardized social image of the body which tends to deform the way adolescents relate to their own bodies," that it is a "'character school' which aims at creating authoritarian, narcissistic, aggressive and obedient personality structures."

I have read now of one female reporter – and other women in other pro rooms – who was sexually harassed in an NFL locker room, who was accused of looking. One commentator suggests the men wanted to punish her for crossing a boundary, for transgressing the accepted/acceptable roles for women and therefore threatening the masculine order/hierarchical system that holds domination of women as key. Her presence became about sex.

Another book details violence and sexual abuse at the Junior level and supplies too many images of team intoxication that leads to gang rape and sodomy and young women who want to be with these amazing boys and then put themselves in danger. The boys know only the team, and women are not a part of the team; they are only a part of a system that must please the privileged – healthy, elite, potentially ultra-moneyed, dominant males – however they want to be pleased. The girls are there to reinforce masculinity, not to complete it and make it more complex.

I watch a period of Boston vs. Detroit and the men seem more menacing tonight, the ageing players kind of seamy and pathetic. Or the hockey's slow: Boston wins 3-0 and the only thing that looks like a hit is when Joe Thornton brings his stick to rest gently across Steve Yzerman's waist and Yzerman goes down, his bionic knees upset at even this small pressure.

Tom remembers the hockey players in Duncan in high school. They were barely in puberty and the same age as other boys, but suddenly they were getting blow jobs at will and having lots of sex with lots of women under lots of circumstances. Suburban guys, not outdoorsy like Tom and his friends, sex in the back seat of a blue Chevelle with full-moon hubcaps in the municipal lot at the Kinsmen Rotary Park. How one guy would have sex in the front seat, another guy in the back, and the two would converse and quip and provide commentary. Even then the camaraderie – the team concept – more important than another intimacy, the one with women. Team(ing) excused rudeness and cruelty, loyalty had a narrow definition, proximate scope.

Tom thinks girls were attracted to hockey boys – the soccer and basketball stars didn't get the same sexual attention – because of the culture of hockey. The boys who played might be stars one day, the town had bred a couple of Courtnalls, after all. And everyone knew someone who knew someone or was related to someone who'd made the NHL or who came close. That system – its history and cachet – is profoundly arousing to certain girls. The violence, too, a turn-on to some.

"Quit talking about what it all represents," Tom snarls from his side of the bed. "Just let it be what it is: some girls like rough guys, simple as that." Money, power, prestige and a very strong community: girls who do not dream of discovering insulin or winning the 100-metre hurdles or reporting live from Afghanistan are aroused by that junk. How complicated can it be? "It sounds like you're just criticizing now. You're not celebrating." And the light goes out.

So what. Trevor Linden has a crush on me because I'm smart, funny, a good teacher and former country singer, because he wants to be tender to me and hear what I have to say because I'm charming and he can't resist. "The lines on your hands," he says and holds them both and has to look way down – a whole foot – to admire them, "the lines make you more." But we don't smooch because he's good and I'm good and we're hooked on each other but only in a shy and safe way that doesn't mean anything bad or disrespectful to the people we've loved longer and deeper. This is the fantasy of an egghead, spinning toward her forty-eighth birthday, badgered by the pranks (ring the doorbell and run) of peri-menopause. Insomnia may think it has me, but once Trevor gets to the part about how his life may never be complete without me and his tears come because he knows I'll never leave my family and disappear into this dream, I'm asleep.

This month, Don Cherry – *Hockey Night in Canada*'s between periods expert, hockey gadfly who resembles a more toned Truman Capote – begins his tough-love tirades about the relative studliness of visors and how only wimpy French Canadians and Europeans wear them. Tampa Bay at Montreal on a Saturday night when kids watch, and Cherry says the reason the games are so loud in Montreal is that it's the only time English-speaking Quebecers are allowed to express themselves. He refers to one player as a suck and others as studs and must – how could he not? – understand the sexual allusions. Two visorless Quebec lads get revenge: Tampa's Martin St. Louis (my father would adore him: the pint-size, the speed, the brains) scores his second hat trick in nine days, and Vincent Lecavalier (my father would love him: the number four, the crush on Béliveau) gets three assists.

So sue me for not celebrating Cherry's profound knowledge of the game, what he adds to the spectacle, and his support of good Canadian boys; I'm not saying get rid of him. If we treat Cherry's appearances as comedy, his bits are entertaining. But I don't think he is clearly – not to children – comic. If it isn't comic, then it's nasty, even hateful and bigoted social commentary. When he theorizes – although he's the expert and makes it sound factual – that only certain wuss players wear face shields, and suggests the good Canadian (read: English-speaking) kids are the real players because they don't need 'em, the level of xenophobia goes even deeper, especially since he's wrong statistically. When he refers to hockey players as "sucks" or "studs" as he did that night, the generalizations are semi-funny because they over-simplify or mock existing stereotypes, or make public the accepted homophobic lingo of the sport. But they are also overtly sexual in nature and push a code of preferable masculine conduct while ridiculing another.

They also present playing hockey as akin to sexual practice (suck or stud: take your pick). Add to those terms his apparent delight in Brendan Shanahan vowing to break the arm of a Junior player should the kid be so foolish as to hot-dog in the NHL – and he repeated "break his arm" for effect – and the masculine model presented to us on a light-hearted Saturday night is one of violent dominance and sexual aggression. The creativity, playfulness, and happy ego-centricity of a teenager, Cherry suggests, will be, and deserves to be, dealt with through extreme physical violence.

If I think of him as a parody of the old school of hockey, I can handle, even enjoy, Cherry. But as soon as I think of the boys and girls – and moms and dads – who watch him and receive his permission by example to be violent and bigoted bullies, I feel ashamed that we allow him to be so visible. And it may even be bad business. I'm sure there are plenty of women who find Cherry attractive and amusing – lots of women choose men like him as husbands – but he sticks to a simplistic narrative that invites only one, over-determined reading of the game. He is hostile to anyone who suggests there may be other ways to view it and its players.

Another night in January, I dream about Jarkko Ruutu. The last time I'd seen him was on the bench in the locker room, bare chest narrow, smooth, and slightly caved. In the dream, I watch him interviewed by an unseen host. In the dream, Ruutu resembles Igor Larionov – the Professor who is a skilled chess player and spectacle-wearer – until he flips one long and graceful leg over the arm of his leather club chair, toe pointed. I realize he's Toller Cranston – gay, artistic, subversive. Last Saturday, Ruutu provoked a Calgary player by first pretending to drop his gloves and then sticking out his tongue, à la Mick Jagger or Gene Simmons. Don Cherry was predictably outraged: "Is this what hockey players have become?" When Scott Stevens hits Paul Kariya so hard his brain swims in his skull, that's a good clean check. When Dion Phaneuf at the World Juniors hits a young Czech player so hard and high that the boy's face is fractured and spinal cord compressed, that's a good clean check. Sticking out a tongue – teasing and taunting – is a contemptuous act that insults the game.

It's also homoerotic, and Don wouldn't like that. Imagine what Don thinks when Turbo Todd lays a big fat wet one on Nazzie's cheek after a timely goal. In my dream, that's the best part.

* * *

Hey Lorna,
Actually, that probably won't be the best day. The schedule has been so crazy that I think the players might get that morning off and it might not be worth the risk.
    Let me know when you think you might be coming over and we'll see about another day.
Thanks,
Chris

ON MY WAY to the ferry, back to the gym after almost three weeks away, to my new worship. The stationary bike pedals feel stiff when I press the pad to reach my usual resistance. Cardio's okay, I'm no more winded than usual, but my legs feel weak. I go through a typical workout, occasionally dropping reps or pounds when things get hard. My legs don't feel good. My arms are fine, even triceps, but hamstrings and calves, back to square one. No they're not. I sit at the end of the weight bench and face the mirror, and even with the clunky black knee brace, I see more muscle around – leading to and away from – both knees. That night, my knee will throb above and under the patella, and the next day will bring louder crunching when I chug upstairs to check my hockey pool (tied for eighth and last night, Ziggy went out with a shoulder separation; am I doomed?). Today, all muscles have soreness. And I'm glad, not despairing. I've been battling the slings and arrows of a stupid headache and heart palpitations for a couple of weeks. Today, both are gone. A nice mix of folks: two women working through obesity, quiet and slow on the bikes, slow and steady on stability balls and curling teensy two-pound weights. They talked quietly to each other, pale and pasty, and never stopped moving. They were pleased with themselves and played together outside the bullshit expectations of those who are slim and taut. I love these funky broads.

It's my birthday on the *Queen of Vancouver*, the one P.M. sailing. She's an old ship. The ceilings hang low, the chairs stand wide on pedestals. Strange riverboat curtains loop back from the windows. It's more intimate, kinder, closer, more like a train across the country. The intercom is thin tin and hard on my ears. The calm water and its warm January air are close in this so-called vessel. The engine rumbles everything and creates tone clusters around my head.

On the ferry, Paula Brook's column in the *Sun* is about middle-aged women and movies that push the fantasy that we are desirable to younger men. Diane Keaton, when gorgeous Keanu Reeves tells her, "You are so sexy" says, "I swear to God I am absolutely not." I'm forty-eight today and I am absolutely not too, I guess, assuming anyone is looking, which they're not. But I absolutely am inside, more so than the last two decades and in a better way than my twenties. Cruel world, you betcha. I have more of these: tone, imagination, desire, wisdom, common sense, willingness to enjoy myself, socio-economic power, retirement funds, good responsibilities, bulbs in the garden, compassion, publications, colleagues, moisturizer, cds in my car and yet . . . Paula says any expectation that a young man would want me is pure fantasy, such an obvious and common one that they're making movies to get my bucks, to feed the fantasy and let me delude myself into thinking it's possible. Watch it: might have a birthday weep on the lovely *Queen of Vancouver*.

In her fourteen years, I've never spent my birthday away from Lily. In the kitchen before I left, she said to Greta Kriegie, the impervious dachshund she held to her face for the comfort of soft ears, "Awww, you don't want her to go either."

"See you tomorrow," I bounced, stressing the shortness of the trip.

My friend Rick meets me at the hotel. It's his birthday, too, and I haven't seen him more than twice since I moved to Vancouver Island almost twenty years ago. We were part of a circle of musician friends in Vancouver and its outskirts in the 1980s who played the bars. The bands and relationships and rental houses we shared shifted shape like amoebas in a Petri dish. Rick's wife/bass player was married first to my guitar player/boyfriend, who loaned his sister to my first love/bass player, who now lives in Nashville with a nice woman from outside the dish. Some were more gifted musicians than others, some had less control over urges and addictions than others. Rick was brilliant, kind and clean.

"The guy in the shopping cart told me how to park on this street," he says in the dark on the cold porch outside the hotel's glass doors. "He said if I paid him two bucks he'd keep an eye on my car, so I paid." There's always been a smirk in Rick's voice. "Wow. You look great."

Rick's wife has ended up with another man and the left-behind teenaged son now lives with Rick on a bar musician's wages which have never been great. Rick recently took courses in counselling, hoping that might be a puzzle-solver at home and also a career for a smart guy who's past fifty and a single dad. A couple of times, I've Express-mailed tickets to games I couldn't come over for, knowing it's a small price to pay for the homeopathic healing qualities of hockey: even a little can cure the blues.

"Thanks. I work out," I say with my own smirk. "Plus, no booze for twenty years. Happy birthday. Sorry it's Florida."

The Canucks, like Rick, are having trouble winning at home. Nazzie scored two against Anaheim a few nights back, reached his 800th career point, but he's not so slick tonight. I'm missing some faves: Cooke, Arvedson and Chubarov out with sore spots. Apart from the spectacle of Valeri Bure jitterbugging all over the ice – but to what end? – the first forty minutes are awful and the boys close the period down two-zip.

Rick's an excellent game companion: alert, happy for goals no matter who scores them, not too chatty except between periods. He never did have a lot of hair, but things have gone sparse in many ways. Perhaps, like dachshunds, skilled pickers shed when under sudden life-threatening stress. His knees, too, are under renovation and the rehab's going well. He and his son have found a quiet, cheap rink near home and often they're the only two superstars on the ice. Between the second and third, he disappears and comes back and hands me a bag: "Happy birthday. Sorry about the wrapping." It's a black Canucks T-shirt, a dozen sizes too big and perfect. We get overtime and the game ends tied, which to everyone but me and Rick is the same as "not a win."

A week later, January 17th, Lily and I are back for her birthday against Anaheim. Party or hockey game, she was asked, and chose Jovo. The team hasn't won at home for ages – they tied Florida to extend to five a home-game "winless streak." I'm sure they'll win tonight. They score – Henrik, a gorgeous goal, end-to-end – in the first period on what J.-S. Giguère will deem "a technical mistake" on his own part. Anaheim gets one in the second that sneaks in behind Clootch. And, okay, then another on a play that seemed offside, but fair enough. The Canucks don't fold, though; they come back with a power play to start the third. And don't score. The chances are everywhere and Giguère is side-of-barn huge and yet agile. A penalty shot by Daniel in the second seemed too slowly executed in real time, but smooth and clever and yet doomed on the replay back in our room. We were on our feet for him, then settled like a falling kite once buoyant.

We have assholes. Pissed and pushy, two guys in front spill beer and try to perfect their loud whistles. They have the look of those always riding the rails to or from drunkenness. They are young and in their own bubble of delirium. Their mouths are foul and they want others to enter the bubble and cure their abrupt loneliness. Lily doesn't like it. One tries to teach the nice black-coated short-haired gentleman next to him to whistle loud. He won't let up, leave off. He's not watching the game and it's hard for the rest of us in our pleasant neighbourhood. His buddy leans forward on the bars, and Lily and I can't see when the Canucks are trying to keep the goals out. Finally, I ask him loud: "Could you sit back please?" He turns smiling, thinking this might be a fun voice, a chick to tease, but sees me and scowls, "No," and leans ahead again.

They lose. So great for the last couple of years, the power play has been scouted and videotaped and dissected, and teams – especially defensive evil geniuses like Anaheim – no longer panic and get burned. Back in our room, emboldened by her new status as teenager, Lily tells me I have butt problems. It's the old style Levi's, she says, that make it look too flat but also wedgied. "*Gluteous Minimus*," she says. "And that short red button-down sweater," she groans, "that's not flattering." She speaks of my only cashmere. "They got some breaks," Marc Crawford is saying of the Ducks in a post-game interview. Where's mine?

Chris,
Yup, I could get to Burnaby. For what I'm working on just now, Linden and Sopel would be best.
LJ

Lorna,
Okay, we're practising on Sat at 10:30 and the players will probably be ready by 11:30 for the interviews. You can hang with the other media types that will be

there and I'll see you.

Take care,

Chris

I GET UP AT THE DARK and cold hour of five and take a seven A.M. ferry, grab the bus to downtown and check a bag at my hotel, hustle down to the Skytrain station, printed trip itinerary, courtesy of the BC Transit website, in hand. I can make it out to Burnaby for 10:30 if I score the right connections, but I'm feeling like a panicked and inept tourist. What am I wearing this time? No clue, who cares. The Skytrain was built during the last years I lived in Vancouver. From my rented house out in Sapperton, I rode it to take in the Everly Brothers at Expo'86 and that was the first and last time. Now I'll need to figure how to get to Burnaby 8 Rinks from my hotel downtown. Bus transfers.

On the train, a young man stands in shorts with his golf bag on his shoulder – it's January 24 – and chats with another guy about his game, about living in downtown and the urban noise. The doors slurp open like Star Trek and an attractive woman with hair so streamlined I suspect wig gets on, notices the golfer and begins to shriek: "Oh my gawd: you're Rod Stewart." He's in shorts, taller than Rod, actually has the wide and shiny face of a hockey player. His hair is blond and he's handsome: end of comparison. "Ex*cuse* me, you *are* Rod Stewart. Oh, I can't believe it," and she looks around at the rest of us, truly thrilled. She has him autograph something. He tries to tell her he's not, tries to be the respectful good-guy athlete, but she explains to us how and why a star would say such a thing. We're in Burnaby; we pass my Grade 7 teacher's street – Semlin. Two young conservative guys try to reason with her: "What would Rod Stewart be doing on Skytrain?" They want her to get logical, reasonable. They don't understand she's nuts. She's on the edge of turning aggressive. "Excuse me," she gets quieter and firm, "He is Rod Stewart" and then she's shrieking it loud and comic but also a brain cell away from provoking us all. One stop later, she's gone, and a laugh is had by the men at her expense.

Sleet falls at Metrotown. I don't have a clue where I am, except there's Kingsway and that's old Vancouver. And then the bus driver drops me at the rink, and I'm there along with every little boy on the planet. It's Saturday and a "Skate with the Pros" deal's going on. A dozen peewee teams line the rink in their gear and wait to meet the players. I can't see anything, except the team's on the ice and Cooke and back-injured Mats Lindgren are up in the weight room, and folks are two deep above the rink. A creepy guy keeps calling to Jovo. Who's media and who isn't? I go back and ask a white-haired, bubble-butted, pink-veloured ice girl at the front doors where I might find media, but she looks at me like I'm a big pile of poo and says with a Valley Girl up-flip, "I really don't know?" And even though I'm here early, clearly the practice is almost over and I've been led astray as to the correct time. It's over, a quick Zamboni scrape and the big-mouthed buggers swarm the ice and crowd the alleyways, smash their sticks in front of my face and hit the glass. I tell a security guy manning the gate to the corridor behind the benches that I'm looking for Chris Brumwell, that I've arranged interviews, "which way do I go?" "Stand right over there," and he points to the end boards, a few feet way. "Just wait there." I do. For a long time. And when I ask him if I shouldn't be going down to the room, he says, "No, you're in the right spot." Twenty minutes pass. A young father bends low because his kid – puffy ice clothes and big floppy skates – is so small and that's what it takes to get close enough to spit "Are you stupid or something?" into his child's face.

Twenty-five minutes and former Canuck Darcy Rota strolls past me and smiles and winks. He, too, born in Vancouver, born of course in 1953 and so older than I am, hence the eye contact. I've obviously underdressed since my knees now ache with the cold and pretty well everyone has gone, including the security man. Adios opportunity. Out back of the rink where I will catch a bus back into Vancouver, two girls about fourteen years old hover outside the skookum players' parking gates, one in her big Linden jersey, standing and waiting.

Vancouver downtown on Saturday is all commerce, and I'm fed up with myself – with my inability to get the fucking job done, to ask questions. I don't even want to windowshop new jeans. Everything is about money, suddenly, even that thrashing horde of hockey tykes waiting to touch the same ice the boys had skated on. Back-to-back hockey games and Chinese food in my hotel room should help, but no.

The next morning, I wake in Room 12. Out the tall window a one-time courtyard is now covered in fibreglass shingles and an empty trellis. A discarded condom flung from my window, or the one above, is now planted between cedar planters of grey on grey alchemilla and rosemary. This room has a desk and I can mark students' stories on a lovely oak surface with good light. I've had fresh orange juice, two cups of strong coffee in a white china mug, a warm blueberry muffin that has only the sweetness of berries and a tub of peach yogurt. I should be calm and happy with a Sunday morning spent this way – a game to go to tonight – but there's a huge mirror a metre from my face. And maybe it's the line from the student's story – about a woman visiting her ex-husband – "in six months she would be seventy-four" – or it's what's in the mirror: my own hair brittle, the tide line of colour that makes the grey and black roots so pronounced, the eyebrows gone sparse, eyelids drooped and pouches that seem more cheek than eye. No colour, even in the eyes. Or it's the migraine coming back to pick me up, or the pressure of the ghost of fertility, or the memory of so many mornings like this when I was a musician and on the road and drinking – waiting for night and work to come, the boys at the bar to pay attention, the owner to pay up and ask me back. Or a mirror is just a mirror, and I see myself in it. This isn't the bit of teariness I had in the shower yesterday afternoon, trying to warm up from two hours at the rink. These are tears I know will puff my face further, but fuck it.

Last night – the mirror is tall and bevelled – I stood on the satin duvet on the king-size bed in my underwear to have a good look at my two legs. At first, they seemed impressive and even equal, the right one finally catching up. There is quadriceps definition in both and the right one no longer looks spindly and sunken around the knee. But look longer and the difference is still there. In fact, the left one looks powerful and built; the right one is the cornstalk that didn't get light, couldn't send out roots for its share of nitrogen. And now the season's past midway: can it recover and catch up? Doubts.

The steam clock in Gastown sings "O Canada" as a dirge. The maid complains down the hall about candle wax on someone's sheets.

> Hey Chris,
> I was at the chaotic 8 Rinks on Saturday but by the time I nailed down where you were, Mr. Security Dude wasn't interested in me being there; I must resemble the dreaded ageing puck bunny or something. I'm over for another few games and will check things out with you before I come.
>   Are short phone interviews ever done with your guys?
> Lorna

Against Nashville, Clea joins me again. Vancouver wins 4-1. But a few minutes in, Jovo is tripped and goes down on his knees and slides low and hard into the boards. The pain shows, he's on his belly and his legs kick like a baby's hissyfit. He lifts his head to see if he got the call – "He's okay," I say to the nice man next to me. And then the pain floods in, and the trainer has him on his back, hand under his jersey – I know the code for shoulder separation. So many out this year already – Ziggy! – having their surgeries, gone for the season (a lovely open phrase). I wonder if Lily's listening on the radio at home. Then he's up and not cradling his elbow, but he's also not lifting his head, no movement in his upper body. He doesn't need help; that's hopeful.

Keane takes a guy into the boards, takes revenge, a Predator takes exception and they fight.

"There's something wrong about a nice balding man throwing his fists," says Clea, still a student of the game.

CHAPTER SIX

OUT OF TIME

So a lightweight hockey player like Paul Kariya, at 180 lbs but skating at full speed, has more kinetic energy than an offensive lineman!
    – Alain Haché, *The Physics of Hockey*

When a guy like Lindros comes out and criticizes the doctors and trainers, he's thinking of himself and not the team.
    – Bob Clark, Philadelphia Flyers GM

February All-Star break and I'm at the gym after two weeks away. It's good here. Wheelchairs, kind men, older women exercising in pink leisure suits. A couple of Surrey chicks strut in, Farrah Fawcett retro hair, booze and drugs written all over them. Skinny, uncoordinated. One has the body of a thirteen-year-old, but up close she's thirty. I watch her on the treadmill, going so fast that limbs splay. Then she's on the stationary rower, technique wrong, the pin still at sixty pounds where I had it, and she can only nudge that weight. She thinks we're watching her – I'm stretching on the mat, beside her now and the only one watching – and she talks loud to get her friend's attention: "Wow, that's a great stretch" – and that's it. She's in the change room washing her face. She lasted twenty minutes.

Also in the room, ladies talking about the Seniors Centre: cribbage, bridge, tai chi, checkers, dinner and dance – "Oh the dinners are lovely" – monthly Las Vegas nights, bingo. Once you're fifty-five you can join!

Holy fuck. I'm in my cubicle peeling off my knee brace and have to sit. That number is so close. And when I stop for coffee at the Tim Horton's, the contractors – boozy eyes, grey mullets, loose jeans – turn their bodies to ogle and try to get me to look back. It's come to this.

THE ALL-STAR GAME is more about the pending potential for a player lockout than about celebrating the ultimate players converging for a parody of competition. Joe Sakic will score a million goals, set up on a line with team captain

Näslund and his chum Bertuzzi. Today, though, is the skills competition. Bert looks puffy. He alludes to drinking shooters the night before. He looks so miserable for any media, his face a mask of control. Have Markus and Todd decided to show nothing to keep out the contamination of media spin? Were they burned so bad last year? Back then, the always upfront Näslund dared suggest he might go back to Sweden, that his friends and family and heart were there, and he felt obligated to finish his career and educate his children in the motherland. Man, he got nailed. Traitor! Turncoat! Ungrateful prick! Tsk fucking tsk! Yet, weeks later, the hypocritical press in Toronto were trying to get Canada's Steve Nash to admit he'd rather play in Canada instead of in Dallas where he'd been paid megadollars and was the town hero. When a Swede wants to go home it's bad; when a Canadian wants to come home we love that.

During the skills contest, the players' children fidget on the benches, some in sweaters with their dad's name on the back. Messier's non-wedlock son, for example. There's a mix of veteran and novice. Messier to Rick Nash, Sundin to Kovalchuk. And Roenick's still with us, claiming respect for the referees, including the one on whom he spat and hit with a water bottle days before.

Martin St. Louis is not of this world as he skates through pylons and keeps the puck on his stick. He is gorgeous to watch, a smile lighting his eyes, determined at every stride to prove his value.

The camera catches Bert on the bench a couple of times, son Tag supported by his dad's huge arms. Daddy is loudly boo-ed each time he appears on the ice because we're in Minnesota, and they remember how he baited them during last year's playoffs. How does the little guy feel about this honour? Bert's face is soft when he does a quick check – his hands are huge – to see if all's well inside Tag's pants. In a game I watched on television last year, the puck disappeared in Vancouver's end after a shot on goal. Players and refs shuffled around, looking up and down, puzzled and bewildered. Where'd it go? Who's got the puck? Bert strolled into the picture, calm and large, picked Dan Cloutier up by the back of the pants, lifted him off the ice and shook him hard. Bloop: the puck fell out of Dan's big pants and Bert went back to the bench, another miracle notched under the Big Top.

When the competition is over, the players are milling, and the voyeuristic camera catches Todd and Tag again at the bench. Todd leans over and kisses his boy's face, long and strong, his eyes lit like St. Louis's. The camera had been seeking – patiently – a moment of incongruity and finally it came.

My skin itches, I reach tears too fast. I imagine a violent end to me in minor conflict situations, a headache flirts with the right side of my head, I've forgotten to bring home some crucial marking, and I'm so wanting sex with a hockey player twenty years younger than I am that tonight during the All-Star festivities, I found Chris Pronger's gap-toothed smile attractive when Sakic and Näslund were probably only steps away. What's happening to me?

ON VALENTINE'S DAY, they lose to Anaheim and I hate their stupid guts. The Mighty Ducks – fuck that fucking name – played, for one night only, as they did last year in the playoffs. In fact, it's like watching Vancouver versus Minnesota last year when any thin opportunity had to be fought for. An accident on some sucker's part would be a goal; little else could lead to one. The second period, Vancouver can't escape their own end. Time and again, Anaheim wins faceoffs, gets the puck to an open winger or Keith Carney at the point, a quick shot on net, another faceoff. Like dancing the cha-cha when you want the smoothness of a waltz. Or the Canucks would try to penetrate the neutral zone and the Carney wall would meet them and push them back, cha-cha-cha. The boys appear inept. I'm ashamed and mad, even while I understand how hard they are playing in a game with no rooms, a house with no hallways. Two games are played – theirs and ours. After recent games, the players sigh deeply, exhausted by the moments of post-game reflection, unable to breathe.

I'm not saying kill the trap; I'm not saying free the game and get more offense; I'm not saying the game is dead if defence rules. I've seen replays of the Edmonton games from the eighties, Gretzky and Messier and Kurri et al. Sure, they were fun to watch – all those goals! – but it's hard to keep interested when every rush is off a turnover because the pass sucked, not because the defence was sharp. I've loved 2-1 games with Minnesota, marvelled at the control and the more offensive team's ability to solve the crossword puzzle of the trap and find a non-existent lane via the unexpected right wing surge from a burly left winger. I'm not saying outlaw the trap; I'm saying on Valentine's Day, tonight, it isn't romantic to watch the Big Line get thwarted by Mighty Ducks.

Yesterday, Jeremy Roenick caught a slapshot with his face, went down and out, and then the blood pooled. Jaw broken in seven places, fifty-odd stitches, another concussion, wires to hold his mouth shut, the only way to close him down. What does pain mean to J.R.?

THE CANUCKS ARE WINLESS since the All-Star break and meet Colorado for the fourth time this season. After the loss to Anaheim, the players agree it is a must win tonight, albeit a tough must win, if there's a hope of winning the Northwest Division. Remember: this matters. There's evidence throughout the scoreless first period and much of the second that the game will be rough. Matt Cooke smears a high stick across Derek Morris's mouth. Ruutu relentlessly sticks and pesters Forsberg; Peter the Great calls for penalties throughout the game. So I'm not sure if it's spur of the moment revenge, or the sportier and premeditated "retaliation," when Näslund goes down.

He's doing that curling stretch where one leg is back and extended and one arm is forward and out, stick attached, to push the puck gently over the Colorado blue line. He's as close to the ice as a curler, pretty and sleek. And then Steve Moore skates from nowhere – he who Bert, in an hour or so, will call a piece of shit or crap (it's hard to read his tight lips) – bends his shoulder low while also bringing it up, and connects hard with Näslund's face. My pretend boyfriend spins and goes down flat, his head – or only his visor – wobbles in the air and then it hits the ice hard. He was unconscious, but he's not now. He tries to get up but there's bewilderment on his face – where *is* this? – and blood. He's alone out there for such a long time. At home, his little girls wonder why no one's helping their dad. He looks over to observe the rough stuff on the boards, Brad May ineptly going after Moore. Jovo's still out with that shoulder, which is what saves Jovo from probable jail time.

This is May's Vietnam. He would have been great then and there; able to spend some of his anger – at what, who knows? – for a just cause, he would have come back a better version of himself, but also changed and shut down. In an hour, May will pledge to semi-alert journalists that it will be fun to get Moore next time. But on the ice, the trainer finally attends Näslund while May nails Moore into the boards, takes a penalty. Moore doesn't. Näslund gets it together slowly, on his knees, his face pressed into the white towel, trainer at his side, having a nice welcome back chat: "Where are you Markus? Who are you? Who's better, you or Peter? When will the Sedins finally break out? Should belt match shoes?" He takes so long and when he rises from his knees, he's still not there, his face cut, his eyes wonky, now childlike.

Neurologists have dispelled the myth that a concussion is a bruise on the brain; it's actually a wicked chemical imbalance within the grey matter. The force of impact causes the head to go fast while the brain stays put. So the brain slams against the skull, neural cells stretch, and then chemical reactions:

the brain panics. Neuroscientist David Hovda calls it "a sinister wave of electrical activity" that spreads across the brain. The cells are desperate to get back to normal. Instead, all that firing causes the neurons to absorb too much calcium and sodium and to reject potassium. "The calcium clogs mitochondria – the cell structures that make energy – preventing them from doing their job" when the neurons need energy the most. At the same time, the calcium and potassium make the brain's blood vessels constrict; the sodium makes the brain cells take in water and "the water swells the cells, pushing them up against the skull. If the swelling is extreme, the expanding brain will start to crush itself against the skull." Neurons can die. Likewise, the whole brain.

Markus's children watch at home and see the pretty birds chirping at their dad's lovely blond hero's head. *Cole-rah-dough* he called the Avalanche, an honest team. "He's our best player," says Bert, "and he's our friend," and then off he goes to the hospital to stay the night with his best friend, his blood brother, a night camped by the river for Lennie and George, *down in the brush by the river.* I dream that night of blowing softly on Näslund's face and head.

OF COURSE, the story is much better. This is behaving like a climax, but those who write stories, or even those who feel them deep in their bones, know this isn't it; this is the beginning of something, not the end. I've seen his head hit the ice thirty times and it's only the next morning. This is the test of my resolve. I don't know if I can commit to a game that thrives on the head shot, that wants and thinks it needs star players horizontal. A friend who played high-level Junior e-mails: "There are moments when I think about turning away and never turning back. That was one of those moments."

By the end of the day, I've watched it sixty times, looking for what? On CKNW, via radio from Colorado, Markus sounds groggy and slow, but no more depressed than usual at this time of the season. The headaches are bothering him, and he's lost a chunk of memory – the hit, for example – but things are coming back and he doesn't have other concussion symptoms. And then he's in Vancouver – crusty Chris Brumwell warns the press to stay away from the airport or else lose your privileges – and then he's at a fancy downtown hotel looking mangled but speaking more clearly and taking questions. "I don't think it was a dirty hit," he says. "I think, um, he took advantage of me being in a vulnerable position, uh, and he obviously looked to hit me there. But, uh, the actual hit itself, it wasn't, to me, it didn't look like a dirty hit." He's asked about the strong words from his teammates after the game. Linden has said we should understand the high tempers post-hit; after all, the team had just seen a man they love (he used that word, "love") lying on a stretcher and unable to come up with his own name. May has said he was only acting in a parody of the movie *Slapshot*, that his remark about getting Moore was a joke. Näslund says, "I dunno. We'll see. I'm sure the guys are gonna talk to him. Uh. I don't know if he's a guy that'll stand up for himself, who'll fight, or what . . ." In retrospect, it seems clear that Näslund has by this time learned Moore is not a guy who will stand up for himself, who'll fight. Here, the honourable and heroic Näslund seems to be taking a cheap shot at Moore, letting him know that other Colorado players have filled him in on what to expect. Moore is a rookie, a college boy, and too old to be a rookie. Allegiances between Forsberg, Sakic and Näslund perhaps go deeper and a code – the one that says don't fuck up the stars or we're all in trouble – has been broken. The code – if interpreted literally – now has Forsberg, Colorado's own star Swede or perhaps captain Sakic, as marked men. In a certain kind of story, one that is predictable and symmetrical in its patterns, Forsberg would be a Vancouver enforcer's target next game. It's interesting to me that the Canucks choose to focus, instead, on Moore. A code within a code.

May is asked again, days later, about the hit and whether a call should have been made by the refs, if part of the fiasco is that the refs lost the handle. He doesn't blame the officials. "The game's so quick," he says. "I think even if you look at the replay, it's questionable, I think, you know, was it dirty? I don't know, but it was certainly on the line of, you know, possibly injuring another player, but um, I'm sure that um, Moore he's . . . he's . . . an upstanding kid and he's probably a good teammate for Colorado, but our job as teammates here in Vancouver is to stick up for our best players, or everybody to a man, and that's the bottom line."

For Näslund's hit, I was by myself, Tom in Toronto and Lily playing her trumpet. When Paul Kariya was hit by Scott Stevens in the playoffs last year, I shrieked because I'd been reading up on concussions and how death can come quickly, believing the oft-bashed Kariya was dead. The camera had followed the puck, as usual, and so Lily and Tom didn't know what I was thundering and rubbing my face about, until the camera came back to find the boyish Kariya – Tom Sawyer in sportier clothes – to pick him up at centre ice, on his back and clearly knocked out of Time.

When Näslund goes down, the same thing: the camera and the play by play follow the puck he was after, and I stay behind with Markus because when he's on the ice, I watch everything he does. I've seen him go down, the way his head hung loose and whapped the ice. It takes forever and I'm alone in the room, so I stay composed, no shrieking, no wailing. Or maybe I was ready for this because I've read so many stories and know there's got to be this magnitude of setback; it has to be this bad if the team is going to learn about itself and get stronger. The action of the last two years was rising too slowly, was following one thread – the long and gently curved road to the Cup – and that's not how good stories are made. The tangent is everything; the subtext and its texture are the true blood of fiction, the throbbing and wandering bass line below a shit-hot vocal, sexy backup singers and punchy horns. Nazzie's scrambled brain will make everything up at the surface have greater meaning. His friendship with Todd will have more colours now that one of them has had death kiss his lips and take him out of Time.

In Calgary to do a reading in a lovely bookstore that is also a restaurant and a mall: stainless steel teapots, leather and linen journals, a great sports section. I'm desperate to discuss Näslund but the city isn't yet Flames crazy. I seem to be the only one predicting Flames and Canucks in round one. The Readings Coordinator tells me there's a great drink special after midnight at my hotel. I tell her, whose parents originate in Africa, that I've been working in the Canucks locker room. "Well, if you're ever in the Flames' room, let me know." She'd like to be there.

"Let me guess," I say, looking at her gorgeous sparkling eyes, her open face. "You have a crush on Jarome Iginla?"

"Oh, I don't know their names," she says and laughs needlessly. "Brett Hull. This is the only thing I know about the Winnipeg Jets. Brett Hull is the first player to make a million dollars and it was for the Winnipeg Jets."

ON TELEVISION against Minnesota, the Canucks are a jury-rigged team, so many new lines, so many babies, and they look like chickens when scraps are tossed: frantic, puck greedy, reluctant to share and make a little go around. Silly plays, useless plays, and nowhere to go because it's Minnesota. It's obvious the players love Näslund, love being with him and don't like it as much when he's not there. They love him and want him, as when an admired teacher – tough but fair – takes a day off with flu: the class falls apart, no one learns anything. In fact, the sub will ask an easy question so they'll prove what they know – "Ms. Jackson says you've been studying fish migration. Who can tell me what kind of fish are spawning right now in the Goldstream River?" –

and they can't even remember what they know, don't want to even take part in learning when their true leader is away. And without their leader, they lack the confidence to guess, so worried to be wrong. Fedor Federov is tonight's sub, he of the humungous attitude problems, discipline problems, team-ing problems.

Things are complicated for the team. Jovo, Matt Cooke and Magnus Arvedson are out with injuries. And although Näslund only misses three games, the retribution circus around the next game with Colorado is outrageous. The media begins to anticipate, they ask us to anticipate, a revenge act and, lacking a more intelligent imagination, make the rematch the focus of their coverage of the Canucks. The story of hockey the media write is a simple one, without complexity, able only to follow the fucking puck, without surprising possibilities, without consideration of their own complicity in what circus-gone-wrong they might succeed in creating; if not the next game, then the one after that. In 1972, Bruce Kidd and John Macfarlane, in *The Death of Hockey*, observed that hockey is "real in a way that most television shows are not, so the fan naturally assumes that a hockey telecast is journalism. He believes that the men in the broadcast booth are 'reporters,' that the men in the remote control unit parked behind the arena are 'editors,' and that together they are 'covering' the game as a television news team would cover a political convention. He is wrong. And that is another indignity television has inflicted on hockey: it has turned it into a show."

Thirty years later, the story is the same. We assume that hockey pundits know their stuff, that they are bringing us the story, not making it up, that when they don't express concern over what this season has been an escalation of the cheap shot and the dangerous hit, there must not be a problem; that when they ask players, "How important was it to start the third period strong?" we understand this to be the most important thing to know after the game, even though the player will, nine times out of ten, respond with, "no question: it was huge." "The hockey writer is the most influential spokesman for sport in the country," warned *The Death of Hockey*. "More than anyone else, he teaches us the meaning of sport. If he is uncritical of capricious violence, if he registers no disapproval of the slashing, interference and boarding for which professional hockey players are no longer penalized, if he fails to challenge such flagrant abuses as the 78-game regular schedule, if he applauds the win-at-all-cost ethic enshrined in professional hockey, he contaminates our attitudes towards all sport." I wonder what they would say when media attempt to create a situation in which extreme violence can thrive, attempt to incite a dramatic turn that doesn't come from within the game. Reporters and fans want "hard and tough hockey between the whistles," Brad May will remind the media; you incite it, you better expect it and take responsibility for the aftermath.

BRUMWELL MUST HAVE his hands full, because he's not getting back to me. The dominant narrative – the one the real hockey writers are building – must be taking his time. But there's talk of no season next year, of a lockout, and I know once the playoffs come I won't get access to the players. I have a month or so to keep talking and asking new questions. I'm anxious and frustrated and pissed off that my story, and the help I need to make it work, doesn't get the priority that the stupid story – star gets hit, code is enforced, perpetrator gets nailed by vengeful teammates – being constructed by lazy media does. I need Linden for questions about the culture of the team and how it has changed since he was drafted; how the NHLPA believes players should be marketed; why fans – especially female ones – are so loyal to him. I'd like to ask Sopel what kind of player, and man, he hoped (living in Saskatchewan) to grow up to be; whether he is becoming the kind of player off-ice he thought he would be; what he thinks of the love/hate fan-base he has in Vancouver. I have one question for Näslund, but it's an important one: how does the off-ice prototype of young male hockey player in Sweden differ from the North American version? Is there the same acceptance and promotion of lots of sex and ego in order to build a hockey player there?

Given the series last year against them, Vancouver could be said to have a nifty rivalry going with St. Louis and though I don't get access to the team, Lily and I enjoy an excellent game. Chubarov scores on a breakaway: comes off the bench, picks up the puck – What's this? – and fires, shocked and reluctant to capitalize on his gift. It looks like the Blues could come back in the third but I tell Lily, "Don't worry. They take bad penalties near the end of the game." And presto! They take three unsportsmanlike and Ohlund scores on their fourth penalty. Hedberg is brilliant in goal, especially a save off a mysterious end of game Pavol Demitra penalty shot in keeping with a rule he didn't know. "Robbed," says Lily. Matt Cooke has been all agitation. Afterwards, Mr. Diplomacy Keith Tkachuk, sounding weary and faux-wise, calls Cooke a "gutless kid. His teammates know it, everybody around the league knows it. When he does something out there, he'll get the respect, but right now he doesn't have the respect from anybody around the league." It's hard to buy this complaint, especially given how the agitated Blues took so many silly penalties – succumbed to agitation – and lost the game because of it. Still, the often nasty and psycho Tkachuk sounds like a fed-up coach's message to Cooke: come on, kid, get with the offence, you're better than the role you've been given; quit yapping start scoring. Fed-up coach, or shitty loser.

Näslund has a million chances but can't finish. After the game, Lily and I snug back in Room 12 with cold pizza and pink grapefruit juice, he takes questions on ice surrounded by kids. He's tired and the scar is ugly, jagged, a beer bottle bar fight scar, not a pretty stick slice. "I look like a real hockey player," he said this week. He admits to being lazy, says his wife does all the work at home. He has a sexy glint and giggle about Swedish nannies with Kelly Hrudey. And he gets agitated over yet another slight directed at the guy for whom he was traded from Pittsburgh. Näslund was taken sixteenth overall by the Penguins in 1991; Alek Stojanov went seventh but was floating around, an enforcer and tough guy, when Pittsburgh GM Craig Patrick pulled the plug on an under-achieving Näslund in 1996 and brought in Stojanov, who has since left the game after a car accident and wants to be a firefighter in Windsor. It could have gone either way, Näslund insists – he could be looking for work in some steel town – and is ashamed that another player would suffer because of his own success. "You've tried to contact him," presses CBC man, trying to get Näslund to fess up to heroism, but he denies that he's been the good guy. For every Näslund, or undrafted Martin St. Louis, there are dozens of guys who went high in the draft and disappeared; players are ethically bound to keep this in mind and Näslund does.

HOCKEY PLAYERS AREN'T BOXERS; their sports differ in form and function. In general, so do their childhoods. Joyce Carol Oates proposes that boxers – usually raised in poverty, in racism, in urban ghettos – choose boxing as "the only sport in which anger is accommodated, ennobled. It is the only human activity in which rage can be transposed without equivocation into art." I have friends who had angry fathers: a surly Saskatchewan farmer who thought girls should be girls; a drunken Mennonite who thought girls should be embarrassed; fathers who chose other women over their wives, and by extension, their daughters. I wasn't tormented or doubted. My father was not an angry man, and since he was the only man in my brotherless life, I am not much of a fighter. My parents did not argue. He treated my mother with respect and affection and good humour. He didn't ridicule or berate us. Once, when at sixteen I had become fed up with my oldest sister, took off my love beads and threw them and shrieked something primeval about hating her, he swatted ineptly at my butt as I stormed past him to my room. That was the extent of the physical aggression in my home. I've never been spanked or struck by either parent. My father would raise his voice at a bad call in a Habs game, and would raise his voice only to say, "Ah come on, fellas" to berate the refs. It angered him when men referred to their wives as "the wife" and didn't use their names. I must have angered him, but he didn't express that anger. Maybe he spent it over Berlin, March 1944. Or in a stalag.

Or when he disappeared, or when he came back suffering from amnesia. My mother tried everything to explain what now looks like a profound act of anger: he was so pissed off he couldn't come home. There had been the head injury a few years before, at a logging camp in Sparwood where he was itemizing the heavy equipment for auction. A crane had swung and knocked off the orange hard hat. Maybe there was an undiagnosed concussion, she theorized. And there was the deep cut over his left eye when he landed in the swamp in Germany; regardless of what he claimed to be no injuries from the bail-out, the flak in his leg and arms would surface throughout his life. But that cut: maybe a head injury. And then when he was seventy, a couple of years into full retirement, he had to pull over to the side of the road on his drive home along the Fraser River delta, his face was twitching so badly. A seizure, a stroke, but mostly the work of eight brain tumors, metastasized from the melanoma on his bicep – the stain of those long tennis matches on grass courts, my mother theorized – and taking over his brain for good.

There was one other angry moment with my dad. We are at Vancouver General Hospital waiting for radiation. My father loved the way I drive – understandable, since he was my teacher and fed me his traffic calm-down mantra, "We all just want to get home, fellas" – and so I've come over from Vancouver Island with my red Mazda and left two-year-old Lily to join Tom in the woods cutting firewood to sell. We are renting a cabin in Becher Bay in Metchosin and have no money. I've finished course work for my Masters degree in English, I've handed in my thesis which discusses the presence of hysteria in the non-fiction writing of three poets, but I haven't yet defended it orally. I earn a few hundred dollars a month as a researcher. I knit sweaters to sell at craft fairs and write book reviews for forty dollars a pop. Tom works occasional sixteen-hour shifts on our landlord's towboat; he earns a hundred or so a week writing country life essays for CBC radio in Vancouver; he's been contracted to write a history of the Union Steamships and the advance is small. We had to go to Social Services to afford Lily's cooperative preschool tuition and almost got kicked off the roster when the government was slow sending the cheque.

Three times I come to drive my father for his radiation, and it's March in this story, too. I have already shouted at his doctor for putting him through this. The aphasia is constant – "day, week, house"; he tries to order things but can't – and it's ridiculous to put a man like my dad through this when death is politely asking for a sweet smooch. He can barely speak. He has many x's drawn on his head where tumors hide within. He's chubby and flaccid and very pale. His face is big, his eyes are small. He's wearing a thin cotton wrap that makes him look like a Ukrainian woman hooked on spuds. We sit for half an hour in the waiting room – his legs are so white and freckled – and he holds the sports page of the *Vancouver Sun* open in front of him, only one page, the one with scores and stats and columns of names and numbers. For half an hour, he holds it there and then suddenly he looks at me, angry, and conveys outrage with a few coherent words and hand gestures: *I can read and understand what's on this page, but I can't talk to you about it.* Why is that moment the one that fills me, and not the one when he's back at home, propped in his bed looking out over the marsh and its snow geese, a couple of days from death, and he puts his soft hand on mine and says, "love" though he's unable to speak?

Oates believes "men and women with no personal or class reason for feeling anger are inclined to dismiss the emotion, if not piously condemn it, in others." People like me, who grew up in relative peace and prosperity, with men who appreciated life's comic potential and strived to make the evening drive-home a time of contemplation, she proposes, may not understand that humans in the flesh are primitive, that "anger is an appropriate response to certain intransigent facts of life, not a motiveless malignancy as in classic tragedy but a fully motivated and socially coherent impulse." I think I do understand.

Is that what the media are expressing? Anger? Anger is not one thing, and it isn't confined to masculinity. I'm angry that Näslund has been so aggressively attacked, and angry that he's not himself, now, on the ice, that aphasia – metaphorical – has taken over his wrist shot and prevents it from going in the net, that his family has to worry about every shift he takes. And I'm angry because the story – its throbbing and pumping bass line – asks me to be angry. And if I were walking down the street in Denver, say, and handsome Steve Moore came toward me and I happened to have had a particularly good workout that morning, maybe increasing the weight to sixty pounds per side on the leg press, I can't say for sure that I wouldn't shove him off the curb as I went by and hope he went down hard on the pavement. I can feel this urge in my muscles. Part of me wants to be the hero who avenges Näslund's outrageous injuries. Or maybe not me, but I could understand and even congratulate the guy behind me who does it instead of me. "Impotence takes many forms," says Oates, "one of them being the reckless physical expenditure of physical potency." Anger and aggression are not caused by hockey; they are a part of the game and a part of me. I'm not saying that hockey is a reflection of life as it is; I'm saying I understand that anger is appropriate and inevitable and ingrained. A punch to the head, it seems to me, is a detail from a small story, whereas a stealth missile is a detail from the same story, only larger.

EARLY MARCH, 2004 versus Detroit, no score after the first period: bad penalties, lazy plays, Bertuzzi again – how many times this season? When will he clue in? – negates a power play by taking a fatuous penalty in the opposition's end. Hey Bert, rate your emotions management from one to ten.

Manny Legace is good, sure, but Detroit looks back to form (so awful and creaky earlier in the year), regardless of a million injuries and other setbacks, including a three-goalie miasma.

Sopel and Ohlund are great and passionate, as is Morrison, but one line is full of retreads, another stocked with weed dwellers, and the unit never comes together. Twice, Näslund tries to superhero up the gut to the net – grab onto my cape, boys – but gets squeezed out of the play.

Linden looks defeated, or pooped from penalty kills. Vancouver needed this game to keep a baby step behind Colorado and giant steps ahead of Dallas.

The towhees are back and scratching the ground for over-wintering bugs. The Airy Fairy rhodo is in bright pink bloom at the front of the house. My friend – one who endured a shitty father – says about my crush on young Näslund, "Pretty soon your vagina will dry up and get sore and then you'll be invisible. Then you're a beluga."

Once again, the season will end in a complicated way.

CHAPTER SEVEN

COLD-COCKED
(AIN'T THAT TUFF ENUFF)

If the opposite of war is peace, the opposite of experiencing moments of war is proposing moments of pastoral.
    – Paul Fussell, *The Great War and Modern Memory*

Anything less than a passionate demonstration of perfection in the plaza is met with jeers, whistles, sarcasm, disdain, and a rain of seat cushions thrown into the ring, aimed at the offending matador's head. The audience's famously gladiator-style demand to be thrilled and stirred often pushes bullfighters to take more dangerous risks than they can manage, just to appease the masses. Either the bull will kill you in Madrid, it has been said, or the crowd will.
    – Elizabeth Gilbert, "Near Death in the Afternoon"

Is the man to be blamed for having been addicted to his body's own adrenaline, or are others to be blamed for indulging him – and exploiting him?
    – Joyce Carol Oates, *On Boxing*

The new routine at seven that morning in a crowded, end-of-week-frenzied gym made me sore, my lower back locked on the left side, and though the exercises seemed easier – sitting on a big blue ball makes it kindergarten – I was more wrecked than after pumping iron. A shower and a strong cup of rec-centre coffee, but, driving to Gail's, it was hard to keep my left leg still to hold in the clutch. At traffic lights, I could either shift into neutral and shake it out, or tempt an embarrassing stall in the middle of the four-lane Island Highway. I shifted.

The morning was all-Sooke: the highway narrows past Willow Wind feed store and tangles south through backhoes-for-hire to ocean and clean westerlies. The wind was high and headed inland. Douglas firs whipped against a digitally blue sky, seagulls floating, getting off on real weather. My red car (my

Mazda Ovary, Tom calls it), a second cup of coffee and loud R & B – Delbert McClinton and his punchy Memphis horns, his "Bright Side of the Road" Van Morrison cover like Martin St. Louis entering the zone with speed. Great weather calls for this kind of road trip through farm start-ups, oceanside resorts, heritage barns and tarpaper wannabes.

Only another few klicks, past the logbooms at Otter Point, and the sky turned cold grey – Delbert goes deep, slow and bluesy: *I got dreams, dreams to remember* – and hailstones attacked my car and the wipers whirred full blast against them. Did the strange light and artillery cause me to overshoot Gail's driveway and head for Jordan River? Come on, I've been coming here for five years.

I crept back along the road, geared down even lower and turned up – way up – her perpendicular drive. To the left: what used to be a dream lot that hugged, shaded and hid her home from the rest of the debased world was now open space, bright even with this cloud cover. No wonder I'd missed my turn. On Wednesday, the municipality's bulldozer smacked down the scrub alder and scraped off the lush salal and bracken. They left the ground a denuded mess.

I hadn't seen her for four months – I've been at hockey games, she's been in South Africa to visit her civic planner husband – and she worked on me for a tough hour in the white room, the rosemary thick in the warm air, trying to unlock my lower back and also explain the defilement next door. Think about how fast they can come and ruin where you live, take away the buffer between you and the craziness and not even knock on the door and say, "guess what we're gonna do next!" SEAPARK – what a pretty acronym – is going to put up a parking lot for the legions who come down here to the ends of the earth to fish Otter Point.

TWO NIGHTS LATER, the game was a cryptic puzzle: how could Colorado score so high when they'd been beaten likewise a few nights before; why was Brad May unhinged and maniacal, so into Aebescher's face and goalie-space; why was Steve Moore on the ice without appropriate back-up; could a run-up score really send a man like Bertuzzi over so steep a cliff; where were the heroic, smooth-faced captains in this game – Näslund and gentleman Joe Sakic, their All-Star Game hat trick (Bert helped, too) only weeks old – and why didn't they stop it; why was Bert on the ice without Näslund; what is it coaches do for young men, if not get them safely through these land-mined years.

Either the bull will kill you in Madrid or the crowd will. The pre-game circus was gross. In August 2005, veteran columnist Cam Cole will write that Bertuzzi is only 50% to blame for what happens; the league and its officials and coaches are responsible for the other 50%. Missing from his equation: media and fan complicity. Airwaves and print welcomed the engorgement of revenge, couldn't wait for this game, thirsty for more conflict, more drama, more dimensions, to hear themselves faux-analyze and smirk in that awful insider way, on pin-striped panels of hockey has-beens. There was the pornography of the phone-in show, "the church of athletic self-opinion," where it all gets said and the appetite for more extreme opinions is whetted. Since when did democracy mean everyone's an expert?

Moore didn't see the hit coming, we're told by the same pundits over the next weeks, and that's what made it so dishonourable and also so dangerous, you see. But they imagined the violence so many times, placed it in the realm of possibilities, saw it coming and even called for it, dialled it up, defined and reinforced the code that would make such an act honourable.

We are all complicit. Duh.

But if he didn't see it coming, he certainly heard the freight train of Bertuzzi, the clanging warnings around the ice, the blast of the horn to pull over, pal, if you know what's good for you. At 8:41 of the third period, Moore decided to drive on. Bertuzzi did a bad and stupid thing and the pile-up was awful to see. May carries the puck, drops it like a clingy girlfriend, and begins his extraneous and automatic punch-up nearby. Hedberg gestures pathetically like a North American traffic cop to Aebescher: *come over to my place, let's throw goalie punches.* Meanwhile, Moore was the worst version of horizontal we've seen. The game was no longer a metaphor for war, to borrow from Joyce Carol Oates; it was the thing itself.

THE NEXT MORNING, the gym is the best place to be, but I don't wear my number 44. It's seven A.M. and cold in here, and oldies radio helps us get at it, for once laying off the puerile anti-motivation of Loggins and Messina, the Doors, the Eagles. On the mat, a blonde, curly-haired Beanie Baby of a woman wears a T-shirt that says "expect miracles" and shiny Batman tights. Two wobbly and tilting stretches on the ball, headphones on her bicep, cd player tangled on the mat and her cellphone goes off, insisting she chat about wall colour and siding dimensions. On the recumbent bike, Honky Tonk Woman continues the debate as to whether her Arab husband in

Marakesh is being targeted by a government that says he only married her for citizenship: "I was 185 pounds when I met him, but I'm in good shape now."

At the lat pulldown machine, the breathless and pumped conversation between a couple of hairy-chested midlifer guys – so much sweat, so early? – is beside the point:

"You can live your life the way you want to – "

"You bet."

"But when you go out to make money – "

"Yes."

"You *gotta* kiss some ass."

"You bet."

"It's still the same."

"Yes."

"That hasn't changed."

"No way."

Kim Wilson and the Fabulous Thunderbirds ask us the musical question, even those trying to drown them out running nowhere fast on the hum-heavy treadmills: *Ain't That Tuff Enuff.* Dave Edmunds' ear for the thrashy and crisp guitar pushes Jimmie Vaughan's stratocaster way forward and it soars with a locomoting and jubilant bass line. Let's dance! I'm suddenly stronger at the seated row, you bet, and now it's a love anthem from all the tuff guys out there to all of us weaklings down on the mat doing crunch sets.

The newspaper mug-shots are everywhere: Colorado's Moore smiles like the captain of his college debating team beside Bert wearing Mr. Surly Logger Face. The media's post-crisis hyperbole matches their pre-game hysteria. March 11, the local paper has Bert crying on one side of the front page, on the other, this headline: "Pickton's meats may hold human remains." *Macleans* names it "the Cheap Shot Heard Around the World" – so Moore's the Archduke and Bertuzzi's a nutty anarchist? You call that an analogy? *Globe and Mail* columnist, Christie Blatchford, reacts to the coverage as I do: "Having spent the past six weeks covering a case where a five-year-old child was killed, then smartly dismembered and beheaded, I remain surprised and even a little touched at how delicate are my colleagues who toil in what the late *Globe and Mail* columnist Dick Beddoes used to call the playpen." In the Bertuzzi case, reporters don't report; analysts get only so far and then resort to emoting. The media world is aghast.

Researchers in Australia have studied "tall poppy syndrome," the tendency, especially in post-colonial countries that are subject to unconscious envy, to scrutinize high-profile types — wealthy, powerful, gifted – and look for reasons to "cut them down to size" and then feel great when the cutting's done. The researchers claim journalists and sports consumers "internalise the conservative values of competitive sport, and they sometimes use them as a standard to evaluate their own behaviour and the behaviour of others." High-profile performers are expected to conform to an idealized social order that we can aspire to, to take us back to kinder, gentler times when fair play and moral conduct meant something. When they violate our expectations – when they do a very naughty thing – out come the snick-snicks and down they go. It might be inevitable, then, that journalists who are paid to be free of bias, who don't self-identify with players, would cut down the tall poppy, especially one like Bert: smart-mouthed, quick-tempered, arrogant and even aggressive towards them (he was reported to have shot a puck at the plexi-glass during practice a few days before the Colorado game in order to send a knock-it-off message to the reporter behind it).

As if violence is the only aspect of the sport nexus worth our outrage. Why no ongoing criticism of the locker room aphorisms: "There is no I in team," or "Defeat is worse than death because you have to live with defeat," and "Winning isn't everything, it's the only thing." Why no lasting network policy changes to correct the message that women journalists know nothing about hockey and that women athletes – or amateurs or disabled athletes – aren't worth our excitement? No, the world wants to be aghast, once again, at violence in sport.

Thanks to Bert reaching what Ken Dryden calls his stupid point, the game, apparently, is disgraced. Quavering mothers phone in to CBC – no less pornographic than its all-sports counterparts – and describe peewee Corey's face as he rips down the poster of Bert from the shrine of his bedroom walls. She irritates me. Lucky for Corey, lady, that sports gives him these moments to reconsider those he worships, to cry big tears in his bedroom and think again about where he wants to fit in the world, who he wants to be. His mother dials in so we'll share her outrage and *Change the game! For chrissakes! We've gotta do it for the kids!* But I'm glad Corey gets to feel and respond. What happens if our children never question their heroes? If they never have to think and debate and defend and accuse and grieve?

We're advised to worry about those kids idolizing players like Bertuzzi who may now try to imitate him. *For chrissakes! The kids!* Wait. Here's what sociologist R. K. Barney famously set out twenty years ago as qualifications for athletic heroes: *physical excellence* comes first, followed by *moral excellence* displayed across life's board – "acting with honesty, humility, generosity, sportsmanship, and self-control." Candidates for hero-worship must "give unselfishly of their energies and talents to assist those less fortunate than themselves" and to have "demonstrated theoretical and practical wisdom." And the most important criteria is that "true hero status should not be accorded an athlete in his or her lifetime," since the truly naughty stuff only comes out posthumously. *Should it be that way?* Brad May said to me rhetorically in the room in December. What kind of parent would allow their child to elevate unquestioned a man like Bertuzzi – talented, comic, beautiful, driven, but also rude and often brainless on ice – to hero?

Sure, children observe and learn from outlaw sport heroes, but what they really notice is whether the behaviour paid off and whether others approved of the lawlessness. In other words, kids learn to be good guys when society approves of good-guy behaviour. Some kids will learn aggressive behaviours and imitate them when Dad or Coach isn't looking, but Bert's screw-up was hardly a national child-rearing disaster. Do the math, and it's more likely that kids – especially little boys – learned this from Turbo Todd: don't hit somebody because you might break their neck and people will hate you and take away your privileges and consider jail. Your pretty young wife will grow old and hard in a heartbeat and media will mock her outfits, as if that matters any more. And if you do make a bad, bad mistake, then shave, dress up, cry because you can't help it, and say sorry even though you feel so terrible about what you did to another guy from your union and you wish you could hide under the covers for a long time, maybe forever. Put another way, act with honesty, humility, generosity, sportsmanship, and self-control as Bert did, eventually.

Some believe *fan* comes from the Latin *fanum*, meaning "the sacred, the beneficial, the salvific, the temple, the consecrated place." *Webster's Sports Dictionary* (1976) sees *fan* growing from *fanatic*, out of the Latin *fanaticus*, meaning frenzied, or "insanely but divinely inspired." We identify with our team and its stars. When miracles happen – a playoff goal in triple overtime – hardcore fans will look within the athlete for reasons: focus, skill, mental toughness. That way, we get to feel good about ourselves, too. But if a sport hero screws the definition of hero – like drives a speeding Ferrari into a brick wall or sucker-punches a smaller, less skilled player – their fans will look for external causes: obscene salaries or inexperienced referees. Fans don't want to identify with a guy who loses it and invites the world's disdain, so they'll blame the world instead of the player.

As long as we make sure players are punished – publicly mortified, too – when their stupid point is reached, peewee Corey and his ilk should be okay because they don't want to be shunned losers. When Dany Heatley's car came apart and killed his friend, though, only one journalist, the veteran Mary Ormsby in Toronto, dared criticize *him* – he's a young thug with lousy values – and she endured the nasty wrath of the rest of the hockey-scribe team, especially the boys on HNIC. *I can only hope her own child never makes a mistake,* they blustered, *She's just wrong.* Another round, bartender.

When Canada's World Cup of Hockey team was announced at the end of May 2004, the event was all pageant. It could have been a rite of forgiveness. But as soon as Wayne Gretzky said they'd chosen thirty players because they not only represent the best in the game but are more importantly the ultimate role models for children, I knew Bertuzzi would get gassed, though he could have made the squad despite his NHL suspension. Gretzky and his crew wanted Canadian tykes to pretend all summer long to be Jarome Iginla or Joe Sakic, he said, and as each player was named, a kid wearing that player's sweater came onto the stage and did a nervous 180 turn.

The first player was Dany Heatley, and Kevin Lowe looked fatherly when he smiled and gushed about the kid's Heatley-esque red hair. Vancouver's contribution was announced penultimately (just before host Calgary's stars) and only Ed Jovanovski's name was read. "Fuck you, assholes," I shouted, and Lily left the room, upset at my anger and attitude, wanting to celebrate Jovo's success. Later, out in the garden, finally getting the Roma tomato plants under plastic and in the ground, I got reasonable: Okay. Wayne-o couldn't suggest that the logical consequence for what Bert did – he almost killed a man with his fist – is representing your country in a prestigious international tournament to play your nation's sport. Fair enough, I thought, point made. But he'd called Theo Fleury in detox two years before. And Dany Heatley *is* invited to play. In May, Heatley was still charged with a felony, vehicular manslaughter, and four other misdemeanors; Bertuzzi was under police investigation (he was later charged with a single count of assault causing bodily harm, pleaded guilty, was granted a conditional discharge and 80 hours of community service, made a cautionary video for kids which I only saw broadcast in full once; life goes on without jail time). One difference is that Heatley's stupid point was reached away from the rink – but only barely, since he was driving home with teammate Dan Snyder from a team event. Bertuzzi broke the rules and more as part of the game, witnessed by 18,000 folks at GM Place and a couple hundred thousand of us at home. No one saw Heatley's accident. Heatley still gets to be a hero who did a bad, bad thing. And here's what those kids who idolized him have been told by The Great One, of all people: when you drive way too fast in a very hot car and you hit brick and wrought iron and your friend dies, you still get to play for your country. Bertuzzi doesn't. Sometimes stupid is forgiveable, sometimes not, but I'm wondering who came up with this sliding scale of forgiveness and who governs it, who's in charge.

MY PUBLICIST PICKS me up at seven P.M. for a reading at a funky Kitsilano chick-bookstore. Boxed in by classes to teach, I flew to Vancouver in the ten-seater float plane in the sun of late afternoon, excited to sit behind the pilot and watch the Gulf Islands from that height, feel the engine vibrate me into sleepiness. If I made eight million dollars, I'd do this trip every day.

In her dark van, my hair smells of conditioner, the zipper on my semi-cashmere orange jacket twinkles. I'm nervous about reading and acting the bigshot and so I say, "Bertuzzi's giving a news conference right now," to make conversation. She fiddles with the radio dial and swooshes through downtown. Way too fast, the van is alive with Bert's disintegrating voice and I hear him cry and cry, the shwick shwick of the cameras' rude shutters. He says he's sorry to the kids and to his teammates and I start to cry, too, regardless of the make-up job. "Oh dear," the publicist says, but she's talking about him, not me. Radio makes it more immediate and beautiful. He's so upset and so are we.

At the shop, a Newfoundlander reads a story about a body, a murder. We did this together a few nights ago back in Victoria, too, and at dinner in a sidestreet Mexican restaurant beforehand, she stopped me when I mocked a hockey player from Newfoundland for his reputation as a dawn to dusk drinker. With the authority of a regional accent so subtle I can't imitate it, she told me that in the young man's extended family, a brother killed a brother.

I can't listen to her read tonight. I hear Bert's voice and lose her story's thread.

The bookstore: posters and prints of women's big jiggly bellies, the out-loud of mastectomies, dead female authors hanging on banners like a division championship. The passage I did had the word "dyke" in it but, fast on my feet, I cut it out.

When we arrived, the nice tweedy women who run the store, once they knew I'm writing about hockey, effused about the women's game. "Oh, the Olympic women's team. You have to watch *them*," and they nodded stridently to each other, like parodies of themselves. How come so bossy, gals? "*They* play the game the way it was meant to be played." I think not. It's weird to suggest women play a purer, less violent game because they are women. Or that less aggression equals pure sport.

I'd rather be with Bert. I can't excuse his rank-out or deny my complicity. I'll point out external reasons like a card-carrying fanatic – coaches, refs, media, fans, Nazzie's wounds, May's hysteria – but I won't let Bert go unexamined. I do want a court to tell me why he did such a terrible thing. And if it turns out his wasn't a spontaneous flip-out, if a nasty plan was hatched by boys on a dare, then peewee Corey and I will think harder.

But he's made me feel so much, as any truly honest character does, and I'm moved by the problems with this story, its contradictions, and grateful to be thinking hard and feeling so much. To watch a man like that cry. At the end of our safe literary night, a fat orange cat waits by the store's heating vent, eager for night's mice.

"Do I watch this game stupidly?" asks a stunned Joan MacLeod, post-Bertuzzi. "Do I celebrate all that goodness and grace and athletic genius and push aside the goon part? Is this all feeding some twenty-something self-destructive love of the bad boy crap? When he flattened Steve Moore we all watched the tape again and again wanting to rewind and change everything desperately. But it also made perfect sense that he did what he did, given who he was and what had happened – the perfect climax and a character-driven one at that. He was within character – the crappy side getting to run the show for those brief moments but fuelled in part by the better half too – loyalty, strength. I read about Kelly Ellard's trial and how her lack of remorse (except at being caught) must be so frustrating for the Virk family when we all know she's guilty. The reporter cited Todd as being the opposite of Ellard – he is someone who did show remorse and we knew it was genuine and because of that we forgave him and want the injured parties to do so as well. We believed him entirely when he said he was sorry. We know he wanted to rewind the tape as badly as we did. We believe in both parts of him. We want, ultimately, for him to succeed. Who is the royal we here? Am I just embarrassed to really own this stuff?"

Alone in my hotel, I watch him again and again – his pretty wife's Chanel jacket and his handsome silk neck tie – well into the night, though I will need to fly early and teach shortly after touching down on the water in Victoria.

Joan tells me, "When Todd went after Steve Moore I had a dream about him the very next night. We were both teenagers. We were visiting other teenagers in some sixties style rec room. The house seemed, well, swanky. Rich parents slept upstairs. Todd had his arm draped around me for hours; I remember the weight of it. And that, as teenagers do, we didn't really talk; we just shuffled around with other teenagers in that time teenagers own in the middle of the night. Everyone was tired and I finally convinced Todd to lie down on a sleeping bag that was stretched out on the wall to wall. He fell asleep and I stood guard over him for what felt like hours. So what's that about? It reminds me of watching my daughter sleep now–she seems to be entirely made up of goodness when silent."

FUKT TELLS ME the guys in our hockey pool are mostly from Boston and Sarnia. I'm tied for second, then third, now today, fourth. PEACHY is on top – six points ahead of me – but he/she has the improbable Steve Sullivan who has been renewed from a trade to Nashville, the screaming Nashville, Nashville the offensive mystery.

After many misses, Brumwell has me visiting Burnaby 8 Rinks again. This time I know the route and I'm slick and speedy. I'm determined and will ask anybody any question if it means I'll find out where to stand, where to go, and talk to Sopel and Linden. This is the last chance. The unspoken rule is no questions about Bert, period, not even sneaky ones or you'll get tossed. It's easier when the place isn't crawling like an ants' nest with peewees, or is it my new resolve that gets me going. I slouch with the media boys at the gates, looking journalistic with my black shoulder bag and dark-rimmed glasses. Try to bounce me, Security Dude, try. He doesn't. The players look drained and bugged from drills (again, it's clear they've been out there for awhile, so again, my arrival time is wrong). They're doing one-on-ones at both ends. At the other end, the stay-at-home Czech d-man, Marek Malik, takes Ruutu out too hard behind the net – Malik is 6'5" and 235 pounds, has three inches and forty pounds on him – and Ruutu shouts at his teammate and then, composure and wit regained, gestures broadly for a mock penalty shot. Back at this end, Malik hits Brad May high and hard and deranged coming into the defensive zone, and Linden barks his name, crosses his forearms in front: what's this? A private "knock it off" from the voice of reason? May's pissed, but Mr. Belligerant Bear only looks at Malik and shakes his head. Team Happy they're not. Malik is leading the league in plus-minus stats, but I smell a trade.

Joan will be choked if that happens. Malik's her favourite player, which makes her the only person on the hockey planet aside from his mother and first grade teacher. "With him," she writes, "my draw to the way he plays the game is entirely personal and because of that, like a true fan, I imbue him with qualities he probably doesn't have but I think we share. I know this is basically stupid but so what. Now he's a big guy, really big. I'm tall and big boned. I almost never feel graceful. Marek Malik reminds me of Frankenstein (flip side – me as Frankenstein). And Lord knows Frankenstein has inspired sympathy over the years, all that gentle monster stuff. But Malik, he has this grace sometimes that is stunning. He inspires me. Maybe I too will come out of the end zone one day with the speed of a hyena and the grace of a ballerina. So I champion that. And, ridiculously, I champion him because no one else will." Certainly, his team isn't doing it today. But by "no one" she means people like me, the gals under five-five, with the delicate bones and the full dance card. "They're all too busy fawning over Markus and other pretty faces," she sniffs. "Ringo was my favourite Beatle."

It's been a hard practice and still they skate sprints for a few minutes. And then they're off the ice, clomp clomp clomp into the room and here we go after them. I greet Brumwell and remind him who I am, who I want. Do I only imagine his smirk as he greets the real reporters, calls a guy-talk "Hi Hughie!" to the handsome Jim Hughson, and slouches into a confident, in-charge pro vibe. I wish he wasn't so much taller than me. Sopel is gone already, he says; his wife had a baby last night. Skunked again. Linden isn't feeling well, but – wait – he's talking to that guy so go ahead. Reporter etiquette is foreign to me, but this is the day I ask questions. I will not be confused: "What, I go over and wait till he's done?" "That's right, go ahead." I do. I'm not the only female today. A very young Asian chick dressed in skimpy everything flits around the room without a tape recorder, stepping over pads and socks a trainer will collect off the floor, without a notebook, talking to peripheral players and looking stressed and busy busy busy. While I wait for Linden to stop speculating on the post-season, the other guys form a tight circle around the neo-healthy Jovo, little tape recorders extended. He stands in his towel, a new spare tire around his middle thanks, we can only hope, to the many games missed. Jovoid. He looks at me from over there, the eye contact, but this is a harder version of the playful puppy. This one's been kicked, teased, left without water, has a thorn in his paw: approach with caution, if at all, because he's afraid. He might lick the hand, or bite off several digits and call that lunch.

Look up. Look way up, and pay no attention to the athletic cup that's level with your chest. Be professional, friendly but not too friendly, and remember to say something nice the way you'd planned, something complimentary even though it contravenes code, like never asking a player for an autograph. "I'm not a reporter; I'm writing a book, and I'm wondering what you think about the public image of today's hockey player."

"Public image?" Okay fuck. I've used the wrong words again, it makes no sense, what an idiot, what a terrible question, he doesn't have a clue what I mean, and why should he? Fucking academic blah-blah. Why not ask him to deconstruct the heteroglossic postcolonial model of slave/owner *vis-à-vis* the NHL? But Trevor lets me try again. My arm must look stupid way up there. I have no neck.

"I mean, what's changed since you were drafted that now we have a bunch of really good guys with great bodies, great citizens, and ten or fifteen years ago that wasn't the case. When you came along, there wasn't that pressure to be a sort of model guy, was there?"

"I don't totally agree with that. I'd say the profile of this team in this market is larger."

"More visible you mean?" I remember this from Brad May. Aren't I smart.

"Absolutely, absolutely. More visible and that brought us, and us as individuals, into people's homes more than just the hockey player on the ice type of thing. And I think kids and young people identify with us more than they did before because we're more accessible now."

"And that was a device, right? A marketing device?"

"No, a lot of it's natural because when I first came in the league there was one TV station and a guy or two covering us, now there's three twenty-four-hour sports channels." Oh, Trevor. I've heard this too many times be-fore, from too many athletes in all professional sports. It's a way for you to avoid having an original thought, a way to stay away from feeling and caring and questioning anything. Eric Duhatschek has told me he believes "NHL players of the modern era have had the personalities leeched out of them, mostly by teams trying to control access and encouraging players to say noth-ing of interest or consequence that could 'rile' up an opponent." Don't do me wrong, Trev. Have a thought.

"So is it just media, or is it the athlete as well? Did you know when you were drafted that you were going to have that kind of pressure to be that pub-lic good guy?"

"I don't really view it as pressure. The team has always been very active in the community. It's the motto when a guy gets here that you're part of this team and you're part of this community. But it's an easy buy-in. It's a natu-ral fit. A lot of the things we're able to do with children is a good fit, a natu-ral fit."

"It's a good fit for you, but is it a natural fit for all players? The eighteen-and nineteen-year-old guys coming in?" I don't even know what 'natural fit' means.

"Oh, you know. It takes a little time. For the most part I think any time an athlete or a hockey player in Canada can work with children it's a natu-ral fit. And I think the team here has been really progressive in helping us to be part of the community and it's just been a natural thing. I think the guys when I started in the late eighties were as giving and as hard-working as they are now. I just think it was less visible and maybe not to the scope it is now."

"A veteran reporter told me that it was because young guys coming in think of themselves as marketable, that they're a corporation, right?"

"No."

"No?"

"No. I think that guys in 1988 when I came in worked hard and did a lot of things in the community on a smaller scale. Now you're seeing bigger events, more dollars raised, and everything's kind of grown. But guys don't have to do anything they don't want to."

"But not with this team, right?"

"No, not with this team, it's expected here. But if they came in here and said, 'Naw, I ain't doin' a thing' they could. If Brian wanted to keep 'em or whatever he would, but maybe he'd trade 'em. But it's got nothing to do with that they look at themselves as corporations. I don't agree. Nope, I disagree with that."

"One last question," I say, panicked and out of breath and knowing he's not feeling well and that my mental egg-timer is almost out of sand. I'm determined to ask a question no one else in this room would care about, to see if there's a place for the personal, for someone like me, and for information that doesn't come with a stat or a play by play. "Why do you think female fans are so loyal to you specifically?" A cluster of reporters nearby breaks into ill-concealed giggles, I assume at my expense, and they mumble answers to my question to each other. I put on my schoolmarm serious face for Trevor, but he gets squeaky and adolescent anyway.

"To me?"

"Ya."

"They are?" I look at his silly face. "Aha. I didn't know that."

"Oh you did so," I say like we've been going out for years, like I'm his wife and I'm both pleased and impatient with the little boy act. He appears miffed that I'd question his honesty. So what, big boy. We go way back, me and Trev.

"I didn't know that."

"Really."

"No."

"You don't see the jerseys and all that suff?"

"Oh ya." His voice is several decibels of twelve-year-old boy squeaking and singing and he's blushing, too. He's hoping no one else is listening, but he clearly knows we're talking about sex. This is a sincere moment, a normal bit of conversation between two people. "Um I didn't, you know, ah, I didn't, you know, ah, I didn't know it was 'female' necessarily, I don't, ah." The air is too thin on this planet and we can't last. Press the button and the Lindenator program is back. His tone changes, full sentences slide into place. He seemed to enjoy that silly minute but wants to give me a good answer. Manvoice: "You know, I talked to a girl yesterday. In the team's lottery, the guy who won the truck's daughter – grandaughter actually – she was telling me how she and her friends grew up watching me, at twelve and thirteen years old, really in love, you know."

"I have a daughter that age; I know how they are."

"She said, 'it's so embarrassing! I sent you letters and everything.' I think it's because they knew me as an eighteen-year-old and a lot of them were watching the game with their dad when they were eight or nine. But I was a young guy and they identified with me and they started following me and I kind of grew up here, and they've kind of grown up with me, so to speak. I think that has something to do with it."

Say we were in a windowless room with a couple of chairs drinking cold bottled water, in our most comfortable and flattering slacks, and we had a half hour together, the only ones in the room and keeping our voices quiet. Or say I was in my office at home, looking out at the chickens and the new lambs, the broad beans coming up, the dogs at my feet, a westerly blowing up off Juan de Fuca Strait, and talking on the phone to Trevor who's also somewhere authentic and calm, a man and not a god. My follow-up questions would be killer. What means 'natural fit'? What of the parking lot girls at 8 Rinks? But the rising and twirling ferris wheel we're riding here at Carnival Canuck suddenly stops and it's over and I'm stranded. "I think you're pretty inspiring on-ice as well."

"I appreciate it."

I know I spoke with defenceman Bryan Allen after that – "that's Bryan over there," Brumwell said as if I didn't know what he looks like. He'd dyed his hair and was bending over and I couldn't see through the crowd – but my questions confused him, he misunderstood what I meant about a player's psychology and told me of that extensive psychological testing they have when drafted. The interview was all my fault; it was hard to go from the easy chatter of Linden to the painful extrusion of a younger, less socially adept player. I quipped later that it was like talking to a Douglas fir, but those are important trees, and it wasn't meant to be the insult it came out as.

"I'm done," I tell Brumwell.

"You are?" He knows something I don't. Nearby, Hughie is saying to another pro, "Markus is going to have to stop talking to those Swedish papers."

"Yup. Thanks a lot."

And then I'm gone, pleased with myself, relieved to have got it – however small – done.

I head up to the dimlit overhead lounge for a celebratory cup of coffee. At the next table, a man with a huge toque around his huge head and awash in a scruffy outfit is eating a sticky bun and slurping tea from a Styrofoam cup and looking down at the ice. On one side of him sits a slightly younger mentally handicapped chap – Leslie – eating a hot dog. On the other side, the man's wife. She looks like Loretta Lynn after the downslide: manic, over-coiffed, wrinkles like lava formations, lacking the more modern shades of hair dye.

The man's voice is loud. "They're bums." Repeat. Repeat.

"It certainly wasn't as exciting as I thought it was going to be," says the wife.

"That wasn't a practice. That was a photo op," her husband carries on.

Leslie chimes in with a cautious and deliberate phrasing. "The most exciting part was when they left." He may be slow, but he's got the debunking down.

"They're not going to beat Dallas that way," says the man. "They're not going to beat Dallas that way, are they Leslie?" And then he gets up from the table – bow legs like an old logger or a cowboy – and takes Leslie by the elbow and leads him downstairs for an autograph with Daniel Sedin, the least the team can do since they've come all this way.

It's Linden's height, his world-on-shoulders face that makes him seem my age. I fell deeply in love for ten minutes and by the time I get back to downtown Vancouver – seeking the consolation of new underwear – I'm sad, lonely, and in tears amid the thongs and push-up bras. Even lingerie is beyond me.

I love that room, the smell, the colours, the noises, the purpling welt on Daniel's (Henrik's?) thigh, the knee brace on Allen's long leg, the fatigue on their faces and how easy it is to make it go away with a girly question. I'm afraid in there, but it's so much more interesting than a square concrete room deep beneath the main branch of the library, with tidy people on hard chairs who argue for a compliance to formality on the part of some poets should they decide to write ghazals, listening to me and two other writers discuss "Love and Loss" and to a moderator who can't shut up and who builds on the thesis that "women feel loss deeper than men do." Ya, sure, buddy. Tell that to Bert, if you can find his tortured land of exile. Tell that to my father and his addled brain. Memory, home, love, loss: these concepts don't interest me tonight. The faces and bodies of athletes at a difficult time – five games to go in the season, key players injured or just way gone – interest me, here in my home town, where memories of love and loss usually reside. Tonight, I feel love and loss simultaneously, and I feel them for Linden, like it or not Trev, in the zone between my newly toned lower abs and my revitalized quadriceps. I hate being forty-eight on a planet that doesn't want me, where I can fall in love and also be pathetic, where my imagination can't be controlled and I want to enter the story, not stay outside it.

At ten o'clock at night I walk the couple of blocks from the library in the hard rain, my head bare as it was for thirty years in this city, back to my hotel. Sleepwear: an extra extra large grey manstyle tent of a T-shirt I got at the Hockey Hall of Fame – *Hockey: Invented by Men, Perfected by Women*. What would JLo wear on a night like this? My smooth achy legs – yes, I shaved for Trev – swish and criss-cross under the white duvet; a bottle of cold Perrier and a carrot stick. According to TV sports highlights, while I was upstairs sipping blech coffee with Leslie et al, Markus, fresh from his shower and talcum, was talking to the real reporters down in the room about the hyperextension of his elbow, the pain, and the new calibrations of his wrist shot. So I did tank. That was my last chance to fill up and I drove right by, didn't even see the neon sign, going too fast and high beams focussed on the road ahead, on that twisty highway deeper into wilderness. What a fucking goof.

TWO WEEKS LATER, I go over – by myself – for their last game, a sunny, calm and gorgeous day on the water. I wear Lily's low rider jeans, Lily's wind-breaker, trying to get with a stomach I've never liked. At the bus counter, some idiot's Gap tag's out at the back of his tidy sweater vest; cargo shorts hug his tanned and taut thighs. His glasses are funky and he's svelte in an upper class kinda way. He steps up to the bus driver and announces, "Howdy. I'm going to the Canucks game and I'm taking the wife so I need two tickets." The bus driver asks how he thinks they'll do tonight. "Oh, they'll be competitive. It'll be about the goalies. Our goalie has to be better than theirs." Everyone's an expert. I want to slap his head. Is that the best he can do? Mime the knobs on sport TV? Why simplify a complex situation? Why pretend you know any-thing about the game? Because you think it's all about you, Mister Narcissist. Maybe it is.

Strangers sit too close. Do they not understand my need to be alone? New underwear to fit the jeans' belly button dip. Chances are, I don't look like an idiot.

At the hotel, the sidewalk has been torn up and fluorescent cones surround the front steps. They are putting me in a room on "the other side." I have to walk out the front doors and around to Pender Street and enter through the Victoria Building entrance, a black door that doesn't seem secure, more like gangsters and heroin. I'm in a construction zone, and although the wooden stairs, plaster walls, chicken wire tile at the side entrance suggest heritage, I feel discarded. The doors upstairs have two numbers, none of which correspond to my key's tag. Two doors are closed and I try my key in one; it opens and the bed is made and there are bright towels and a new television. But the phone's unplugged, the tile job isn't finished, and there's no Victorian trim around the door. The heritage fire alarm dangles from the wall. No worry: there's Leafs and Sens, I have a bag of trail mix, and they're fighting for playoff home ice (Leafs 5-0). It's hard to wait for six o'clock with no one to talk to. I miss Lily, my true companion.

Halfway through Ontario's third period, same jeans, I leave the room and am immediately disoriented. The large door to my right – the one to the stairs – is closed now and locked. I go the other way, but the building is less and less done. I'm heading into a deeper zone of construction. Turn back. The door opens if I haul on the lock. This doesn't seem right but I make it out of the dusty labyrinth.

At the front desk, Shannon's puzzled by all the sudden doors but says she'll go check. The night is ridiculously warm; blossoms already. Even at 6:10 jerseys pose at every street corner.

A different seat for this one, between centre and the blue line: closer to the ice but not so close I can't see the visitors' end boards. I'm next to a nice elderly lady with a smoking cough and crop-dusted cologne, season tickets since day one and the Coliseum. It's too crowded here, she thinks. It used to be that she and her husband were right behind the players' bench and she felt close to them. She has a high and breathy giggle whenever anything goes wrong. She's a blamer, but a sweet one: "Oh, that goal was your fault, Malik, you pushed your goalie," and she ignores the mess Linden has made of checking his man. I have to talk. I thought I could keep still and quiet, that I wouldn't need to cheer so much by myself, would look like a goof if I did.

The period ends 2-1 Canucks, and extreme optimism is tempting. The team could win their division at last. "Where are you from?" she asks between periods. She has to cough every time she speaks. She's from Dawson Creek originally. She has opera glasses but doesn't use them right: "Why's Nazzie holding his back like that?" I'd asked in period one, but we weren't paying attention to the same things.

She tells me, "It was just down here," and she lays her hand on the cold air to show where Todd did his movie. She's angry that Colorado have been so smug, have "made the most of it." She suspects damage was done by a

Colorado player who flew in and dove on Bertuzzi, fists flying. "As soon as he was taken off the ice, I said to my husband, 'Let's go.' And we left. I'd had enough."

Moore should have shown compassion during his neck-braced news conference, she believes, since he could have been in the same position as Bert had the headshot on Näslund been more muscled. "He *must* feel compassion," she says, outraged still and loyal. We both know there's too much room on the ice tonight without him.

The second period is fast and hard. Ryan Smyth appears bewildered, loitering like a delinquent alone along the boards awaiting the right pass, the cough-up. I'm concerned that no one checks him, but maybe he's not so dangerous. 3-1 end of second. The refs seem overly kind to the do-or-die Oilers, but Keane is flying, as is Chubarov and they'll be okay. I can relax for the first time in two seasons.

Or not. Near the end of the third, it's 4-2 and our deadline rental Rucinsky takes a penalty. Slick-suited coach McTavish is up and shouting across the ice. "The ref's got Rucinsky's stick," I tell the woman next to me.

"What?"

"They're gonna measure it for an extra two minutes." She doesn't understand. And they do – its curve is illegal – and so an extra two, a faint hope clause for the desperate Oilers. Whatever happened to using the legal ones for the third? Did Ranger GM Glen Sather make a friendly call to his old team, the Oilers, about recently former Ranger Rucinsky's stick? "Do you enjoy the game more now than you did, say, ten years ago?" I ask while we wait for the measure and the sorting out. "Yes, because I understand it more now," she says and away we go.

Raffi "Baby Beluga" Torres boards Keane – those naughty redheads – for the second time, and Keane – bloodied and swelling along his brow bone, goes in on goal with Linden, two on one, and snaps it past the goalie. Morrison steals and scores. Ohlund, too. It's sad the Oilers' year is done, but we stand for the final minute, applauding and cheering. I'm happy. The boys are happy. Smyth gives one last hangdog look at the Canucks' happy faces as the Oilers leave the ice.

"Good luck with your book," my friend says and struggles down the aisle with her husband the old farmer. She wasn't impressed that I'd chatted up players in the room; she wanted to know if Linden's marriage was intact since his return to the team. "We knew he'd had troubles when he came back and she wasn't with him." She's not staying for the jersey giveaway, she who is guaranteed seats to all playoff games. Lifelong fan?

Thousands stay, way more than last year – diehards waiting to witness Nazzie put his foot in it probably – and they're a few names into the order – drawn from big envelopes – when I realize Bert must be here. They wouldn't do this without him. There's a dark-suited Brumwell down there on the ice talking into his little phone and a flurry of serious-looking suits mingle in the tunnel with walkie-talkies. And then a tiny elderly woman on the carpet – she's got her Drafted by Canucks T-shirt on and a new hairdo – opens her envelope: Bertuzzi 44. Crawford holds his press conference while this happens; most press are off with him while Todd faces a few bars of the music. The boys on the bench twist toward the tunnel; they seem surprised and paled by this news and then there's Todd: slighter than before his mortification, clean-shaven, a young man trying to hold it together. He walks out in his nice trousers, past the burly guy holding a tiny baby, wraps the old lady in a glorious hug – head office must have picked her: brilliant – and then strips off his jersey, signs it, hugs her again. His face is composed. Näslund is up and applauding. The crowd goes nuts. We've missed him so much.

BACK AT THE HOTEL, Shannon tells me I've gone to the wrong room; the keys are inexplicably the same. She escorts me upstairs, along the ruin of unfinished new rooms – "The plumber's been sick," she says. Through another door, one I didn't think to open, and, presto, there's a lovely carpet on the fir-floored hallway, the doors have golden numbers and my room, when we open it, has a king bed, marble tile on the floor, a fridge and a comfy chair. The molding is mostly done. The fixtures are porcelain. We move my things – like an absurd passage into another state – and settle me in.

It's ten o'clock and the sports news comes on as I lie back into the big satin pillows. I watch highlights until eleven, seeing Todd over and over. I bless the old lady for holding him so close, for kissing him the way I want to, not just once. The newspaper will quote her: "I told him, 'Todd, I just love you with all my heart. You take good care of yourself.'"

ON MONDAY, our field is desperate with life and death. The night before, Alfie gave birth to four lambs – like last year, only this time they live. But she doesn't want to live. She can barely stand, won't eat, not even the imported alfalfa we borrowed from a horsey friend. She is bleeding from the anus and is all bone and skin. We inject her with a long-acting antibiotic and shoot liquid nutrients down her gullet several times a day. The lambs need bottle-feeding while we wait for her to die.

Monday morning is sunny and still and at seven, another healthy ewe – Blue Tag – is in labour and we want to graft one of Alfie's lambs onto her. So we watch her do it herself and when she's had one lamb, I lift the smallest of Alfie's quads and wipe Blue Tag's placenta over the wee one's head and shoulders and tail, hoping to fool the mum into accepting him. The rest of the flock – larger this year and a better lambing percentage – are in the next field over, slurping up the lush grass while we finish the births on our own field. They're noisy this morning, one ewe in particular is more bellow than baa. I can see her from where I'm kneeling at the side of the lambing shed, through the hanging branches of an old-old red cedar that separates the fields, the dappled light. A lamb limps. Mishaps happen when the flock is big and the lambs, especially at dusk, race around the field as a pack, and limping lambs are commonplace. But all that noise?

While I attended the last game, two farmer friends lost sheep to a cougar. This, too, is commonplace and to be expected in the still-wild terrain we monopolize. There have been sheep in Metchosin since 1843 and the cougars must have been pleased that year. This year, though, the cougar isn't eating its kills. Instead, he kills, panics, and runs off to the next innocent to kill again. Metchosin's cougar lady – mid-ninety-year-old Joan Yates who has dozens of cougar kills in her stat book – believes this happened: last year, a mother and cub were shot by the wildlife officer in nearby East Sooke Park, but they didn't get the second cub. Mrs. Yates believes these killings have the look of a cub who didn't get trained and now doesn't understand the rules of nature. They call these rogue cougars.

Tom's in the house making tea, and I leave Blue Tag to do what she needs to. Under the cedar, I can see the limping lamb and the bright red of blood. And another lamb, too. Ewe #10 – who had healthy triplets a couple of weeks ago – is wandering and she's covered in black, filthy from Grecian nose to bobbed tail. Two bloody lambs follow her. Only two. The bawling is coming from Flathead, who had birthed an inefficient single early on.

"There's blood," I say to Tom and refuse the mug of tea. He's over the fence quickly and we start the search. "10 should have three," I, our official scorekeeper, tell him.

A burn pile in the neighbour's field, a hill of charcoal, must have been where #10 tried to hide or went down and then got up. Who knows. "Here it is," Tom shouts from the edge of the field, under a stand of Douglas firs, near where we lost Alfie's last year. The dead lamb has only a few marks on the neck. I put my hand on its belly. "Still warm," I announce and Tom and I both look up into the trees above, stunned but not stupid. "This isn't hers, it's too big. This one's Flathead's."

The injured lambs are a mess: bite marks on all four haunches, scrapes of claws along their sides, flaps of flesh hanging, and we decide to treat those wounds before we keep looking. They're easy to catch and the bright blue antibiotic spray stinks like poison and makes them look like a child's spotted toy.

Meanwhile, Blue Tag is now nursing three lambs, two of her own and the runt from Alfie. I have to give a final exam to a class of clever fiction writers, and I'm tidied and washed getting into my car at nine o'clock when Tom comes from behind the woodshed and says, "I found it." Not ten feet from where we park our cars, the neck marked, too, but cold.

When the wildlife officer comes with the tracking dogs, we'll learn that the cougar left our place and went down the hill, stopped at one neighbour's farm and killed a couple, then carried on down William Head Road and took out a couple more at about the time I'm driving through the gravel pit toward town.

For the next few days, the trackers and the TV news guys will invade our field and everybody else's. The local anchor – tall and tanned and fedora-ed, his Aussie coat beading up the rain – will chat amiably about getting sheep for his young daughter, about doing a little hobby farming out in Saanich. *Are you fucking nuts, pretty boy?* I want to shriek, but smile and let the hard rain make my hair look terrible. We'll lead our flock into the chicken coop compound near the house every night, blast Radio Australia from a plugged-in box out there all night, a weird ethnic song that sounds like *keithtkachuk-keithtkachukkeithtkachuk*, and take calls from a network of sheep farmers who see or hear of the cougar. Alfie will be injected with twenty-four subcutaneous doses of vitamins, looking as skinny, pocked, and big-eyed as East Vancouver, a local shepherd's last-ditch attempt to save her. Then we'll blast her with a dose of short-term antibiotic, and the next morning she'll nibble alfalfa from my hand and sip from the water bucket. Blue Tag will ultimately reject Alfie's runt; the lamb is deaf, we realize, and can't keep up the way a real lamb should. The bottle will bond us.

Saturday at five: "The music teacher just chased it off her goats up the road from you and it's coming your way." We gather our sheep and lock them in. An hour later, another call: "They shot it," and Tom drives the couple of blocks up the road, in behind the elementary school, to have a look at the young, skinny male, limp in the back of the trackers' pick-up. Neighbours and lookie-loos and a photographer from our local paper drink from beer bottles and observe the clean and careful hole in the head. The dogs are still going apeshit. Only Tom kneels close and lays his small hand over the cougar's huge paw, glad he's dead, you bet, but sorry too.

CHAPTER EIGHT

A DAY WITH TODD BERTUZZI

Carla Funk

I'd make him take a watercolour lesson . . . go to a poetry reading . . . bake bread. But then I'd want to see some of that aggression, so I would get him to butcher some chickens, too.

Marilyn Bowering

I'd like Todd to cook dinner and I'd like to watch and talk to him while he did so. This after a day on the pond, with his kids/my kids when they were small, but with me picking up some hockey tips, too. I'd just like to watch him skate, go through his skills, because it's such a pleasure to watch somebody so gifted. I'd like him to talk about his childhood . . . And yes, of course, in some way to acknowledge his physical beauty . . . .

FUKT

I have a garage that really needs cleaning out, plus I'd want to see how many samwiches he could eat. During his break, I'd get him to see if he could throw my old couch up onto a neighbour I don't like's roof.

Joan MacLeod

I have spent enough time pondering Todd, rooting and worrying about the whole bunch of them. It's time for all of them to think about me. Todd and I would attend one of my plays – a really good one that I haven't written yet. He would laugh, cry, come to know himself in a whole new way. It would be at once life altering, soothing and cleansing for Todd. He would also get all my jokes, in fact tap into this whole witty part of himself for the very first time. Then he would tell me to go lie down, get some sleep, I've been working too hard, just stop worrying about it all. He'll watch over me.

Lily

I'd spend it like I was his own child. Do things that I would do with my own dad. Help him stack firewood in the morning, eat some gross-sounding lunch that he picked up the recipe for when he was playing in St. Louis. And admit reluctantly that it was good. Then take the two huge dogs that are half the size of him down to the beach. And lastly – of course – go watch him splatter somebody against the glass like a fruit fly at the game.

What I'm saying is that, while you might be asking what a normal fan would do during an ideal day with him, my ideal day would be the above, me actually BEING his child. That's the only way that the experience I described could be valued for me. Otherwise, the thought that I'm "Just A Fan" would be stuck in the back of my head.

My GOD! I'm starting to sound like a writer myself. EEEEW! It feels so dirty! GET IT OOOOOFF!! **Scrubs furiously** IT'S NOT COMING OFF! AH!

CHAPTER NINE

HOCKEY TOUGH

And grief itself be mortal! Woe is me!
Whence are we, and why are we? Of what scene
The actors or spectators? Great and mean
Meet massed in death, who lends what life must borrow.
As long as skies are blue, and fields are green,
Evening must usher night, night urge the morrow,
Month follow month with woe, and year wake year to sorrow.
  – Percy Bysshe Shelley, "Adonais"

When the hero or the villain of the drama, the man who was seen a few
minutes earlier possessed by moral rage, magnified into a sort of metaphys-
ical sign, leaves the wrestling hall, impassive, anonymous, carrying a small
suitcase and arm-in-arm with his wife, no one can doubt that wrestling
holds that power of transmutation which is common to the Spectacle and
to Religious Worship.
  – Roland Barthes, "The World of Wrestling," 1952

Your goalie
in his frightening mask
dreams perhaps
of gentleness.
  – Michael Ondaatje, "To a Sad Daughter"

I don't feel like working out, don't even get why I'm doing this. Maybe, in the vernacular, I've plateaued; a new routine would inspire me, but what's the point. I'm stronger all over – sure, how can I not be? – and the back – mid, lower, upper – and neck are stable and predictable; I can wake and stretch with a topnote of optimism about the day's promise without the risk of physical cubism. When I've done an hour at the gym in the morning, I feel satisfied come afternoon when the muscles sizzle, that I've accomplished something strenuous. I go three times a week and that feels lazy. My throat is wrinkled like an old hen's whattle; I see my father's jowls in the mirror and they look stupid with this haircut. But I never said it was about beauty, did I? Where am I going with this?

"I can't stop," I say to Tom over organic muesli. "If I stop, it'll turn to fat."

"You'll turn into Brad Park: one big face."

"Right."

"Or Marcel Dionne. You'd look like him."

"Okay, I'm going."

"God, those guys."

"Yes. Okay. I'm off."

City girls just seem to find out early . . . Fuck those fucking Eagles. The gym is busy with mentally handicapped youth this morning and it's rocking hard even without a good soundtrack. Down Syndrome athletes in bright colours – tank tops, flippy tennis skirts, tattered sweat pants. One young and stubby guy is particularly stoked with his reps; he can't be quiet, can't stop moving and shouting and squatting and leaping and twirling and laughing. *One two three ouchouch Ha! Ha! six twelve eighteen* go the speed demon overhead presses. He's repeatedly told to keep it down by the huge, bellied and cranky team leader, but forget it. *This is great!* is all his mouth can think about, his arms similarly enthused.

My cousin David suffered from Down Syndrome. A guy I was dating got a job at his group home. In his thirties, and with the excess weight and sloth typical of activity-resistant Down males, David had a reputation for moodiness. My boyfriend took him outside, threw a football, and made him play full-contact: David got happy, at least the boyfriend bragged he did. His uncles – one of whom was my father – were athletes with championships and cups and division titles in their scrapbooks. David's sister has a silver medal in rowing from the 1984 Olympics. His mother – my aunt – now a decade after his death, still plays tennis a few times a week.

Over in the corner by the blue stat cards and weigh scale, a woman in her fifties – pretty patio shorts and a pastel loose-fitting short-sleeved T-shirt, cropped hair dyed strawberry blonde, a skim of make-up to even things out – is overwhelmed. No visible muscle tone; knees of mush. It's likely her first time here, and she confers with her tall and taut husband while fiddling with a towel she pats to her clavicle. This gesture is symbolic only: no sweat, no high colour, no tense mouth to suggest recovery from exertion. "I don't think I can do this," she says quietly, a self-preservatory smile. "Why do you think that?" says kind and cooling hubbie. "It's too much," she says and smiles at him, nearly losing it but unable to walk herself to the change room to fall apart. The towel dabs the corner of her eye, in case of leakage.

Step aside buddy, I'll handle this! But no. Hers is a private moment in a public place and I shouldn't witness her surrender.

She picked a bad day to try hard. The room is one big internal combustion beast and if you're not already part of the four-stroke system, a smooth piston or crankshaft or camshaft or a hard-pumping valve all fired up, it'll be difficult to see yourself as part of the room's clean, efficient engine. Is she induction or exhaustion? Even the handicapped know how to do everything, and the pin weights and pec deck and the leg press seem too complicated for a gal who likely never learned to check the oil in her car.

I'm finally part of the machine. I'm fortunate to be here and lucky to balance on my knees on the big purple Swiss ball for as long as I want, to pretend the hard-cored Matt Cooke is my mocking coach. "Here's a water bottle for you. There's lots," says the largest member of Team Special. His shorts are tangled up into his crotch and reveal a certain pinkness of the upper thigh. He offers me a spray bottle of blue disinfectant. I'd have to take one hand off the ball to accept it, and it's still too soon for that skill set.

For Game 5 last night, Brian Burke channeled Winston Churchill into GM Place before the game, the booming audio of his famous June 4, 1940 speech. *Whatever the cost may be, we shall fight on the beaches.* The towels waved in tight formation, and Canada watched Vancouver get behind the war effort. *We shall fight in the fields and in the streets, we shall fight in the hills.* Between periods, Don Cherry – fully behind Calgary now, as all the CBCsters are – said he was moved by the selection *we shall never surrender.* It was a powerful moment, he conceded, but possibly the wrong strategy: Burkie might have frightened The Twins. We shall never forget to diss Sweden's non-role in WWII or miss an opportunity to reinforce the masculine ideal. Still, I laughed. Cherry's remark had some subtlety, and it deflated the pompousness of the war analogy and its role in the marketplace of hockey.

* * *

Success in hockey – and in life – is about learning to manage your mind effectively. By managing the mind effectively I mean setting clear, challenging goals;

defining specific on-ice tasks; maintaining a positive focus; creating and using power thoughts and high-performance images; tuning out negativity, fear, anger, doubt, and distraction; creating empowering feelings; and nurturing a positive, winning attitude. All of these elements are building blocks to becoming hockey tough.

   – Saul L. Miller, *Hockey Tough: A Winning Mental Game*

THE HOCKEY NEWS will goat-horn Jovo because he goes apeshit with a couple of minutes to go, Game 7, Vancouver down a goal and on the power play. He bangs Kiprusoff, then crosschecks d-man Robin Regehr, then whacks Rhett Warrener three times with cross-checks, and the ref calls him, has to, because it's so flagrant and out of control. With less than thirty seconds to play, the Vancouver net is empty and so the sides are even with Jovo bewildered in the box. Iginla picks up the puck and heads in to shoot for an open-netter to put the game away, confident this is how it should be, already celebrating in his mind and heading out: *Yes! I know the way to San Jose!* Not so fast, pal. Just as he shoots, a desperate fan tosses their jacket from the stands and it must catch the corner of Jarome's eye as it floats. The shot bumbles wide, the jacket comes down, the ref picks it up, and Näslund darts behind the net to grab the puck and bring it out: time for one last-ditch rush, the Nordic hop/skip as he skims away from his own net. He hits centre ice, heading up the left wing. A trailing Morrison gets his naughty stick tangled in the skates – whoopsie! – of the barrelling Iginla and down goes Jarome. Ten seconds to go. Näslund heads hard to the net. Grab my cape, boys! He shoots from in close and presto! There's Matt Cooke where he's supposed to be, covering his captain, on top of the goalie, and there's the puck in the net, 5.7 seconds left on the clock. Fans weep throughout the arena. The towels flap now like a flock of delirious and startled shorebirds. Jovo's in the box, towel in one hand and stick in the other, jumping in his skates and slamming the glass with his gloves, shrieking at his teammates, weeping with glee, the happiest of off-leash black Labs at the beach, ready to leap from the truck, bark at birds and chase that stick into the deepest water.

    They go for a break before overtime and the high must be the highest they've had. Followed by the lowest of lows when Malik misses his check and Martin Gélinas, one-time Canuck, scores while Jovo's still in the bin and the team's out of time.

    Woe is me.

THE NEXT MORNING, before the first power surge woke me with its blast of clearheadedness and mild panic, I dreamed of my father. I don't dream this way. Usually, my dreams contain merely a surreal image, a Magritte moment of meaningless originality. Or they are sexual and quiet: often marine mammals – orcas or Pacific white-sided dolphins – surface in a quiet bay upcoast and sheltered. Or there's an embedded pun I have to untangle and the dream's like an inside joke at the expense of the vulnerable me.

The dream of my father was unusual. For one thing, I don't often dream about the dead, not counting the frequent scenes where my recently gone tabby sits at the top of the driveway and waits for me to call her in. My sister appears now only every few years and I wake grateful to have had a visit, a catch-up. She's always still older than I am, still black-haired and beautiful. Rex has been dead eleven years, and I bet he's only turned up a half dozen times. Where do these people get to?

Even without the shapeshift of a potent dream, my dad looks a lot like Brian Burke. This resemblance has affected my take on Burke. Regardless of his warmongering, his preference for the Braveheart model of citizenship, his shoulder-chip attitude toward journalists (aka "maggots"), because he looks so much like my dad, Burke is kinder, gentler, smoother and funnier than he really is. My dad was not aggressive or violent or arrogant; I underplay those qualities in Burke and love to watch him talk.

In the dream, I'm at a fancy gathering of writer-types. I chat uncomfortably and look over to spot my dad doing likewise. I become short of breath and excuse myself from the small talk, "Sorry, I see someone I have to speak to." I part the crowd and walk over. *He's alive, he's not dead,* I think. The dream is very clear: there's no question he's my dad and that he's been – by choice – elsewhere for eleven years. He's not shocked to see me, more amused. He's smiling and I see the familiar overlap of his front teeth. And he's honest.

"Why did you do this?" I ask him. My chest hurts.

He says, "I wanted a little tenderness." I understand that, even in the dream, he's been with someone happy and tender and lighthearted. Someone unlike me.

I don't want to be a good sport about this. I cry and cry and shout. "How could you leave her? How could you? What about Lily?" She who *is* happy and tender and lighthearted.

"Well yes," he smiles, and I'm in such pain by then I wake myself up. And so he's disappeared again.

IN HER BOOK, *The Mourner's Dance: What We Do When People Die*, Katherine Ashenburg explains one therapist's explanation of what a mourner does in the first days – when there's "a powerfully diminished capacity to be involved in the world of real relationships or activities" – after loss: The mourner "needs time to sort through his complicated feelings about the death, to experience and express his loss, to be angry with the dead for abandonment, to long for the dead, to endure a temporary depression. Ultimately his task will be to accept that his living relationship to the dead is over, while he builds a new internal relationship with the beloved."

While it has always felt most like an obsessive/compulsive medieval romance – magical numbers, an enchanted landscape, pompous ceremonies, constant and tireless practice – not long into this examination of hockey, I began to think of it as elegy. Traditionally, an elegy is a poem written to contemplate, lament and praise a person after their death. It also expresses grief; it's the ultimate consolation, both for the poem's writer and for those who survive the loss of a loved one. It's a healing act, one that uses the magic of art to both memorialize and get over death, a creation that says, "sure he's dead, but look what was generated from that lousy theft: a beautiful thing! A growing thing! We're lucky there's art!" In pastoral elegies, everybody's a shepherd or a nymph and all nature joins in to witness and to grieve and celebrate.

> *Ah, woe is me! Winter is come and gone,*
> *But grief returns with the revolving year;*
> *The airs and streams renew their joyous tone;*
> *The ants, the bees, the swallows reappear*

The death of the Derek Sanderson style of hockey player; the death of offence and the deadly birth of the trap; the end of my hibernation away from sports, that long and serious sleep; the passing of my fertility; the death of fighter pilots in WWII.

Or hockey – the game itself – is the elegy: the ultimate consolation for the loss of childhood, loss of the endless celebration of play and rivalry and freedom and learning that is childhood.

The scar on my knee is an elegy: a sign of violence and pain, but also a consolation, a sign of healing.

Or, yes, this book is elegy: the ultimate consolation for the loss of my youth, the death of a hope I held that hockey had changed enough to welcome women like me. If the team didn't win the Cup, I thought, the book would be an elegy for this season, these two seasons and the teams they grew and how they grew me.

An elegy to Orr, to Linden. To sexuality, self, my sister, certain sheep, Vancouver and my youth there, the body, the brain, the ego, Vancouver Island as an undeveloped paradise. The ultimate consolation for the loss of my dad.

The last ten seconds of regulation, Game 7, were so full of life that death, it seemed, would be cheated. But no. Still, the death of a season is only a mimicking of death, a rehearsal, as when the family spaniel dies before the more human loved ones do the same.

ONE AFTERNOON after the playoffs had moved on to other cities, I visited the bookstore and bought two books: *The Wisdom of Menopause* and *Hockey Tough*. In the first, Christiane Northrup, who is also a doctor, explains the positive transformations she went through at the change: among other things, she called in a feng shui pro, ordered new furniture with a credit card online to create "a potential space for all the new energy that was beginning to stream into" her life, took control of her money, dumped her husband, and left the door to the woodstove open so she could see the flames. "Coming Home to Yourself." "The Power of Vulnerability." Were I to leave the woodstove open, the cat would catch fire. I had to stop reading.

Hockey Tough became my guide, feng shui for my brain. Menopause is a mental game, see, and you can manage it. It's all about thinking in Saul Miller's power zone, controlling emotions, battling through injury and fatigue. Am I right? Yes. I transferred several basic premises of sport psychology onto the problems of menopause. Instead of whining about heat, and confusion, and the loss of youth, I could choose to have the right focus, the right feeling and the right attitude. Hockey tough is "about having a clear direction, working hard, and following through," says Miller. "It's also about having a winning attitude. It's about being committed, confident, mentally tough or resilient, and having a passion for the game." Sure, blah blah. But while Dr. Northrup is all about going inward to heal past hurts, to listen to your body's messages and decode them, Dr. Miller is all about *the winning mindset*. I finished fourth in the hockey pool and won thirty-six bucks. FUKT was next to last. "A lot of the guys live in Boston," he had told me, and I felt like I'd played with the big boys and beat them.

BACK AT GAME 1, Stanley Cup Finals 2004, rough and ready Calgary Flames, having dumped the Dan- and Todd-less Canucks and the depthless San Jose Sharks, played the slick and sleek Tampa Bay Lightning in Florida. Wrestler Hulk Hogan flaunts his pornographic muscles rinkside as his long, blonde daughter, Brooke, her tight Tampa T-shirt tucked high into her rib cage, tarts-up "O Canada." The glitz-rock light show strobes the Flames' white jerseys; Calgary coach Darryl Sutter – one of six Sutter brothers grain-fed on the farm in Viking, Alberta – paces behind the bench looking bemused – or amused, who knows with that face? – by the night's hyperbole. The hype has indeed changed since Béliveau and Orr. What happens when we let anybody have a franchise? A circus breaks out. Vincent Lecavalier and Martin St. Louis seemed like Steinbeck characters trapped in a Danielle Steele novel, pale and French Canadian under the Tampa Bay Big Top, but they won and the game's story is more interesting for the incongruity.

Across the globe at the World Championship, Canada won the final 5-3 over Sweden and Ryan "Captain Canada" Smyth climbed over the seats in his skates to bring baby Isabella onto the ice. So, too, did Matt Cooke, his baby – Jackson – even smaller. Steve Staios had a toddler in each arm. It's been almost forty years since Canada's won gold two years in a row and I'm not sure how they did it this time, so awful were they early in the tournament.

In the locker room, Smyth pointed to the inspirational motto above the stalls – For Our Kids – and said not just our kids (those of the team) but also the kids back in Canada who will grow up to play international hockey. His mother was there, his dad, too, but Smyth wrapped an arm around Mom and leaned his head over onto hers. His crossed eyes crossed more elaborately. End of interview, he embraced his lovely wife, gave her a huge smooch and the baby Isabella was pressed like a daisy between their bodies.

Mother Niedermayer hugged all the boys, who kissed their wives and smoked cigars and drank champagne and beer all on television.

DURING THE NHL's lockout of players, Markus Näslund had a go at his dream to finish his career in Sweden. I watched his televised first game back with Modo. An unpenalized butt end into Näslund's sternum on his first shift told me enough. *Vancouver Sun* columnist Iain MacIntyre summarized Näslund's time in Sweden this way: "The concept: humble prodigal son comes home, embraced by his grateful nation, and honourably finishes his career as hockey statesman, validating the Swedish game and showing everyone he is a decent guy." Reality played out differently. "Prodigal son comes home, gets whacked, hooked and held into submission by opponents who want to take down an NHLer, then blasted in the press for failing to live up to his supposed stardom – the level of stardom defined by his obese NHL salary." Näslund will ultimately choose to end his career in Vancouver and say it feels more like home for his family. When Steve Moore decided to sue Bertuzzi and a number from the Canuck fold – including soon-to-be ex-Canuck Brad May – Näslund chirped from Sweden that he has no respect for a low-skill player trying to get top dollar through the courts. "If it was me," Näslund said, "I'd be doing everything I could to get back and play and show everyone the character I have, instead of trying to sue everyone." It's hard to be a diplomat, I suppose, with bone chips flaking from your elbow, a contused sternum, and an untidy scar above your right eye to remind your lovely wife that the mood might not get better, your game may never be high octane again.

On August 8, 2005, Commissioner Gary Bettman reinstated Todd Bertuzzi, noting in his decision that he believed the player felt genuine remorse. So Bert would be back for the 05/06 season in Vancouver. Wayne Gretzky immediately extended to Todd an invitation to the Olympic camp in Vancouver. Sport psychologists have predicted hard and haunted times for Todd in this city, that it would be better for him to start fresh in another market, that he will always be confused by what he did and wonder if he might be capable of such a mistake again. His play might suffer. His mind might wander. "I've had a lot of sleepless nights trying to think of things," Bertuzzi told reporters in his first press conference. When asked by a television reporter why he should be allowed to play hockey again while Moore still recovers, Bertuzzi fought to compose himself. But he did. "I'm a firm believer," he said, "in second chances. If we're going to go through life not giving anyone second chances, what kind of life are we going to have around here. People make mistakes in life. I was under a microscope and on TV when my mistake happened."

Post-lockout (and left with a CBA and season some believe we owe to Players Association president Trevor Linden's diplomacy, intelligence and heart, or to his innocence, lack of resolve and willingness to sacrifice bottom-feeders in the NHLPA), we were promised a freshened up game: rule changes or better enforcement to loosen an increasingly tight game; smaller goalie gear and less wander-room around their crease; a shoot-out to decide games left tied in regulation; the two-line pass, despite the opinion of the game's best left-winger, Markus Näslund.

Other sports have tried to adjust to woo snoozing fans: the NBA's three-point shot and time limits to thwart that game's defensive traps, for example. Audience numbers are still low; violence in basketball and in its stands is on the rise. In the late sixties, tennis's new Big Game of serve and volley cut so severely the number of strokes – offence – per game that reform was called for: eliminate the first serve, make the server stand several feet behind the baseline, don't let the server play the return unless it bounces. The game stayed the same. Time passed. Players got creative just to keep from being bored and the game changed on its own. Besides, wrote John McPhee, plenty of folks liked the power game. "It is the megagame. It has the spectral charm of a Joe Louis stalking a Billy Conn in silence and then dropping him with a few echoing thuds."

The rules are not the problem with the game, unless you count the still-missing rule that applies significant penalties for head shots, particularly those visited on star players. The problem is what *Globe and Mail* business columnist – and usually my conservative nemesis Saturday mornings – Jeffrey Simpson calls "the Don Cherry-fication of the product." The problem is not the game, but how the product has been sold. Simpson characterizes it as a "coarse way" of giving us the game, one that portrays it – falsely – as "the epitome of manliness." This tactic may have "pleased the faithful, much the way large gas-guzzling cars satisfied a certain share of the car market, but turned off new buyers who wanted a better product at a lower price." Cherryfication is a "false gospel" worshipped by a league that believes the erosion of product quality can be disguised by "ever-louder rock music, new uniforms, new franchises, fresh gimmicks such as bobblehead-doll giveaways."

Reverend Gary Bettman says the game will look better on television. More access to players, more microphones, more talking to coaches. During the lockout, I'd seen an interview with Bruce McNall, formerly LA Kings owner and Gretzky pal, subsequently jailed for fraud. He suggested hockey broadcasts should be more like reality TV; that hockey players are too nice; that they put the game ahead of themselves and that's just boring. Put a mike on them at the bench and let us hear all that aggression.

I asked Chris Brumwell by phone what kind of changes this shift in perspective will bring. "Will it mean a change to that awful half-hour in the locker room thing?"

"If you were a beat reporter, travelling with the guys on the road, you'd get lots of time in the room to have a conversation." Out of town, the intense media pressure dissipates and Markus Näslund can sit on the bench for half an hour and talk to the *Sun*'s hockey writer. There's no time and space in the home town. Okay okay, it was all my fault. But will that change now?

Brumwell said with the new schedule that emphasizes inter-division rivalries and limits visits from Eastern teams – we won't be seeing Sidney Crosby here for a hundred years – it will be necessary to arrange more access for local media. If Sid the Kid's in town for only one day, more availability will be needed.

There is now a Competition Committee to improve the game, made up of players, execs, and anyone else deemed needed to weigh in on aspects of the game. No women sit on that committee, no fans. Brendan Shanahan had said, post new CBA, that hockey players have traditionally been conservative when it comes to talking about the game; that will have to change now, he said. Brumwell thinks hockey players have grown up in a sport culture that tells them the team comes first. A good basketball player in high school is a star in high school. A good hockey player in high school is part of a team that doesn't brag, or hot-dog, or talk about how good you are. NHL players are mostly raised in working class small towns, too, and when your dad works overtime night shift at the pulp mill and your mom tries to feed five boys on one salary and hasn't bought lipstick since you were born, you learn to shut up about yourself. What do they mean, then, when they say we'll see a different game?

"More stories," said Brumwell.

I knew it.

"More stories about players, their lives off the ice. That's what they did with Nascar and viewership went up forty percent. It won't change right away. But you'll see a lot more stories."

Some of us were already seeing stories. The stories have always been there, especially when the camera lets us be voyeurs, illicitly noticing the gestures and habits of players. My worry is that someone who knows zilch about narrative, about the need for artful incongruity and the beauty of ambiguity, about what constitutes a surprising detail, will emphasize the simplicity of the staged spectacle. Instead of a voyeuristic camera to catch Todd Bertuzzi kiss his little boy's mouth, some announcer hooked on being the über-narrator will explain: here's an image that proves he can be naughty and nice. It will be like that icky Jim McKay's "Up Close and Personal" bullshit the Americans do for the Olympics, more propaganda than art. Finding a story doesn't automatically increase and improve pleasure. A good story is also what gets left out, the gaps and spaces left for alert readers.

THE LAST BOOK my father read was John McPhee's *Levels of the Game*, a brilliant narrative replay of a key tennis match between young Arthur Ashe (then an army lieutenant at the U.S. Military Academy and whom McPhee describes as "a trim arrangement of sinews") and Clark Graebner at Forest Hills. Published in 1969, it's been called "the high point of American sports journalism" and it was a Christmas gift from Tom, then my new live-in boyfriend and father-to-be, to my father whom Tom adored, trusted and admired on first meeting. "A person's tennis game begins with his nature and background and comes out through his motor mechanisms into shot patterns and characteristics of play," writes McPhee. "If he is deliberate, he is a deliberate tennis player; and if he is flamboyant, his game probably is, too." I don't have a memory of watching my father play; I have clear memories, though, of him in the middle of the kitchen playing air tennis. He is singing the Mills Brothers, "Up a Lazy River" – his favourite song – and he bounces on his toes *Blue skies up above* and sways his hips and says "boom" in a light way every time he nails a backhand *Everyone's in love*. And then he's back smiling, dancing and floating in ready position *Up a lazy river, so happy we will be* a-boom *Up a lazy river with me*. My dad loved McPhee's book and shared it with his pals at the tennis club. His name and phone number still appear inside the cover.

I'm re-reading the book, late in August. Last evening, I played tennis with Lily at Juan de Fuca Recreation Centre to get her loose for a round robin tournament today. Usually we play on courts deep in the forest, on the grounds of Hatley Park and Royal Roads University, halfway between Metchosin and Victoria. We bicker there, when the sun is hot and Lily wants more competition, and I've had to say "Let's go home then" when she tosses her racquet to motivate me. My father grew up near here. The Juan de Fuca courts border a Par 3 and share a parking lot with the new hockey arena. Last year during the lockout, we came and watched the Salmon Kings play Alaska, front row, and wondered why Scott Gomez's big hairy thighs were visible where he hadn't zipped the inseam of his hockey pants. She's tough to figure: part of her wants to enter tourneys and part of her fears them.

Like her grandfather's, Lily's nature is also clear from her game: she is fierce, thrilled with success, sickened by failure, aware of the handsome, brown cadets on the next court and how she appears when she blows on her hand, amused by the toddler whacking balls at his dad, alert to the osprey that nests in a light standard over on the soccer pitch. Though I've told her I can't chase down her signature shot – a hard spinning cross-court forehand – she nails me there whenever she can. I have to be careful. My arms are much stronger, I can bend deeper at the knee, my core is more solid: occasionally I risk before I can stop myself. I chase that ball and feel rivets pop below my knee.

She does not like to be coached, so when she decides to finish the hour with serves, I say quietly so the cadets don't hear, "Maybe hit a couple without thinking, see what happens." She obeys. When propelled only by her grandfather's genes and superb rhythm, her serve toss goes high and straight, and she nails a liner with spin. When interviewed about her tennis by the Metchosin paper last summer, she said, "I think my grandpa would be proud of me."

Tom dropped her off in Victoria this morning for the tourney, a long Saturday drive into the now-swanky neighbourhood where my parents first lived, near the university. There will be six players in her group; four are boys. An hour before she's scheduled for pick-up I'm reading McPhee in my office, dogs on loveseat: "Ashe turns, in the cascade of applause for his sensationally incautious shot, and walks away from the court. He withdraws into himself, his back to the court and to Graebner. Thirty-forty. Set point."

Her voice is young and small on the phone. "Hi, Mom, it's me."

"Hey Loo-Loo."

"We're done."

"Okay. I'll send Dad."

"Thanks."

The dogs need water. I'm about to hang up but remember the day's point. "Lily: how'd you do?"

"I won," she says.

THEN, IT'S THE END of October, the convoluted post-lockout hockey season underway, and next week I'm scheduled to see a game in Ottawa versus Tampa Bay, to witness at last the Vinnie and Marty show, to admire Alfie in the slot and see Heatley's bi-coloured eyes light up as he crosses the blue line still a little wonky on those car-wrecked legs. I want to visit the new War Museum there, and step inside, I hope, yet another Lancaster at the aviation museum.

It is the last Friday of October, and I'm in my office in the stone house on our property that overlooks the garden, the field, and beyond it, the Galloping Goose Trail. The garden is still semi-lush. The tomato plants are gone, and I've planted next spring's garlic; I have yet to scrap the cantaloupe vines now black and thin. Tom has loaded the woodshed early for once, and several walls of the main house's shingles have been re-stained against the prevailing westerlies. The lambs are big after a bad summer of intestinal worms and scant grass. The farm looks tidy, green, almost prosperous.

At ten A.M. on the last Friday of October, Tom climbs the steps to my office. For the last year, he's worked two minutes away, in an oceanside heritage cabin that is now headquarters for a farm magazine he edits and publishes. "It's not too bad in here," he says about the temperature. A few years ago, we finally had this house rewired, and while Tom has written several books here bundled into overcoat, toque and gloves, I can now write in soft jeans, sweatshirt, and stocking feet, dogs deep-snoozing on the loveseat, in relative warmth. I get sleepy, too, intoxicated by the scent of eighty-year-old rat piss and bat guano infusing in this warmth.

"Why are you here?" I ask and hope he's come for tea, that he'll hike down to the main house and bring back two mugs, a cookie, that it will be that way again.

"To talk." He leans, still in his jacket, against the cold fireplace. His face is pale. "It's rough," he warns.

He tells me he's in a relationship with someone else. "I want out," he says.

THAT WAS FRIDAY. Monday is Halloween. I go to the gym. Gridlocked. My gym buddy, who is everyone's buddy here, doesn't tease me about the relative weight of my medicine ball sit-ups, probably because of my eyes. If I have learned one thing in the last two years, it is this: pain subsides. I have learned to trust and redefine pain: call it growth. I have learned that upping my cardio will help me sleep through even the wild wind, cold rain and falling branches of this freak storm. My body is a good place to live. I can trust it to be strong. My body.

Back home, before the bath, the weep, and long nap, I let the dogs out and they race up to my office and disappear around the side of the little house. The rain is hard and cold. "Not today," I shout, but they're gone and I follow. They've sniffed a small white-tailed deer under my office window. It leans on the other side of the gate next to the old coop, curved into a patch of salal and against the red trunk of my blighted arbutus. The deer tries to stand, startled by this crowd, but stumbles back down. I grab Greta and growl at Max to come up to the office where I call the conservation officer.

Within an hour, his big truck diesels in the driveway, and I show him where the calm deer still lies. "Oh yeah," he says with tenderness. "Well. I'll come from above and get him that way." He gumboots back to the truck and meets me on the driveway with his rifle. His hair's a mess and his uniform is wrinkled. "Just make sure if he tries to get up, he doesn't go out to the road."

I watch the officer circle from the road verge above, creep through the Indian plum and vine maples, both scantily clad this time of year. He raises the rifle with such diligence and care. The shot is a small sound against the hiss of cars on wet pavement.

"Too bad. He's in good shape." We stand in the rain, both bare-headed westcoasters, and look at him a long time. The muscles that now spasm are smooth. Despite the beautiful blood oozing from his huge nose, the coat is clean and rich brown. The eyes glaze. Two small horns, single points. "You had a cougar here last year," he says.

"Very naughty."

"I just got the hide back from the tanner. Gorgeous animal. Wrong place, wrong time."

He drags the deer to the truck, drags him up and in. We look for wounds and I hold one back leg in my hands. "Look at this," he says, and shows me the bone protruding from a front leg. The back one I hold, also broken.

* * *

you OK . . . ? . . . ridiculous question, I know.

. . . spoke to Trevor for you . . . definite interest there. He says he sees his free time opening up . . . especially during games.

rick

FUKT STARTED the 05/06 season as BESTASS and leads the pool, thanks to a prescient selection of Jaromir Jagr. Joan MacLeod is the ill-spelt TALON and chose Shane Doan because she imagines her name should they marry. Lily is JOVOPERM and doesn't pay attention. I – LUCINDA – was doing okay until Ziggy Palffy retired and now I am fukt.

I keep in infrequent touch with a high school chum who teaches pediatrics in Belfast. On hearing of The Troubles here, he cautioned kindly, "As you know, adolescents have a lot of trouble linking psychological pain with physical symptoms and there can be trouble downstream." Maybe that's what this book has been about: linking psychological pain with physical symptoms. Or is it about the trouble downstream?

If Tom had died, Lily and I would be allowed to grieve, publicly and privately. Death is clean. This loss has jagged edges that cut anew and keep cutting, so healing is continuous and yet unable to keep up with the fresh wounds. Tom's new woman is blue-blooded, younger, owns more sheep, has a larger, more prosperous farm nearby, has two teenage daughters. Also – I have known her for most of my thirteen years here – she is happy, tender and lighthearted, or so I've always imagined. Hates hockey. Her daughters will attend private school. Her mother will serve on municipal council. Perhaps she will cut even more trees from her parents' waterfront farm in order to build yet another riding ring for the horses. Meanwhile, Tom will live with her, and with the fifteen-year-old daughter who is now in most of Lily's classes at school. So much change so quickly.

November 11 also pours rain. Lily's booked to play "Last Post" on her trumpet. Our cenotaph is modest, halfway between the white heritage church and the co-op preschool Lily attended. She will play from the shelter of the preschool porch, where ten years ago her nervous father cursed the women in fast cars who sped past regardless of zone.

My mother attends, my father's air force wings pinned to her jacket as if she wears his number, his jersey: is she taking power from my father, or showing off her own, masquerading as a soldier? Three old men surround her; one tells of his many missions with Bomber Command, another of his horrors in the South Pacific. The trumpet begins. My mother tells these men, "that's my granddaughter" and they shoulder her forward, take her arm and lead her past the municipal candidates and farmers, the Boy Scouts and other paramilitary kids, to the front of the crowd so that Lily can see her. Lily winks.

Tom, as usual, is emcee for this ceremony. And as he begins to say a few words – maybe, like last year, he reads from the Governor General's message *They came home scarred by their experiences, of which they often will not speak.* As he begins, my mother turns her back on him and walks past St. Mary's graveyard to her car.

This year – the first in the thirteen years we've been in Metchosin – I don't attend. I don't lead the group in the singing of "O Canada." I'm at home with a mug of tea. This morning, my mother brought me a few things from a scrap book she'd found, wanting to set my mind to more troubled times, to the promise of a heart's endurance.

Her exam marks from second year at UBC May, 1944. The grades are fine, but not high; her sweetheart, after all, was MIA. Also, a notice from the flight training school in Claresholm, Alberta: "The station Basketball teams playing last night split a double-header series. The Men's team took the top honours in the second game by defeating the Pearce quintet 38-28. Paced by L/C Norman who was closely followed by P. O. Jackson, in the matter of point making our team really looked swell."

There are newspaper clips and letters that report my father as first missing, and then a prisoner of war. March 26, 1944: *It is with great regret that I have to confirm the news you will already have received that your friend, Flight Lieutenant William Rex Jackson, is missing from air operations.* And a clipping: *Flt. Lt. Jackson, recently listed as missing . . . was well known as a basketball, softball, and tennis player. Brothers are P.O. "Busher" Jackson, RCAF, former Domino basketballer and P.O. Allan Jackson, RCNVR.* Then June 11, 1944, *PLEASED TO CONFIRM YOUR SON FLIGHT LIEUTENANT WILLIAM REX JACKSON IS PRISONER OF WAR.* And on May 1, 1945, *Flt. Lt. Rex Jackson, a prisoner in German hands for the past 14 months, has been freed from Stalag-Luft I.* Followed by a string of cryptic telegrams to my mother as to when the train would arrive, asking her to be his Valentine, always signed, Joe, the name she called my father in the early years of their romance and throughout their long marriage.

IT'S FEBRUARY, I'm fifty, and yesterday early at the gym, Janis Joplin sang "Mercedes Benz" as I rested between bench press sets and watched my dogs watch me from the car out the window, across the grass, parked under the Douglas firs. "Good thing she killed herself," said the man I don't like, "So we don't have to listen to any more of that." I thought of Joplin alone for eighteen hours, beside her bed on the floor of the Landmark Hotel, the balloon of heroin releasing her from life's tortures, her body's final contortions. Greta's paws on the steering wheel; Max tall and handsome in the back seat. Time to go.

Three hours later, the Canadian hockey men were eliminated from the Olympics after losing to a team loaded with eager boys and sensible, proud veterans from Russia. I will allow the analysis to come from the frenzied, finger-pointing pundits – we will never agree and I'm tired of the banter. It no longer surprises or outrages me that for the CBC boys and their counterparts on screen and in print, the right answer to the pathetic question *why?* is a "thuggish" and "undisciplined" penalty – he set a pick on a featherweight Russian like a million other picks in the tournament that weren't called – taken by Todd Bertuzzi to begin the third period. On this penalty a dancing, dazzling Alexander Ovechkin – he who blew coach Wayne Gretzky a kiss after scoring on his new team, the Phoenix Coyotes – capitalized, left alone like a dumped wife in the crease. Were all the other penalties – one taken by coach Pat Quinn to start the second period – somehow less psychotic? Should Bert take the blame when the team and all its multi-millionaire stars could not score one goal in the remaining eighteen minutes to cover his big Baloo butt?

Though I was hungry for the thrill of international hockey I'd experienced in 2002, this time the Olympics did not supply it. Hooking, slashing, holding. Joe Sakic's broken cheekbone and cut open face. Chris Chelios's elbow connects hard and fast with the face of the player who skates innocently behind him, post-whistle. Jarkko Ruutu smashes Jagr's head into the boards. Derian Hatcher knocks out Teemu Selänne's teeth. Evgeni Malkin takes a swing at Vincent Lecavalier's handsome neck with his skate blade. Xenophobe Don Cherry conveniently forgets that Lecavalier himself was suspended in January 2004 for the same obscenely violent act.

That last game against Russia, it was clear the Canadians had lost their most admirable gift: the ability to improve incrementally and quickly under intense pressure. While I had been ecstatic with the gold-medal win in 2002 and watched it twice just to feel it again, I didn't grieve during this game, since defeat seemed an incongruous and interesting way to end the tournament's compressed narrative. It is not shameful to lose, nor is the pain of loss an empty pain. While the faces of the team looked terrible – the sad-eyed and 6'6" Chris Pronger had only that morning been my pretend boyfriend in my garden, shirt off, blue jeans low on his hips, spreading yet another load of goat manure on the tomato beds – they didn't choke me up.

Until, with about a minute left, the ambulance-chasing camera panned down the Canadian bench and found Todd Bertuzzi, his head hung so low and motionless that his own neck seemed broken by hockey's cruel, beautiful and relentless weight.

STAY AT HOME DEFENCE

I've had almost two full seasons to dance with this new game; some nights it's hard to get going and get out there for a few twirls. The first season post-lockout, players who'd been a large part of the story I constructed had moved on: Hedberg, May, Keane, Sopel, Chubarov, Malik; Brian Burke was off to California and those Ducks. Others suffered from the break and seemed less graceful, less gleeful. Linden averaged about seven minutes a game and, thanks to more infractions called, became a five-on-three penalty-kill specialist. Not a sexy role. Only the Sedin twins seemed better, and the incongruity of Anson Carter's black skin between their porcelain faces made the story better. Called the Brothers Line by those who dared, they were the most fastidious in the league. Nazzie seemed torn.

I was embarrassed by the television advertising package – the narcissistically named *My NHL* – that once again equated hockey players with warriors, this time even more explicitly, with the intention of wooing an elusive American audience with rump-roast pecs (hockey players don't have them, trust me), unbridled aggression, Oriental rugs in the locker room, and mystery women who recite Chinese proverbs and wait at home in gauzy nighties for the soldier to return from battle only to send him out again, red fingernails stroking those pecs, with that familiar and really breathy call to arms, "It's time." I suppose the whole thing was meant to get men to identify with the players and thereby see themselves in the game blah blah. Another case of market research gone terribly stupid. That's the story we've been waiting for? Not me.

And the shoot-out: the fans want and deserve an outcome, the testochrats say, and so the shoot-out was added to *really* resolve the conflict. That last frontier of undecideability and ambiguity, that moment of anti-closure – the tie game – has been eliminated. I object, although it does seem to rightly celebrate the boyishness of players, the egocentric piece of their hockey player puzzle, the part of themselves that can keep puck on stick and simultaneously lift one leg to do a fancy little back kick while pulling it to the backhand, cocking a pimply boy-band head fake, and then flipping the bugger top shelf, all in three seconds while sucking a mouth guard that makes their lips fat. Marek Malik, to Joan MacLeod's delight, scored the shoot-out goal of the century for the Rangers, between his legs and backwards, after a couple dozen other, more skilled players had missed. The very definition of monstrous grace.

The only story we've been given is the saga of the Staal brothers and their turf-farmer parents, and it has been told to death. Players are wired, sure, but that means now we can hear teenaged Alex Ovechkin sing badly during warm-up, or the occasional whoo-hoo! from a perennially pumped-up veteran, or maybe a sketched-out strategy between a left winger and a centre, but we can't see it anyway since the camera follows the puck and the right winger has it. Reality TV, indeed. Headshots. Cuts to the face. Retribution. Ontario and its jock-sniffing media believe their teams are the only great ones on the planet; Ontario teams under-perform yet again.

Meanwhile, in 05/06, the Canucks fell apart: Cooke was injured twice in practice and the team stunk without him; Jovo, out again; Cloutier's body betrayed him again and Alex Auld was fine, but not fine enough; Bertuzzi could not give or take a check and often seemed to wear a body cast around his fragile core; Morrison could barely skate by the end of the season and his hip required mega-major surgery once the playoffs were missed. They could have made the post-season, given heart and grit, but the team seemed to know they wouldn't last with all those broken bodies and so they let it all fall down. The locker room, we are told, was a sick swamp of me-first egos, deep resentments, and hierarchies: the opposite of team chemistry. Did they not realize I needed them more than ever? Talk about selfish.

Spring 2006, the season already on the downslide, I knew that the strong daughter I had built would turn on herself. She was fifteen – the age I was when my sister died – and I knew how grief and swallowed anger could choreograph a young woman's next thirty years. Trouble downstream. She could not fathom her father's choices, his new life, and so she and I rebuilt the team mostly together and alone. A million hearty soups and fragrant scones and steam-ironed pillowcases; the latest gigabytes and downloaded tunes – Queens of the Stone Age and Swedish death metal now; Johnny Depp on perpetual replay: these intoxicants would not keep her from looking inside and finding reason to doubt herself, to give in to pessimism, to fly into enemy territory and blow up or just disappear and never come back. I promised her we wouldn't leave her home until the end of high school. I didn't know what else to do, except the obvious and automatic: love. Talk about selfish.

One cold and windy evening, Lily interrupted a mean-nothing hockey game. "I want to try a triathlon."

Sure. Why do only one easy thing you're good at, say tennis, when you can do three really hard things, all at the same time? "Three sports."

"I want something I can do here, at home, in Metchosin. I want to run the Goose and swim Matheson Lake. I'll get a wetsuit."

She got permission to join an adult twelve-week training course at Juan de Fuca Recreation. She trained six days a week. She swam before school and biked after band practice. The adults in her group wished she could join them in the bar after conditioning, they loved her that much. And in August, one bright Sunday morning at the Naden Canadian Forces Base in nearby Esquimalt, she competed for three hours in the adult grouping of the Triathlon of Compassion and finished the race to the hoots and hollers and hugs of her team. Imagine that.

Then, Bert was traded for the mellifluous Roberto Luongo (aka Bobby Lou); Jovo gone; also Bryan Allen, Dan Cloutier, uthuh bruthuh Anson Carter, coach Marc Crawford. The Canucks are in rebuild mode, too, and being a fan here is a little like cutting carbs and fat while the rest of the world gorges on apple fritters and Ben & Jerry's Chunky Monkey ice cream.

It is the era of the small forward, the born-again vet, the punk rocker. Each team is quarterbacked and driven by speedy little bastards with soft hands and giant thighs – Martin St. Louis, Paul Kariya, Daniel Briere. Retro-stars have the time and space to be the players they used to be: Teemu Selänne, Rod Brind'Amour, Brendan Shanahan. And the league is slick and shiny with maniac boys who can dish, deke, and score, sometimes on their backs while sliding across the goal line: Sidney Crosby, Alex Ovechkin, Evgeni Malkin. The new NHL spots on TV are more comic and self-mocking and go for the "players are regular people" identification angle: Crosby turns up in someone's bathroom, chats with the wife, and flushes the toilet while the husband's in the shower; Jonathan Cheechoo swims horizontal on a surf board; an inept Joe Thornton makes toast. The story lines are goofy, but some of these ads have women in them, and they are not wearing gauze or flaunting a sub-100 IQ.

Midway through the season, BESTASS – he who cellar-dwelled for the first four months – is challenging JOVOPERM in the pool's top ten. Lily was too sad to pick her own team (do not mention Jovo; she weeps), so I did it for her and gave her the best players, including Los Angeles's snazzy offensive d-man Lubomir Visnovsky. LUCINDA made choices based only on those players with whom she would have sex on the first date; she believes that an obsession with statistics is only one form of objectification and not necessarily the most satisfying. The Hottie Team, she terms it, is four spots out of last place, mostly because neither Sedin made the team and the chatty but ice-cold Craig Conroy did.

On the occasional Thursday afternoon, a sore-backed BESTASS droops in the doorway of my office at the university, sweater-vested like Perry Como, and we dare each other to hope. What has been a complex season, a slow-developing narrative, under a new coach and with new and renewed loves — Kevin Bieksa, you surly college boy! Trevor 'Backdoor' Linden on the PP! — may turn into a miraculous one. We've been jilted before, though, and can't afford to feel much; we are the shut down line.

The winter in Metchosin has been spectacular, though really just an authentic winter, like those I remember growing up in Vancouver, the one that broke my kneecap. The snow has been deep, the ice relentless, the power and phones have gone out for days. For a few minus seven days in December, backyard rinks took over pumpkin fields. Just before Christmas, the forecasted windstorm stayed true to course. I lay in bed, one dog under the covers, the other on the floor by my desk, and heard the wind at midnight shift from west to east and move up from the Goose Trail where all is safe, to the road above my house where all is precarious. At 1:45 I lay there still and imagined how I would be a hero and rescue Max from under the 100-year-old balsam that would surely come through the roof and onto my bed. I knew where the little handsaw was. I could dress his wounds. At 2 A.M. the tree pulled up at the roots and fell ten metres from my bed and came to rest across the hood of my Mazda Ovary. My next thought: *I'm glad to live where nature makes me afraid.*

I have kept three sheep: Rose the matriarch, her sister Alfie, and Alfie's deaf runt, now named Buddy, who greets me at the gate each afternoon, lifts up on his stubby back legs and sniffs my breath. I tried to keep Buddy's bottlefed brother, but once I'd named him Todd — the day he chased his Aunt Rose around and around the manger before finally head-butting her across the paddock — and once he'd had me in the chicken coop and taken a run at my quadriceps with his hard little polled horns, it was time to send him away. This morning, back from the gym and a million medicine ball squats on the wobble board, I gumbooted out to the coop to release my young hens into the cold and bright morning. Usually, I can hear them gurgle and cluck and bliss-out at the promise of a day picking worms from wet earth before they explode through the little hatch when I open it. This morning, though, no sound. All ten lay inside, their necks bloodied and broken, beautiful bodies stiff but intact. That's my first mink visit in ten years in this house – mink will bleed a bird and leave the body. The turkey vultures aren't back from holiday yet, or I'd toss one hen into the field and watch them clean up all afternoon, and then I'd describe it for you and help you understand even better – the right details, the colours, the expanse of wing – that there is bounty in death. My next thought: *I can't do this any more.*

My own mother. While she may not get Gretzky, I discovered so much about her through the writing of this book, all of it astonishing and inspiring. I came to understand just how much and how many she has lost, and the grace, intelligence, dignity and optimism she has needed to carry on her life. It was a hard winter for an eighty-one-year-old woman in the country, and she has lived without my father for fourteen years. But she's been lucky to find companionship and love with a kind, lifelong friend. He is 86. And when my mother came to my living room to tell me she would soon move into Victoria, into his house across from the golf course on the water side of Beach Drive, I was inspired again and thrilled for her happiness because she deserves to spend her last years in a warm home, sipping scotch and water in the evening with a handsome man who likes to laugh.

My next thought: *My father's not coming back.*

SOURCES

These are listed in order of their approximate appearance, or when they influenced a chapter, but many appear more than once.

Prologue

BOOKS

Bruce Kidd and John Macfarlane, *The Death of Hockey* (New Press, 1972); Barbara Gowdy, *We So Seldom Look on Love* (Harpercollins, 2001); Roy MacGregor, *The Home Team: Fathers, Sons and Hockey* (Penguin, 1997); Doug Beardsley, *Country on Ice* (Polestar, 1987); Joyce Carol Oates, *On Boxing* (Ecco Press, 1994); Marni Jackson, *Pain: The Science and Culture of Why We Hurt* (Vintage, 2002)

ARTICLES

Laura Mulvey, "Visual Pleasure and Narrative Cinema" (*Screen* 16.3, 1975); Margaret Carlisle Duncan and Barry Brummett, "Types and Sources of Spectating Pleasure in Televised Sports" (*Sociology of Sport Journal* 6, 1989); Damien Cox, "Orr's Left Knee Gone for Good" (in *The Way it Looks from Here: Contemporary Canadian Writing on Sports,* ed. Stephen Brunt, Knopf Canada, 2004); Michael Farber, "Down and Dirty" (*Sports Illustrated,* 6 May 2002); Brian Cazeneueve, Kostya Kennedy, Richard Deitsch, "Out of the Fog" *Sports Illustrated,* 23 September 2002)

ETC.

www.canucks.com

Chapter One

BOOKS

Georges Santayana, *Reason in Society* (Dover, 1990); A.L. Kennedy, *On Bullfighting* (Yellow Jersey Press, 2000); Phil Jackson, *Sacred Hoops: Spiritual Lessons of a Hardwood Warrior* (Hyperion, 1995); Daniel L. Wann, Merrill J. Melnick, Gordon W. Russell, Dale G. Pease, *Sport Fans: The Psychology and Social Impact of Spectators* (Routledge, 2001); Martin Middlebrook, *The Berlin Raids: R.A.F. Bomber Command Winter 1943-44* (Viking, 1998); Lawrence Scanlan, *Grace Under Fire: The State of our Sweet and*

Savage Game (Penguin, 2002); Mordecai Richler, *On Snooker: The Game and the Characters Who Play It* (Knopf Canada, 2001); David Adams Richards, *Hockey Dreams: Memories of a Man Who Couldn't Play* (Anchor, 1996)

ARTICLES

George Orwell, "The Sporting Spirit" (*Shooting an Elephant and Other Essays*, Penguin, 2003); Rona Murray, "Militantly Rural" (*Western Living*, October 1997); Sue Curry Jansen and Don Sabo, "The Sport/War Metaphor: Hegemonic Masculinity, the Persian Gulf War, and the New World Order" (*Sociology of Sport Journal* 11, 1994); Walter Gantz and Lawrence A. Wenner, "Fanship and the Television Sports Viewing Experience" (*Sociology of Sport Journal* 12, 1995); Michael R. Real and Robert A. Mechikoff, "Deep Fan: Mythic Identification, Technology, and Advertising in Spectator Sports" (*Sociology of Sport Journal* 9, 1992); Daniel L. Wann and Nyla R. Branscombe, "Sports Fans: Measuring Degree of Identification with Their Team" (*International Journal of Sport Psychology* 24, 1993); Susan Tyler Eastman and Karen E. Riggs, "Televised Sports and Ritual: Fan Experiences" (*Sociology of Sport Journal* 11, 1994; Michael J. Shapiro, "Representing World Politics: The Sport/War Intertext" (in *International/ Intertextual Relations: Postmodern Readings of World Text*, edited by James Derian and Michael J. Shapiro, Lexington Books, 1989); Laura Eggertson, "Recounting the day she cheated death" (*Globe and Mail*, 12 April 2004)

Chapter Two

BOOKS

Germaine Greer, *The Change: Women, Ageing and the Menopause* (Ballantine, 1991); Martin O'Malley, *Gross Misconduct: The Life of Spinner Spencer* (Viking, 1998); Derek Sanderson with Stan Fischler, *I've Got to Be Me* (Dodd, Meade and Co., 1970); Gerald Eskenazi, *The Derek Sanderson Nobody Knows: At 26 the World's Highest Paid Athlete* (Follett, 1973); Andrew Podnieks, *Players: The Ultimate A-Z Guide of Everyone Who Has Ever Played in the NHL* (Doubleday Canada, 2003)

ARTICLES

William Faulkner, "An Innocent at Rinkside" (*Essays, Speeches, and Public Letters by William Faulkner*, Random House, 1965); Shelley Fralic, "It's that time of year to cheer – baseball's back" (*Vancouver Sun,* 9 April 2004); Mark Schatzker, "Save Me, Gary Roberts (*Toro,* Oct/Nov 2003)

SOURCES

Chapter Three

BOOKS

John Steinbeck, *Of Mice and Men* (Penguin, 1993); Douglas Glover, *Notes Home From a Prodigal Son* (Oberon, 1999); Bill Gaston, *The Good Body* (Cormorant, 2000); Hans Ulrich Gumbrecht, *In Praise of Athletic Beauty* (Harvard UP, 2006); Allen Guttman, *The Erotics in Sport* (Columbia UP, 1996)

ARTICLES

Christopher Cordner, "Differences Between Sport and Art" (*Journal of the Philosophy of Sport* XV, 1988); Donald W. Calhoun, "Athlete and Spectator" (in *Sport, Culture, and Personality*, 2nd edition, Human Kinetics, 1987); Robert Rinehart, "Dropping Hierarchies: Toward the Study of a Contemporary Sporting Avant-Garde" (*Sociology of Sport Journal* 13, 1990); Spencer K. Wertz, "Representation and Expression in Sport and Art" (*Journal of the Philosophy of Sport* XII, 1985); David Kirk, "The Aesthetic Experience in Sport" (*Journal of Human Movement Studies* 12, 1986); Alphonso Lingis, "Orchids and Muscles" (*Journal of the Philosophy of Sport* XIII, 1986); Philip Preville, "Todd Bertuzzi: the King of Mooks" (*Enroute*, October 2003); Eric Adelson, "Force of Nature" (*ESPN Magazine*, 30 September 2002)

ETC.

Al Purdy, "Hockey Players" (in *The Caribou Horses*, McLelland and Stewart, 1976); Jim Hughson, *Snapshots* (interview with Markus Näslund) Rogers Sportsnet; www.splendidezine.ocm; Jack Shadbolt, "Hockey Owl": www.maltwood uvic.ca/mcwvancouver/artists/shadbolt_j.html; Todd Bertuzzi, Great Canadian Male *EnRoute* cover: www.enroute mag.com/e/archives/september03/index.html

Chapter Four

BOOKS

Varda Burstyn, *The Rites of Men: Manhood, Politics, and the Culture of Sport* (U of Toronto P, 1999); David Cruise and Alison Griffiths, *Net Worth* (Penguin, 1995); Eduardo Galeano, *Soccer in Sun and Shadow* (Verso, 2003); Jeff Klein, *Messier* (Doubleday Canada, 2003); Phil Esposito and Peter Golenbock, *Thunder and Lightning: A No-B.S. Hockey Memoir* (McLelland and Stewart, 2003); Steve Wilstein, *Associated Press Sports Writing Handbook* (McGraw-Hill, 2002); Steve Craig, *Sports Writing: A Beginner's Guide* (Discover Writing Press, 2002)

ARTICLES

Alison Griffiths and David Cruise, "The last thing you need to know about Alan Eagleson" (*Toronto Life,* July 1998); Lisa Disch and Mary Jo Kane, "When a Looker is Really a Bitch: Lisa Olson, Sport, and the Heterosexual Matrix" (in *Reading Sport: Critical Essays in Power and Representation,* ed. Susan Birrell and Mary G. McDonald, Northeastern UP, 2000); Paul Sloca, "Way Out of Bounds" (*Ryerson Review of Journalism,* Spring/Summer 2004); Lawrence Wenner, "In Search of the Sports Bar: Masculinity, Alcohol, Sports, and the Mediation of Public Space" (in *Sport and Postmodern Times*, State U of New York P, 1998)

ETC.

www.salmingunderwear.com/historia.html

Chapter Five

BOOKS

Dorothy Gronwall, Philip Wrightson, and Peter Waddel, *Head Injury: The Facts* (Oxford UP, 1998)

ARTICLES

Polly Shulman, "Blowing the Whistle on Concussions" (*Scientific American,* 2002)

Chapter Six

BOOKS

Alain Haché, *The Physics of Hockey* (Johns Hopkins UP, 2002)

Chapter Seven

BOOKS

Paul Fussell, *The Great War and Modern Memory* (Oxford UP, 1975); Saul L. Miller, *Hockey Tough: A Winning Mental Game* (Human Kinetics, 2003); Katherine Ashenburg, *The Mourner's Dance: What We Do When People Die* (Macfarlane, Walter and Ross, 2002); Christiane Northrup, M.D., *The Wisdom of Menopause: Creating Physical and Emotional Health and Healing During the Change* (Bantam, 2003); John McPhee, *Levels of the Game* (Farrar, Straus and Giroux, 1969)

ARTICLES

Elizabeth Gilbert, "Near Death in the Afternoon" (in *Best American Sports Writing 2002,* Houghton Mifflin); R. K. Barney, "The Hailed, the Haloed and the Hallowed:

Sport Heroes and Their Qualities" (in N. Muller and J. Ruhl eds., *Sport History*, Schors-Verlag, 1985); J. Robert Grove and Michelle Paccagnella, "Tall Poppies in Sport: Attitudes and Ascribed Personality Traits" (*Australian Psychologist*, July 1995); Roland Barthes, "The World of Wrestling" (in *A Barthes Reader*, ed. by Susan Sontag, Farrar, Straus and Giroux, 1982)

ETC.

Michael Ondaatje, "To A Sad Daughter" (in *The Cinnamon Peeler*, McLelland and Stewart, 1992)

Other Sources

Here's a partial and eclectic list of books and articles read – or read in the past – which were inspirational, educational, and otherwise indicative of what sports writing can do:

GONZOID

Dave Bidini, *Tropic of Hockey: My Search for the Game in Unlikely Places* (McLelland and Stewart, 2000), *Baseballissimo: My Summer in the Italian Minor Leagues* (M&S, 2004); *The Best Game You Can Name* (M&S, 2005); Peter Gzowski, *The Game of Our Lives* (M&S, 1981); George Plimpton, *Open Net: The Professional Amateur in the World of Big-time Hockey* (W.W. Norton, 1985); *Trent Frayne's Allstars: An Anthology of Canada's Best Sportswriting* (esp. Brian Preston's "Nasty", Doubleday, 1996); Jason Cohen, *Zamboni Rodeo: Chasing Hockey Dreams from Austin to Albuquerque* (Greystone, 2001); Ken Dryden, *The Game: A Thoughtful and Provocative Look At a Life in Hockey* (McMillan, 1983), Melissa Holbrook Pierson, *The Perfect Vehicle: What it is About Motorcycles* (W.W. Norton, 1997); David Shields, *Black Planet: Facing Race During an NBA Season* (Crown, 1991)

OTHER

Ed Willes, *The Rebel League: The Short and Unruly Life of the World Hockey Association* (M&S, 2004); Debbie Elicksen, *Inside the NHL Dream: Take a Tour from Inside the Locker Room* (Freelance Communications, 2002); Nick Hornby, *My Favourite Year: A Collection of Football Writing* (Phoenix, 2003); Alfie Kohn, *No Contest: The Case Against Competition* (Houghton Mifflin, 1992); Jim Denison and Pirkko Markula eds., *Moving Writing: Crafting Movement in Sport Research* (Peter Lang, 2003); C.L.R. James, *Beyond a Boundary* (Pantheon, 1983); Bruce Dowbiggin, *Moneyplayers: How Hockey's Greatest Stars Beat the NHL at its Own Game* (M&S, 2003), *The Stick*

(Macfarlane, Walter and Ross, 2001); Brian Pronger, *The Arena of Masculinity: Sports, Homosexuality and the Meaning of Sex* (St. Martin's, 1990)

ALSO

Iain MacIntrye, Elliot Pap, and Gary Mason at the *Vancouver Sun*; the photographs of Jeff Vinnick www.jeffvinnick.com

ACKNOWLEDGMENTS

Some were willing to talk hockey with me, even when the talk got rough or boring, and I'm grateful. Let's see: BESTASS, John Burns (who also attended a game with me, versus Dallas, and came armed with French bread and a stinky cheese the shape of a puck, neither of which were confiscated by security. "They look like the Berenstain Bears!" he remarked about the Canucks during warm-up, before they won the game), Joaner MacLeod, Carla Hesketh (Funk), Marilyn Bowering, Rick Leather, John Gould, Daniel Hogg, my students and colleagues at the University of Victoria.

Others helped as part of their job description, but still, they were generous and welcoming and I'm grateful: obviously, Chris Brumwell then of Orca Bay and now of the 2010 Olympics media department; the staff and weight room crowd at Juan de Fuca Recreation, especially Rob Wilson; Dan O'Connell, Gail Abernethy, Barbara Pendergast, Eric Duhatschek, John Metcalf. Also obviously, the players who gave so willingly their time and attention.

Ally Hack researched; Jamie Fitzpatrick prevented embarrassing mishaps and was a most ingenious, engaged and thoughtful editor; as was Marjorie Celona. Remaining bloopers or missed calls are mine.

Others inspired, educated, amused and consoled: Dave Bidini, Lucy Bashford, Ruth Allison, Arley McNency, Max Jackson, Edith Jackson, and the remarkable Lily Jackson.

Vancouver-raised **Lorna Jackson** began her working life as a musician and travelled throughout British Columbia for nine years as a bass player and singer. She has published a collection of short stories, *Dressing for Hope*, and a novel, *A Game To Play on the Tracks*. As well, her non-fiction and literary journalism have appeared in *Brick, Quill & Quire, The Georgia Straight*, and *Malahat Review*. She teaches Writing at the University of Victoria. Her next collection of fictions, *Flirt: The Interviews*, will be published by Biblioasis in 2008.
(PHOTO: www.diananethercott.com)